Gavin Jarret's low, gravelly voice sent her heart rate tap-dancing.

He was the last person she'd expected to see here.

"Don't tell me you're in trouble again?" she blurted out.

The corners of his mouth rose slightly. "I'm on the other side of the desk now. You did tell me to make something of myself, remember?"

Heat flamed in her cheeks. "You're a lawyer?" The word didn't make sense. Though he dressed like a lawyer, the bad boy of the county still lingered in his relaxed, confident pose. His eyes pinned her where she sat.

"You and I will need to work closely together. Will you be all right with that?"

Her heartbeat stuttered again. She lifted her chin and met his gaze. "Of course. Will you?"

Dear Harlequin Intrigue Reader,

Take a very well-deserved break from Thanksgiving preparations and rejuvenate yourself with Harlequin Intrigue's tempting offerings this month!

To start off the festivities, Harper Allen brings you *Covert Cowboy*—the next riveting installment of COLORADO CONFIDENTIAL. Watch the sparks fly when a Native American secret agent teams up with the headstrong mother of his unborn child to catch a slippery criminal. Looking to live on the edge? Then enter the dark and somber HEARTSKEEP estate—with caution!—when Dani Sinclair brings you *The Second Sister*—the next book in her gothic trilogy.

The thrills don't stop there! *His Mysterious Ways* pairs a ruthless mercenary with a secretive seductress as they ward off evil forces. Don't miss this new series in Amanda Stevens's extraordinary QUANTUM MEN books. Join Mallory Kane for an action-packed story about a heroine who must turn to a tough-hearted FBI operative when she's targeted by a stalker in *Bodyguard/Husband.*

A homecoming unveils a deadly conspiracy in *Unmarked Man* by Darlene Scalera—the latest offering in our new theme promotion BACHELORS AT LARGE. And finally this month, 'tis the season for some spine-tingling suspense in *The Christmas Target* by Charlotte Douglas when a sexy cowboy cop must ride to the rescue as a twisted Santa sets his sights on a beautiful businesswoman.

So gather your loved ones all around and warm up by the fire with some steamy romantic suspense!

Enjoy,

Denise O'Sullivan
Senior Editor
Harlequin Intrigue

THE SECOND SISTER

DANI SINCLAIR

TORONTO • NEW YORK • LONDON
AMSTERDAM • PARIS • SYDNEY • HAMBURG
STOCKHOLM • ATHENS • TOKYO • MILAN • MADRID
PRAGUE • WARSAW • BUDAPEST • AUCKLAND

For Natashya Wilson, who challenges me to do the impossible,
and is nearly always right, darn it.
Many thanks.

For Roger, who always listens. I love you.
And for Chip and Dan, who ignore the insanity
and get me through the graphics. You guys are terrific.

ISBN 0-373-22736-1

THE SECOND SISTER

This edition published by arrangement with Harlequin Books S.A.

Visit us at www.eHarlequin.com

Printed in U.S.A.

ABOUT THE AUTHOR

An avid reader, Dani Sinclair didn't discover romance novels until her mother lent her one when she had come for a visit. Dani's been hooked on the genre ever since. But she didn't take up writing seriously until her two sons were grown. Since the premiere of *Mystery Baby* for Harlequin Intrigue in 1996, Dani has kept her computer busy. Her third novel, *Better Watch Out*, was a RITA® Award finalist in 1998. Dani lives outside Washington, D.C., a place she's found to be a great source for both intrigue and humor!

You can write to her in care of the Harlequin Reader Service.

Books by Dani Sinclair

HARLEQUIN INTRIGUE
371—MYSTERY BABY
401—MAN WITHOUT A BADGE
448—BETTER WATCH OUT
481—MARRIED IN HASTE
507—THE MAN SHE MARRIED
539—FOR HIS DAUGHTER*
551—MY BABY, MY LOVE*
565—THE SILENT WITNESS*
589—THE SPECIALIST
602—BEST-KEPT SECRETS*
613—SOMEONE'S BABY
658—SCARLET VOWS
730—THE FIRSTBORN†
736—THE SECOND SISTER†

HARLEQUIN TEMPTATION
690—THE NAKED TRUTH

*Fools Point/Mystery Junction
†Heartskeep

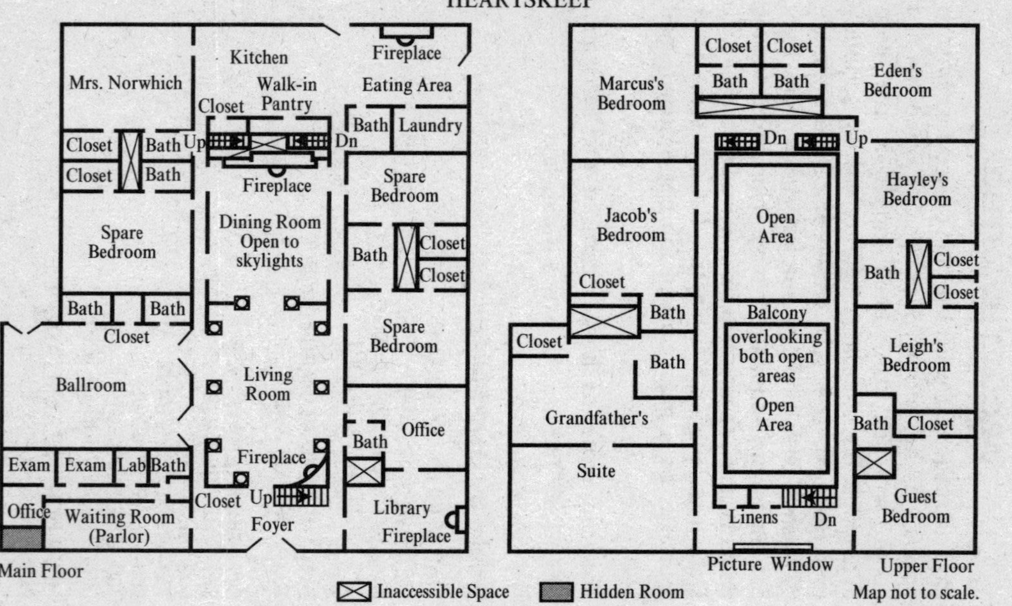
HEARTSKEEP
Mrs. Norwhich
Kitchen
Walk-in Pantry
Closet
Fireplace
Eating Area
Bath
Laundry
Closet
Bath
Up
Dn
Closet
Bath
Fireplace
Spare Bedroom
Dining Room Open to skylights
Spare Bedroom
Bath
Closet
Closet
Bath
Bath
Closet
Spare Bedroom
Ballroom
Living Room
Office
Bath
Exam
Exam
Lab
Bath
Fireplace
Office
Waiting Room (Parlor)
Closet
Up
Foyer
Library
Fireplace
Main Floor
Closet
Closet
Marcus's Bedroom
Bath
Bath
Eden's Bedroom
Dn
Up
Jacob's Bedroom
Open Area
Hayley's Bedroom
Bath
Closet
Closet
Closet
Bath
Balcony overlooking both open areas
Closet
Leigh's Bedroom
Bath
Open Area
Grandfather's
Bath
Closet
Suite
Guest Bedroom
Linens
Dn
Picture Window
Upper Floor
Inaccessible Space
Hidden Room
Map not to scale.

CAST OF CHARACTERS

Dennison Hart—He made sure Heartskeep stayed in the family. He never anticipated that no one would want the place.

Amy Hart Thomas—She disappeared seven years ago without a trace.

Hayley Hart Thomas—As Leigh's twin and the oldest child, Heartskeep should have belonged to her.

Leigh Hart Thomas—She thought she'd put the past behind her, until she returned to Heartskeep and discovered the past refused to stay buried.

Marcus Thomas—His evil reaches beyond the grave.

Eden Voxx Thomas—Marcus's widow knows more than she'll admit.

Jacob Voxx—Does being Eden's son mean he's out to cause trouble?

Gavin Jarret—The former bad boy of the county is now the estate's lawyer.

Bram Myers—His heart belongs to Hayley, and keeping her from harm is his goal.

Nolan Ducort III—He has a secret to keep and a score to settle.

Martin Pepperton—This member of the prominent Pepperton family was stomped to death by one of his own horses—after he was shot.

Keith Earlwood—He always liked hanging with the rich and famous.

George and Emily Walken—Gavin's foster parents have been friends and neighbors of Heartskeep for years.

Dear Harlequin Intrigue Reader,

Welcome back to Heartskeep. The somber estate has only just begun to yield its many secrets. The doorway to the past is open now, and anything can happen.

Seven years ago, tough guy Gavin Jarret cultivated his dark reputation to keep people at a distance. He never backed down, and made it a point to never let anyone close enough to matter. Until a sultry, summer night when he offered a tempting seductress a ride on the back of his motorcycle, and changed both their lives forever.

Leigh Thomas is the quiet twin, forever in her sister's shadow. Her one attempt to break that mold ended in disaster—and a night she could never forget. She thought she'd put the past behind her, but fate and Heartskeep have other plans.

Happy reading!

Dani Sinclair

Chapter One

Seven years ago

Leigh Thomas gulped the soda her date handed her, looking for a way out. She didn't know a soul in the noisy crowd and the live rock band prevented conversation even if she'd found someone interesting to talk with. College age and older, everyone seemed to be drinking, openly using drugs and making out. The beer she'd managed to force down was threatening to make an ignoble return and suddenly, her flashy new image seemed downright stupid.

She might look like part of this crowd tonight, but despite the fact that she had raided her identical twin sister's more daring wardrobe for this outfit, inside Leigh beat the heart of a fairly naive seventeen-year-old. She should never have gone out with Nolan Ducort III.

A party at the elite Pepperton estate had sounded so enticing. The perfect way to change her mousy image. Of course, if Leigh's mother had still been alive, she would have warned Leigh that Martin Pepperton's family was out of the country, and that Nolan, Martin and their buddy, Keith Earlwood, all had questionable reputations. But Amy Thomas wasn't there to warn her, and Leigh hadn't listened to her sister.

Their mother's disappearance a few months ago, coming

only months after the unexpected death of Leigh's beloved grandfather, was still tearing Leigh apart. Amy Hart Thomas hadn't voluntarily vanished right before Leigh's high school graduation. Their mother was dead. They knew it, they simply couldn't prove it.

The police tended to agree, but they believed Amy had been the victim of a robbery gone bad. She'd withdrawn a surprising amount of cash for a trip to New York City when she generally used credit cards for everything. Officers were quick to point out that Amy's fondness for wearing expensive jewelry to complement her designer clothing was something any thief would notice right away. Even her expensive luxury car marked her as a potential target.

Only, Amy Thomas was no fool. She'd grown up wealthy. She knew how to protect herself. Besides, a robbery gone bad didn't explain why neither her car nor her body had been found. And contrary to the local police chief's suggestion, there was absolutely no way their mother had run off with a secret lover. The idea was ludicrous.

Leigh took another sip of the soda. Nolan grinned at her and ran his hand possessively down her arm. Leigh shivered. His touch repulsed her. Definitely, going out with Nolan had been a bad mistake. She'd have been better off at home in her room with her customary book in hand, reining in her all-too-vivid imagination. The family estate of Heartskeep was large enough that she would have had no trouble avoiding her father tonight. She'd had years of practice, after all.

But she'd been so tired of thinking and wondering—so tired of stifling sobs for the mother she missed so much. Going out, being with new people, had seemed like such a good idea at the time.

Nolan was wealthy and model handsome. His sporty new convertible was the talk of everyone she knew. Even

Leigh's sister, Hayley, had been green with envy when he'd singled Leigh out after they were introduced. Being an identical twin, Leigh was used to guys flocking around her out of curiosity, but it was Hayley they were generally drawn to. Hayley knew how to flirt and tease. Outgoing, friendly and smart, her sister wasn't intimidated by anything. Everyone always said Leigh was the quiet twin, perfectly content to let her "older" sister take the lead in most things. It was a real coup to have someone more interested in her than in Hayley. Her sister hadn't been able to conceal her surprise or her disappointment. Hayley had really liked Nolan's car. She had been quick to point out that Nolan was older and more worldly than other guys Leigh had dated. Which, of course, had made going with him tonight a given.

Now, Leigh sincerely wished she had listened to her sister and her own instincts. She was starting to feel dizzy and strange. Must be the effects of that beer she'd forced herself to drink. All she wanted now was to get out of this house and away from this noisy party. She didn't like the way Nolan and his two friends kept looking at her.

Hayley would have known exactly how to handle the situation. No—Hayley would never have let herself be placed in this situation. Leigh was out of her depth and sinking fast.

When a boisterous group of people approached, Leigh seized the opportunity to slip away unnoticed. Outside, the humid night air didn't help the muzzy sensation buzzing inside her head. She felt strange, as if she was melting from the inside out. From one beer? That and the flat-tasting soda were the only things she'd had. Maybe if she'd eaten something today she wouldn't feel so strange. Reaching out a hand for a nearby tree, she tried to shake off the weird sensations.

"You okay?"

A dark shape detached itself from the side of a parked pickup truck nearby. The spark from a cigarette was ground beneath a large booted foot.

Her heart stopped, then jumped to vigorous life as her gaze traveled up the tight jeans, across the flat abdomen clearly visible beneath the open shirt, to reach his face, carved from the shadows. She knew his eyes were deep gray, with a penetrating stare that unnerved some people. Leigh had always found it incredibly sexy. His wavy dark hair was thick and perpetually in need of a trim—as untamable as the man himself.

She was face-to-face with her own private fantasy come true. Gavin Jarret, bad boy of the county, stood close enough that by simply extending her hand, she could slide her fingers over the hard, flat planes of the exposed skin on his chest.

Tempting.

Very tempting.

Which only went to prove how muddled her thinking had become. Gavin was no boy. He was five years older than her and carried himself with a dangerous air of sensuality that had nothing to do with money, clothes or cars. If this had been the era of the Wild West, he'd have a gun strapped on one lean hip and a hat with the brim pulled low over his forehead. He wasn't cocky. He didn't need to be. He moved with the easy assurance of a man who had no need to prove anything to anyone, but wouldn't back down from a challenge.

Gavin had starred in many of Leigh's wishful dreams since she'd first glimpsed him working at Wickert's gas station in town. Rumor had it he'd been arrested, thrown out of several schools, and that he kissed like nobody's business. She could believe the latter. His mouth fascinated her. Everything about Gavin fascinated her.

He'd been one of the many foster youths her neighbors,

Emily and George Walken, had taken on. Everyone told them it was a mistake. Gavin was a loner who liked it that way. Whenever there was trouble, the police came knocking on his door first. But like so many others the Walkens had helped, Gavin had settled down under their guidance. Now he used their place as his home base when he wasn't away at college.

"Heat getting to you?" he asked.

The slow glide of his words ignited a tingling flame low in her belly. His gaze seemed to linger on her cleavage and the daringly bared expanse of midriff over the jeans that just barely covered her navel. She'd regretted the choice almost immediately after leaving her room earlier that night, but had decided to brazen the situation out. She'd felt naked ever since—especially when Nolan had gazed at her with a predator's hunger.

Funny, but Gavin's appreciative gaze had just the opposite effect. It stirred something to life inside her, something daring and exciting and strange. Tipping her head to one side, she smiled up at him.

"It's terribly hot inside."

He proffered an open bottle of beer. She'd been so focused on the rest of him, she hadn't even noticed his hands. They were big, solid hands, with long, tapered fingers.

"Want a sip?"

Her heart fluttered madly. His voice was deep and gravelly. Sexy, like the rest of him. "Sure. Thanks."

Their hands touched.

Hot and wild, a surge of energy flowed through her. Leigh tried not to shiver at that contact. The pads of his fingers were rough and callused from working at the garage, not baby soft like Nolan's.

Taking the bottle, she put her mouth where his had been. The sensation was deliciously naughty. From somewhere came the courage to look him in the eye as she took a long swallow. The beer trickled down her dry throat, icy cold.

She sensed approval as his gaze slipped away to travel the length of her throat, then lingered on the swell of her breasts. Her nipples tightened along with the rest of her. A prickly restlessness enveloped her.

The moon skittered behind a wispy cloud, plunging his features into deeper shadow. As she handed him back the bottle, she dared a tiny caress over his knuckles.

Gavin studied her with dark, unfathomable eyes. With deliberate slowness, he raised the neck of the bottle and covered its mouth with his lips. Tilting the neck back, he took a long, slow drink.

Leigh couldn't tear her gaze away. She followed the path of the liquid down his throat, feeling as if that mouth was on her rather than on the bottle in his hand.

His eyes stared deeply into hers. "Want to take a ride?"

He gestured toward a sleek black motorcycle waiting in the shadows beside the pickup truck.

Her body hummed with energy. The prickling sensation centered itself between her legs, charging her with unbearable excitement. Her fantasy was coming to life. Did she have the nerve to see it through?

She strove to mimic her sister's easy tone, smiling with false confidence. "Sure. Why not?"

"I don't have an extra helmet," he cautioned. "That fancy hairdo of yours is going to get messed."

"Not if I take it down first."

The brazen words seemed to have a life of their own. So did her hands as they reached for the clip holding the carefully styled mass of hair on top of her head. His sensual hunger was tangible, bonding them together in the night. He watched every motion through heavy-lidded eyes.

Freed, the golden-brown mass spilled over her shoulders and down her back. Her fingers threaded the strands as he watched. She trembled when his hand came up, reaching out to lift a section and rub it between those long callused fingers. His eyes went darker still, with unmistakable desire.

Leigh couldn't breathe.

"Come on," he said abruptly.

She had never been on a motorcycle in her life. Amazingly, she slid behind him as though she'd been doing it all her life.

"Hold on to me," he told her.

The buzzing in her head was almost welcome as she wrapped her arms around his trim waist. The tingly feeling became a burning ache of need. They took off with a deafening roar.

Hair whipped around her face, tossing streamers behind as they raced along the twisty road. Her fingers tightened spasmodically around him, but she quickly found the rhythm of moving with his body and the bike. Wind whistled in her ears as trees rushed past. Her fingers sought a better grip, brushing his zipper. He was aroused.

Part of her registered that fact in shock, but the shock was quickly overwhelmed by a yearning she had never experienced before. Tentatively, her fingers traced that bulge, feeling it swell and pulse.

A tiny core of sanity screamed in alarm. Her body no longer listened. It was as if she was acting under dictates she had no control over. She pressed an openmouthed kiss against the shirt on his back. The bike swerved slightly as he reacted.

Gavin steered them down a side road. More of a path, really. She had no idea where they were. She didn't care. Touching him had become a drug of liberation.

They tore up the narrow dirt road, raising a plume of dust around them. Leigh closed her eyes. She slid her hands wantonly over his bare skin. Nothing had ever felt this incredible. He was hard planes and supple skin and she was breathing fast and shallow when he pulled the bike into a copse of trees and stopped. He came off the bike in a smooth motion, then whisked her off before she knew what he was doing. She stood on legs of rubber as he crushed her against his body. His mouth sought hers in a kiss that demanded a total response.

And she gave it, kissing him back with a fervor that astonished the tiny portion of her brain still functioning. She felt branded as his tongue plunged into her mouth, mimicking an action her body seemed to crave. He tasted of cigarettes and beer, with a subtle hint of peppermint, of all things.

It took her several seconds to realize tiny, animal sounds of need were issuing from her throat. She couldn't get enough of the feel and taste of him. She wanted more. Her body seemed to be catapulting her toward some precipice, demanding that she hurry.

She uttered a small cry of protest when he pulled back. His eyes gleamed, dark and hot and wild like the night. His teeth glinted in the dancing moonlight as he smiled.

''Slow down, baby, we've got all the time in the world.''

But she couldn't slow down. She wanted to scream at him to hurry. Yet the only sound she seemed capable of making was a ridiculous, yearning whimper. He yanked a blanket from his saddlebag and spread it in the clearing. Her brain felt muzzy and disoriented, yet the incredible need continued to build inside her, overwhelming conscious thought.

''You're going to burn me alive, looking at me like that.''

Yes! Exactly! She was burning with a need only he could satisfy. ''Hurry. Please.''

He grinned wickedly. ''I intend to do both.''

His mouth claimed hers in a hot, wet duel as he drew

them down on the thin blanket. Every fiber of her was on fire. Grass pricked at her skin through the thin material, acting as yet another spur to the incredible tension stretching inside her.

Leigh never felt his deft fingers bare her breasts to the night sky. She was lost in a tidal wave of sensations that pushed her ever closer to the waiting precipice. Then his mouth closed over one nipple. She free-fell in shudders of exhilaration.

Dimly, she heard his sound of satisfaction. ''Sing for me, baby.''

She should have been mortified to know he watched her lose control. But he gave her no time to recover. Using that incredibly talented mouth, he set about igniting the fire all over again. Her mouth, the sensitive skin of her throat, nibbling on an earlobe until she quivered. With a low sound of satisfaction, he set a new path with his lips, placing light kisses along her throat, her collarbone, her breast, until he could draw the nipple deeply into his mouth. Her body arched in supplication.

A tiny kernel of sanity watched in stunned amazement as she went completely wild, tearing at his clothing, covering his skin with kisses and tiny nips that elicited surprise and a few startled groans of pleasure. Somehow they were both nude. It was shocking, yet intensely exciting. His lips forged a new path down her tummy and lower still. He paused, his breath stirring the hairs at the junction of her legs, making her moan in anticipation. Then he settled there, his mouth doing incredibly naughty things she'd only read about, until now.

He chuckled as her hands strained to touch him, this incredible, fascinating shadowy shape in the dark. He assumed the role of teacher as he showed her untutored body how to please them both. The wild clamoring filled her once more and she wondered if she'd gone mad.

Finally, he stretched out over her. Butter soft, yet uncompromisingly hard. Their sweat-slicked skin came together and he claimed her with one hard thrust. He swallowed her shocked cry with his mouth. The stab of pain was almost immediately lost in the extraordinary sense of fullness.

She thought she heard him swear, but when she began to move against him, he shuddered and began to move as well, withdrawing, almost completely, only to surge against her once more, faster, harder, perfect.

Leigh was beyond words, beyond thought. She clenched around him, demanding more insistently as she pushed her body against his. With a curse and a groan, he began to move, harder, faster, deeper. The pleasure returned, driving her toward some incredible goal until the world exploded in a pleasure beyond description.

"WAKE UP. Damn it, Hayley, wake up."

Confused, her mind tried to make sense of the masculine voice and the hand shaking her none too gently.

"I'm Leigh," she muttered, unable to lift her heavy eyelids. The shaking sensation stopped. She felt the hard rocky ground at her back. Vaguely, she wondered if she'd ever stop trembling.

Gavin cursed again. She should say something, but it was far too difficult to battle the fatigue pressing shut her eyes.

Something wet covered her face. She batted uselessly at the cloth, but hands pinned her arms over her head to the blanket. She blinked as the cloth fell away, trying to make out his features in the dark.

"That's it. Snap out of it. How much did you have to drink?"

The rough demand reached past the haze. "One. Beer."

He swore viciously. "Are you lying?"

"Never. Lie. So tired."

"You're drugged."

The words ripped at the curtain fogging her mind. "No."

"Hell, yes," he said grimly. "Open your eyes and look at me!"

"Stop swearing!" She blinked open blurry eyes, battling the residual haze shrouding her brain. Gavin was holding her down. She tried to remember why that was all wrong.

"That's it, fight back." One hand let her go. Her head lolled to the side. It was so hard to keep her eyes open. His hand slid beneath the tangle of her hair, cupping the back of her head. The tingling sensations were starting all over. There was something incredibly sensual in the touch of that large hand against her scalp.

"Sit up, come on. That's it. Open your eyes, Leigh."

She struggled to obey. He was the sexiest man she'd ever seen. "Fantasy man," she whispered.

Gavin cursed. "We'll see how you feel about that tomorrow. Here, swallow this."

A bottle of liquid was thrust to her lips. It clicked against her teeth, but he gave her no chance to protest. Warm water dribbled down her chin, but some of the fluid made it down her parched throat. The water had a chemical taste, like bottled water that had been sitting in a hot car too long. She choked. Her stomach roiled in protest. Feebly, she tried to push aside his hand.

"Drink some more."

"I'm going to be sick."

"That's the idea. We need to get that drug out of your system."

To her acute mortification, he held her while her stomach made good on the threat. He continued holding her gently even after she was reduced to dry heaves. Almost tenderly, he pulled aside the heavy mass of her hair and rubbed her bare back as if she were a child.

Weak and spent, she let him. Desperately, her brain tried to make sense of it all.

"Take another sip."

"I'll throw up again."

"Swish it around in your mouth and spit it out. Don't swallow it. I know it's warm, but it's the only water I have with me."

She obeyed, totally ashamed as memory played back the things they'd done. He let her go and fished in his pocket. She heard the crinkle of paper as Gavin unwrapped something and handed it to her.

"It's okay. It's a peppermint hard candy. It will take the taste out of your mouth."

His expression was so sweet she wanted to cry. The candy had an odd taste on her tongue.

"Think you can get back on the bike?"

"Bike?"

Memory trickled past. A wild ride. Wanton need. Her breasts were bare, the nipples hard, but tender and sore. The rest of her body was equally bare. Moonlight peered through the trees overhead to dapple her skin. She focused on his face, horror growing as images ghosted through her mind.

"Did we…? Were we…?"

His features hardened, making her flinch.

"Were we intimate? Oh, yeah, baby. We were as intimate as it gets."

His finger lightly traced her collarbone. She had a memory of his lips doing the same. Leigh trembled—hard.

"How much do you remember?"

The knot that formed in her stomach threatened to turn her inside out.

"I don't… I'm not sure."

Lifting her chin, Gavin forced her to meet his eyes.

"Tell me you weren't a virgin."

She lost the battle with her stomach once more. He turned her head in time as her insides twisted in an attempt to escape. Dry heaves wracked her. Gavin swore, but he held her until she finally sagged against his chest, utterly spent. His shirt smelled of cigarette smoke and fabric softener. That he was fully dressed while she was naked made it all the worse somehow. His hands were gentle as he wiped her face, tucking her hair behind her ear.

"Let's get you dressed."

She tried, but her fingers were useless. He skipped the bra and panties and helped her with her sister's blouse.

"Can you stand?"

She wasn't sure. Gavin didn't give her a choice. Her body still vibrated in reaction to his touch as he slid the jeans back up her legs. Her stomach fluttered helplessly at the feel of his fingers trying to fasten the snap. She stepped into her brand-new deck shoes while he held her so that she didn't fall over. Tugging her toward the large black motorcycle, he lifted her up, settling her in place.

"Hold on to me."

A flashback of her hands roaming his bare skin hit her with electric force. Leigh closed her eyes, fighting tears of shame. She didn't open them until the bike stopped. Helplessly, she gazed at the dark building of Wickert's garage.

"What are we doing here?"

"I have a key and I know the alarm system. I thought you'd want to clean up before I took you home."

Home. She had no home. Not anymore. Only an empty house where people waited without hope.

Her stomach knotted. She wanted to cry. His features were harsh. She swallowed her tears, feeling mortified and ashamed.

She barely recognized herself in the mirror of the ladies' room. Her hair hung about her face in tangled strands. Her eyes were huge dark pits against the ghostly white pallor of her skin. Streaks of mascara gave her a raccoon appearance, and there was more than one dark bruise forming on the skin of her neck. Leigh remembered his mouth there and whimpered. The temperature could have been below freezing instead of the high seventies she knew it to be even at this hour of the night.

Holding the comb he'd thrust into her hand after unlocking the door, she sank onto the dirty tile floor and sobbed until there were no tears left. Shame paralyzed her. How could she go back out there and face him?

He claimed she'd been drugged, but that didn't matter. Neither did the fact that she'd had a crush on him since she was fifteen. What mattered was that she'd given her virginity to a man who couldn't even tell her apart from her sister.

Given? She'd practically demanded that he take her.

And that was more demeaning than all the rest.

His knock on the door brought her scrambling to her feet. She brushed at her tear-stained face.

"Are you okay in there?"

"Yes." It came out as a croak of sound. Her voice was thick from crying. "I'll be out in a minute."

"Do you need anything?"

Her mother. She would have given anything she possessed to have her mother here beside her right this minute.

"I'll be out in a minute," she repeated.

Leigh waited until she heard him move away from the door. Splashing water on her face, she used the rough paper towels to rub fiercely at her face, trying to remove all traces of her smeared makeup. Her sister's blouse was buttoned all wrong and her fingers still didn't want to cooperate, but finally, she managed that small task. Trying to tame her hair with his comb proved impossible.

She tried not to think about the marks on her skin or the puffy appearance of her lips, or the strange, small ache between her legs and elsewhere. She could smell him on her skin, and still feel him pulsing inside her. And the shaking started again in earnest, because she still wanted him. It was all she could do to pull herself together and exit the ladies' room.

Gavin came away from the dirty wall with a primitive grace she still found compelling. Worse, a part of her longed for him to pull her into his arms and hold her. She needed to hear that things were going to be okay, that he wasn't disgusted with her. But he made no move to touch her and his stern expression was angry.

With her?

"Come into the office. I made some tea."

"Tea?" There was a surreal feel to everything.

"Mrs. Walken claims tea with sugar is good for shock. I suspect we both need a cup. Besides, the coffeemaker's broken again, so it's tea or soda."

"I'm not thirsty."

"Drink it anyway."

She was so cold inside, she didn't think even a gallon of hot tea would help. She'd probably just embarrass herself further by vomiting it right back up. Leigh looked quickly away from the cookies he'd bought from the vending machine.

"Try to eat one. We need to give your system something to absorb besides the drug."

A protest formed in her head, but she blocked the words before they could slip past. Sipping tea and nibbling on a cookie gave her something to do, a focus other than looking at him.

"What were you doing at that party?"

Leigh cringed. "I went with Nolan."

"Ducort?" he asked in obvious disbelief. "What's a kid like you doing with a creep like that?"

Forcing herself to meet his eyes she said simply, "He asked me out."

Gavin muttered something under his breath. A pulse in his neck began to throb. He looked as if he wanted to hit someone. She cringed. Instantly, his features transformed, softening.

"Listen to me, Leigh, I'm sorrier than I can say about what happened. I swear I didn't recognize you at first or I would have taken you straight home."

She swallowed the hurt, refusing to cry in front of him. The old desk chair she'd sat down on squeaked in protest. "Thanks a lot," she managed to say.

Gavin didn't seem to hear her. "You are not to blame. Do you understa—"

Leigh stood so fast that the cookies scattered across the desktop. "Don't you *dare* patronize me. I'm not twelve."

"At least tell me I didn't seduce a minor."

"It was consensual sex, not seduction," she told him, shaking from head to toe.

"You were drugged," he said bluntly. "And you were a virgin."

"Well, I don't have to worry about that problem anymore, now, do I?"

Headlights bathed the interior of the gas station. A car was pulling up out front.

"Your sister's here."

Horrified, she stared at him. "You called my house?"

"No, I called the Walkens. I wanted advice before we go to the police."

She gaped at him. "We aren't going to the police!"

"You were drugged. Don't you understand? Ducort slipped something in your drink. He intended to rape you. Only, I got to you first," he added grimly.

For a second she thought she would pass out. Dimly, she heard him opening the door at her back.

"Bad luck for you, huh?" she spit at him. A clamoring anger filled her. "Well, don't give it another thought. I sure don't plan to. I'm not going to the police. But if either one of you ever comes near me again, I'll make you rue the day you were born."

Gavin stepped aside. Hayley and the Walkens stood in the doorway with mingled expressions of shock and concern. Leigh's humiliation was complete.

Pivoting, she held her tears in check with fierce effort as she gazed at the man she had dreamed about for so long.

"I will never, ever forgive you for this."

EIGHTEEN HOURS LATER, Gavin sat in jail contemplating his bruised knuckles and wondering why he'd felt obligated to play the hero. All he had to do was tell the police the truth—and ruin Leigh's reputation completely.

Besides, what was the point? The cops thought they already knew the truth. An anonymous tip put his bike outside his employer's house last night. The house had been burgled. Old man Wickert had been struck a couple of times, tied up, then left there to suffer a heart attack. If he died, the cops would add murder to the charge, and Gavin knew the police chief was just itching to do exactly that.

Gavin had been allowed one phone call. He'd used it to call George Walken. He'd elicited a reluctant promise from the man to keep Leigh out of this no matter what. He'd pointed out that telling the truth would only get him in deeper. The cops would claim Gavin had given her the drug and there was no point in dragging her name through the mud. He'd told George's attorney, Ira Rosencroft, the same thing.

Gavin opened his eyes when his cell door suddenly clanged open. A fresh-faced officer not much older than he was took a step back and waited.

"Let's go, Jarret."

"Go where?"

"You need to sign for your things. You're being released."

"Why?"

"You like it here so much you want to stay?"

"Did Mr. Wickert regain consciousness?"

Hope filled him. The old man had been a demanding boss, as crotchety as a bear coming out of hibernation. He'd turned grumbling into an art form, but he'd given Gavin a job and a chance when no one else would, and over time, the two of them had come to like and respect each other.

The cop shook his head. "He died about an hour ago."

"Damn."

Their eyes met in shared sympathy. Gavin swallowed his grief. "So, why are you letting me go?"

"Your alibi came in. You know, you could have saved us all a lot of work if you'd just told us where you were last night."

George had promised him! So had the attorney. Gavin scrawled his name on the paper he was handed and stuffed his nearly empty wallet into his back pocket. Livid that one of them had betrayed him, he started walking away. The interrogation-room door swung open.

The police chief stood in the doorway, glaring at a slim figure sitting on the hard wooden chair. She stared back with wide, unblinking eyes.

"You should reconsider," Chief Crossley growled.

Leigh Thomas rose with the grace of a queen. Her long, golden-brown hair swung halfway down her back. She faced the man with a composure few could have matched.

"No, *you* should reconsider." She spoke with quiet force. "I know you don't like me and my sister, and you don't like Gavin or the Walkens, but if you let that stand in your way, you won't solve this murder, either. Gavin was with me last night, and I'll swear to that in court. There is nothing you can say or do that will change that simple truth.''

She stared him in the eye without flinching. A slip of a girl really, yet she faced that six-foot-five-inch pompous ass with a dignity that shrunk him right down to size.

''You listen to me, girl. If we find one piece of evidence to link Jarret to that crime, I'll have you up on an accessory to murder charge so fast it will make your head swim.''

''No. You won't. You'd have to fabricate evidence, and you may be incompetent, but I don't think you're dishonest.''

''Get her out of here,'' the chief snarled, turning dark angry red. Pivoting, he spied Gavin. ''Get them both out of my sight,'' he told the young cop standing silently to one side.

Gavin fell into pace beside Leigh. She wouldn't look at him as they walked outside. Her chin was up, her shoulders back, and she stared straight ahead as she moved. She flinched when he touched her shoulder, and his gut tightened in pain.

''Why did you come here?'' he demanded. ''I told that lawyer and the Walkens to leave you out of this!''

''They don't even know I'm here,'' she told his shirtfront.

He needed to see her eyes, to know what she was thinking. Did she hate him for what had happened last night?

''Then, why come here today?''

She didn't raise her head. ''Because you were with me when the robbery happened.''

Gavin swore. ''Precisely. There wasn't any evidence against me, just some anonymous phone call. All I had to do was sit tight and they would have released me sooner or later. Don't you realize what you've done to your reputation by coming here?''

That brought her pointed little chin up. She faced him squarely without a flicker of emotion.

"Enhanced it or ruined it depending on who you talk to." Her shoulders rose and fell. "Want to know how much I don't care? If I hadn't come forward, the police would have stopped looking for the real criminal, just like they stopped looking for my mother. Mr. Wickert was a nice old man. He deserves better. Now, take your hand off me before I kick you in the shins."

Gavin dropped his hand, still trying to read her expression without success. "Are you okay? I mean after last night—"

"After last night, you owe me, right?"

Surprised, he managed a nod. Beyond her, he saw her sister running up the sidewalk toward them.

"If you owe me, then do us both a favor, Gavin. Grow up. Make something of yourself. That bad-boy reputation could have cost you a prison term just now. And you made Mrs. Walken cry. She deserves better, too."

The words lashed him with their simple truth. "I thought you were supposed to be the quiet twin," he muttered.

"Leigh!" Hayley called to her.

Leigh narrowed her eyes. "I am. Stick around. My sister will tear a strip off you that will make you wish you were back inside with Chief Crossley. As for last night, forget it, Gavin. I plan to."

"You won't forget," he said softly as she turned to meet her sister. "And neither will I."

Chapter Two

The present

Marcus Thomas had been murdered over the roses he'd so carefully tended. Shouldn't she be able to summon some emotion other than relief? He'd been her father after all. Admittedly that had been a technicality as far as he'd been concerned, but it was biological fact, nonetheless.

Leigh Hart Thomas found herself standing slightly apart from the small group gathered under the hot summer sun. She wondered how the minister could find any kind words to eulogize a man like Marcus. She would have been unequal to the task. Even his widow, Eden, stood there without expression as the mercifully short service was concluded.

Eden's son, Jacob Voxx, looked decidedly ill at ease at her side. Of course, it was broiling hot beneath the sun and he was dressed in a somber black suit and tie. One sleeve dangled uselessly at his side. Since his left arm had provided passage for one of the killer's bullets, it was still in a sling to restrict its movement. That would be enough to make anyone uncomfortable, but Leigh suspected it was only part of the reason Jacob glanced once more to his left.

Leigh's twin sister, Hayley, stood beside Bram Myers. His large, strong hand rested lightly—protectively—on her shoulder. Hayley looked incredibly good for someone who had twice nearly died at the same murderer's hands.

Leigh decided it was hard not to feel a twinge of envy looking at the couple. She and her sister had always shared a special bond—that would never really change. But while Leigh had been in England visiting friends, her sister had forged a new bond—one Leigh couldn't share.

Bram Myers was a large, rawboned man, handsome in a dark, intense sort of way. Ten years older than her sister, he might not think he wanted to marry again, but it was a foregone conclusion for everyone else. If there was ever a couple that belonged together, it was the two of them. Leigh wondered if Bram was aware that he maintained a subtle, physical contact with Hayley whenever they were together.

While Leigh envied her sister, she doubted she could ever open herself emotionally to another person so completely. Trust came a lot harder to her than it did to Hayley.

Restlessly, Leigh tucked a long strand of hair behind her ear and decided she was definitely going to adopt her sister's new, carefree hairstyle as soon as she could get into town to see the beautician. Not only was her current style hot and heavy in the summer heat and humidity, the shorter, sleeker look was a much better image for someone about to embark on a new dream job as a computer programmer for an exciting start-up company involved in the telecommunications industry.

As Hayley and Bram exchanged a private look, Leigh's gaze skated to the couple standing slightly behind them. George and Emily Walken stood side by side. They had been family friends, and Heartskeep's closest neighbors, since before Leigh had been born. The childless couple had always taken in troubled foster youths, and since her grandfather's death and her mother's disappearance, they'd taken in Hayley and Leigh as well.

When Marcus had been murdered, the couple had shielded them from the media. They'd run interference with the authorities, offered them a place to stay, and helped in every way they could. Leigh would never forget their kindness. Being around them was the next best thing to having her mother and grandfather back.

Off to one side, Odette Norwhich scowled darkly at everyone and no one. Eden had recently hired the woman as Heartskeep's live-in housekeeper. While Leigh had only seen Mrs. Norwhich a few times since she'd been back, she'd concluded the woman always looked like that. Hayley assured her that Mrs. Norwhich actually had a softer side, but Leigh had yet to see one.

Leigh let her gaze travel around the circle to the other people who now walked forward to offer their condolences. Since the service had been private, there were blessedly few of them. She pasted a smile on her face and spoke briefly to each person, relieved when it was finally time to go. Marcus had been their father, in fact, but never in deed. And while he'd lived at Heartskeep as long as they had, he had never belonged there.

Leigh started to follow her sister and Bram, when a gust of chilled air swept her body. Except there wasn't the faintest trace of a breeze. As she turned slowly, her gaze skipped over the abandoned coffin and the scattered grave sites surrounding it. A solitary figure stood several yards away. Her breath constricted painfully in her chest and her heart began to pound.

What was he doing here?

Riveted in place, she stared helplessly as memories ambushed her without mercy. It wasn't fair. She'd dealt with these emotions years ago.

"Leigh? Is something wrong?" Hayley asked.

Everything. The mere sight of Gavin Jarret shouldn't affect her so deeply after all these years.

"Leigh?"

She focused on Hayley's hand, warm against the bare skin of her arm. Bram's dark eyes mirrored her sister's concern. Leigh managed to shake her head. Quickly, she sent her gaze to the coffin.

"I should be feeling something, shouldn't I?" she asked, relieved that her voice sounded normal.

Hayley's features tightened. She barely gave the coffin a glance. "Relief?"

After a second, Leigh nodded sadly. "He was still our father."

"'It takes more than a biological act to be a father' isn't just a saying, it's a fact. You know as well as I do that the only thing Marcus loved was his roses. Come on, we need to get out of this heat."

Leigh let her sister lead her away. When she cast a final look over her shoulder, Gavin was gone, but she glimpsed another figure darting between the headstones. Definitely not a mourner. Maybe a celebrant who'd come to make sure Marcus was really dead?

She chided herself for the nasty thought. More than likely, a photojournalist had been snapping pictures for some tabloid. The recent events at Heartskeep had made the Hart family headline news once more. Marcus would have hated that.

As far as Leigh was concerned, the media could print whatever they liked. Still, as they reached the car, she couldn't prevent her gaze from sweeping the cemetery once more. Gavin was gone. She told herself she was relieved. He was the last person she wanted to talk with.

Was his presence the reason she couldn't shake the uneasy feeling that something bad was about to happen?

"YOU *WILL* HELP ME," Martin Pepperton snarled. The horse at his back danced several steps sideways and snorted, reacting to his angry tone.

Nolan backed to the stall opening to give the large animal more space. He shot a quick glance around the empty barn, feeling dangerously exposed.

"This is no place for this discussion," he told Martin, noting the too-wide pupils and the man's sagging jowls. Martin Pepperton was Nolan's age, but at twenty-nine, Martin was not aging with grace. The youngest member of the illustrious Pepperton family was beginning to show the effects of his years of substance abuse.

Martin sneered. "What's the matter, Nolan? Afraid of a little horse? Panteena won't hurt you. Will you, girl? You should put some money on her next time she runs."

The high-strung animal stomped its hoof, jerking hard on the lead Martin held. Nolan had a strong urge to walk away and not look back. It was unfortunate that he was still tied to Martin with bonds only death would sever.

"I've got to get back to my group," he told Martin. "The answer is no."

"Remember old man Wickert?"

Nolan glanced wildly around again to make sure the barn was still empty. "Shut up, Martin. That was a long time ago, and it was an accident. The old man wasn't supposed to die."

"Think the police will care?"

"What's wrong with you? Even your drug-soaked brain ought to know if one of us goes down for that, all three of us go down."

Stepping away from the horse, Martin scowled at him. "You want a bigger cut, is that it?"

Nolan swore. "I don't want your money," Nolan told him, seriously worried now. Martin was crazy—and dangerous. More dangerous than Nolan had realized.

Martin took a menacing step forward, startling the horse

into almost rearing. He yanked hard on the beast's halter. The animal kicked out and whinnied in protest.

"I've already transferred ownership of Sunset Pride to you. Except, of course, the horse isn't really Sunset Pride," he said with a vicious chortle. "Anyhow, I need you to front for me on this deal."

"Why the hell did you put that nag in my name? I told you on the phone that I didn't want any part of your scheme."

"My family's been part of the racing circuit here at Saratoga Springs since the early 1900s. That bastard made a fool of me when he sold me that worthless colt. But I'll show him. I have a reputation to protect."

"What about my reputation?"

"You aren't in racing," Martin scoffed.

"Exactly. No one's going to believe I bought a racehorse. Why would I? I don't even like the blasted animals."

"Businessmen buy racehorses all the time. They're investments, a simple business transaction. All you need to say is that you bought the horse and now you need the cash for something else. The paperwork on this deal won't be challenged. Until they run a DNA sample, no one can prove a thing. And they won't. Why should they? Besides, no one will be surprised that someone outside the racing world was fooled into buying a worthless horse. The only one who will look like a fool is Tyrone Briggs."

Nolan shook his head. "No way, Martin. I told you, the risk is too high. I want no part in selling Briggs or anyone else a worthless horse. They're going to trace it right back to you anyhow. You aren't thinking clear."

Martin's face underwent a dark change. "I'm thinking just fine," he snarled. "You're the one who isn't thinking. I need you to do this for me. You act as owner on this sale or, so help me, I tip the cops about what really happened seven years ago."

Fear sent Nolan's pulse racing. His friend wasn't bluffing.

''Will you listen to yourself? You're so high you're acting nuts, Martin.'' A trickle of sweat started down his forehead.

When a gun appeared in Martin's hand, Nolan's mouth went dry. Martin had become unpredictable at the best of times, but now, as Martin's generally florid cheeks flushed a brilliant shade of red, Nolan knew real fear. The bastard was just crazy enough to pull the trigger.

''Don't be a fool, Martin. The minute you fire a gun in here, people will come running.''

''Maybe I don't care.''

His eyes glittered with a drug-induced sheen. Nolan had no doubt Martin was high enough to pull the damn trigger and worry about the consequences later.

''You don't need this kind of petty vengeance,'' Nolan said in an effort to placate him.

''The guy screwed with me. He's going to pay. No one's going to make me look like a laughingstock. By the time Briggs learns the horse is worthless, he's the one people are going to laugh at.''

Reason wasn't going to work. The drug was in charge. Nolan took a half step forward into the cramped stall and tried not to look at the nervous animal shifting restlessly.

''Okay, okay. If it's that important to you I'll make the call.''

Martin grinned. Sensing victory, he lowered the gun. Nolan sprang forward. Panteena squealed and kicked the wood sharply as the men came together, struggling for possession of the weapon. The gun discharged, muffled by the press of their bodies.

Nolan wrenched it free. For a second, Martin stood there with a blank look of surprise on his face. Then he folded with a groan. That was too much for the frightened animal.

The horse reared with a loud shriek of protest. Nolan jumped back just in time. The wicked hooves came down with deadly accuracy. He heard the crunch of bone even as he hurried out of the stall and closed the gate.

He didn't waste time fooling with the lock as Panteena reared again. In a maddened effort to escape, the horse put all fifteen hundred pounds behind the blows it inflicted on the mangled form at its feet. Nolan ran toward the opening at the far end of the barn and heard the splintering sound of hooves against wood.

Any second now, the horse would hit the gate and be free. That was fine with him. At least he wouldn't have to worry about Martin Pepperton again. No way could he have survived those hooves. A quick glance over his shoulder nearly stopped Nolan's heart cold.

A woman stood framed in the opening at the opposite end of the barn, looking right at him. She turned away quickly and at that moment, the horse kicked open the unlatched gate and erupted from its stall. With a sinking feeling, Nolan began to run.

She must have recognized him. He hadn't changed that much in the last few years. And he realized Martin's gun was still clenched in his fist.

Nolan shoved the weapon in the belt under his jacket and altered his course. He needed to establish an alibi—fast. There was a chance the cops wouldn't listen to the bitch, especially if he could produce a solid alibi.

Hell. Maybe he'd get lucky. Maybe the horse would run her down and kill her too, saving him the effort.

LEIGH STEPPED from the beauty shop and swung her hair experimentally. Her head felt several pounds lighter. The sensation was strange. She couldn't ever remember having short hair, but she liked the feeling. And as a bonus, all those long, golden-brown strands were going to be put to good use. The beautician had suggested donating her hair to a local group that made wigs for people undergoing chemotherapy. She'd been only too happy to agree.

All in all, she felt pretty good as she walked down the street to meet her sister at Rosencroft and Associates. The lawyer's office had called Hayley right after Marcus's funeral. Eden had announced her intention to attend the meeting and Hayley hadn't argued.

"Let Mr. Rosencroft explain that she has no authority at Heartskeep anymore. It isn't worth an argument."

Leigh agreed. She'd never understood the relationship between Eden and Marcus, any more than she'd understood the relationship between Marcus and her mother. There had been no affection between any of them. Yet Marcus had married both women.

She shook off the perplexing thought and looked down the street, relieved to see that Eden had brought Jacob with her this afternoon. His presence might have a calming effect on the high-strung woman. The two were waiting on the sidewalk outside the narrow brick building that housed the lawyer's office.

"Hi, Jacob," she greeted. "Eden."

Jacob turned, his boyishly handsome face breaking into a wide smile. "Hey, Hayley! Where's your shadow?"

Though he'd grown up with them, Jacob still couldn't tell Leigh from her sister. Leigh was used to it, so she offered him a cheeky grin.

"Wrong as usual. Here comes Hayley and Bram."

The couple had taken a walk through the town of Stony Ridge while Leigh was having her hair cut. Now they strolled up, hand in hand. Jacob groaned.

"You cut your hair too? I could finally tell you two apart."

Eden sniffed imperiously, patting at her stiff, bleached blond hair. "I'm going inside, out of this heat." Without waiting for a response, she reached for the door handle. Jacob rolled his eyes behind her back, but hurried to hold the door for his mother.

Leigh smiled. Everyone liked Jacob. Even Bram, who'd been understandably territorial when they first met, had come to terms with the younger man after Jacob took a bullet while trying to protect Hayley. Leigh still found it hard to believe Jacob had actually proposed to her sister, but Hayley was convinced Jacob had done so to protect her from Bram.

Jacob had taken on the role of unofficial older brother to them right from the start. Eden had worked as their father's nurse and assistant since before they were born, so Jacob had spent a lot of time at the estate when they were growing up, especially during the summer and school breaks.

Initially, Jacob and Eden had viewed Bram as a fortune hunter. To protect Hayley, Jacob had asked her to marry him. This made perfect sense to Hayley and Leigh, but Leigh still wasn't sure Bram understood. The truce between the two men still seemed a bit uneasy to her.

Inside the brick building they discovered someone had gone to great lengths to give the law office a cozy appearance. Comfortable chairs and a coffeepot with a tray of cookies beckoned visitors to relax while they waited. As usual, Eden wasn't interested in relaxing. She strode up to the receptionist as if she hadn't a second to wait. Hayley shook her head at the maneuver and winked at Leigh.

"So what do you think of the shorter style?" Hayley asked, sotto voce, ignoring the woman.

Leigh swung her head and grinned back. "I love it."

"Me too. I'm not sure Bram's thrilled though."

"Hey, I told you I liked it," he protested.

"Uh-huh. You also told me you loved my hair long."

"And I did." His eyes took on a smoky look. "It wouldn't matter to me if you were bald."

Oh, yeah, he was a goner, all right, Leigh thought happily. Hayley had picked her mate with the same single-minded determination that she used on everything else in her life. Leigh wished she shared a bit more of her sister's assertiveness. She was tired of being known as the quiet twin. On the other hand, her one attempt at being bold and daring had led to an unmitigated disaster, and that was one lesson she would never forget.

"Yo, Leigh, wake up," Hayley said, giving her a nudge.

The receptionist was ushering them down a short hall to an open door. Bram stepped back, letting Hayley, then Leigh, precede him into the room past the cheerful receptionist.

Leigh came to a dead stop one step inside the room. Bram bumped into her, but Leigh barely noticed. She only had eyes for the man standing behind the desk.

"Hello, Leigh."

Gavin Jarret's gravelly low voice sent her heart rate tap-dancing. She'd barely been able to stop thinking about him since that glimpse across the cemetery, but he was the last person she'd expected to see in here.

"Don't tell me you're in trouble again?" she blurted out.

The corners of his mouth lifted slightly. "I'm on the other side of the desk now. You did tell me to make something of myself, remember?"

Heat flamed her cheeks. He *was* standing behind the gleaming walnut desk, dressed in a dark conservative suit instead of jeans. His thick, wavy hair had been cropped into a stylish business cut, though that didn't stop a few of the unruly strands from straying toward his forehead.

"You're a lawyer?"

His lips slanted wryly. "Sometimes I have trouble believing it myself."

A lawyer. The word didn't make sense. Though he dressed like a lawyer, the bad boy of the county still lingered in his relaxed, confident pose. And as those restless eyes skimmed over her, they still seemed to have the power to penetrate beneath the surface and read her very thoughts.

"Leigh?"

Her sister had moved to her side protectively. Aware of the sudden undercurrent, Bram also took a protective step forward on the other side of her. Wry humor sparked in Gavin's eyes at her unexpected buffer. While touched by their concern, Leigh didn't need anyone to protect her from Gavin. Not anymore.

"Why don't you all have a seat?" Gavin invited.

"Really, Leigh, pay attention. Didn't you just hear that girl tell us Mr. Rosencroft died last week?" Eden demanded.

Leigh blinked. Every eye focused on Marcus's widow. Eden had usurped the chair front and center of the desk and was staring at Leigh with obvious impatience.

"No, actually, I didn't," she told Eden quietly.

"Well, sit down. I have things to do today. You and Mr. Jarret can have your personal discussion after we conclude this meeting."

Gavin's silence spoke louder than words. He regarded Eden as if she was an unpleasant curiosity. Which wasn't far off the mark, unfortunately. Leigh had never cared for Eden, and the antipathy was mutual. In the past, Eden had been careful not to let her aversion show when other people were around.

At Gavin's silence, the woman's sharp expression faltered a bit. Jacob shifted uncomfortably at her side. After a long pause, Gavin turned to Hayley.

"Ms. Thomas, if—"

"I think formality is a bit pretentious under the circumstances, don't you? I'm still Hayley," she told him.

Gavin inclined his head. "If you'll all take seats we'll see if we can't hurry Mrs. Thomas on her way."

The gibe was so deftly accomplished, Eden didn't catch on. Jacob's puzzled expression turned speculative. His gaze went from Leigh to Gavin and back again. If he didn't already know about their brief moment of notoriety, someone in town would undoubtedly fill him in as soon as he asked a question.

Hayley was still in her protective mode, so Leigh mustered what she hoped was a reassuring smile. The sight of Gavin might be doing crazy things to her insides, but she could handle the situation. Especially since Gavin was no longer looking directly at her.

She claimed the seat farthest from his desk and reminded herself that she was no longer seventeen. On the outside, at least, she would appear cool and sophisticated and ready to handle whatever came her way. She was very glad she'd had her hair cut before coming in here today.

Gavin began passing out paper folders. When he came to her, Leigh even managed an impersonal smile. Was that a hint of admiration she glimpsed in his eyes, or amusement at her pretense? He returned to his desk before she could be sure.

"Mr. Rosencroft had been ill for some time preceding his death. For the past several months, I've been the only associate in Rosencroft and Associates. I'm familiar with the estate and the various wills involved and am fully prepared to administer the estate, but you may, of course, wish to petition the court to assign the function to someone else. If you wish to do so, I'll understand."

Leigh held his gaze without blinking. No one said a word.

"The packets I just handed each of you contain copies of the agreement set forth between your grandfather, Denison Barkley Hart, and this firm. There is a copy of his will as well as a copy of the one we have on file from your mother, Amy Lynn Hart Thomas."

"What about Marcus?" Eden demanded sharply.

"I've included that as well. However, it is a very old will and it might be a good idea to be certain he didn't have another will drawn up somewhere else that might supersede this one."

"Ridiculous. This was the family firm."

But Marcus had never been part of the family in any real sense. Leigh looked to where Eden sat stiffly in the soft leather chair.

"I'm sorry, Mrs. Thomas. I checked our records thoroughly. This is the most recent will we have on file for him."

Eden leaned forward. "Let's get something clear right now, Mr. Jarret, this is a community-property state and I'm not going to be done out of what's mine. My husband was married to Amy Hart for more than twenty years and he didn't divorce her until after she disappeared. He's entitled to half her estate because they were married when she disappeared."

"Mrs. Thomas—"

"I intend to contest Amy's will if you attempt to cut me out of what's mine," she continued angrily.

"That's certainly your right, Mrs. Thomas. But I will tell you that these wills were set up to withstand just such a challenge. If you'll look—"

Her expression turned sly. "I doubt Amy's will allowed for the fact that she wasn't in her right mind."

Hayley leaped to her feet. "How dare you!"

"I mean no disrespect, Hayley," Eden lied, "but everyone knows your mother was devastated by her father's death. Even the police think that's why she disappeared in New York City. She was too upset to be as careful as she should have been."

Bram laid a hand on Hayley's arm as Gavin's rough voice swung every eye in his direction.

''Amy Thomas's mental health makes no difference to the Heartskeep estate.''

''Of course it does. As her husband, Marcus was entitled to at least half of her estate.''

''Before we dispute that, let me explain that Amy Thomas's estate did not include Heartskeep,'' Gavin said smoothly.

Eden paled. ''What are you talking about?''

''Mother, if you'd be quiet and listen for five minutes, we'd all know,'' Jacob burst out.

Eden gaped at her son, as surprised as the rest of them by his uncharacteristic outburst. Bram tugged Hayley back down in her seat and kept a firm grip on her arm.

''Prior to his death, Dennison Hart was under a doctor's care,'' Gavin told them. ''A sworn statement is included attesting to his mental state at the time this will was signed and witnessed. The conditions and bequests set out are quite explicit. Amy Hart Thomas was disinherited the day she married Marcus Thomas.''

''That can't be!''

''I'm afraid it is, Mrs. Thomas. That clause was never revoked, even though Mr. Hart's will was revised several times since the original will was drawn up. Amy was to have a generous allowance for as long as she lived. Heartskeep and its grounds were left in their entirety to Amy's firstborn child, in this case, Hayley Hart Thomas.''

''This is outrageous!'' Eden jumped to her feet. Her plump, stubby fingers curled into tight fists of anger. ''My lawyer will be looking into this.''

''Of course, that's certainly your right. I was going to advise you to seek legal counsel of your own. My card is enclosed,'' Gavin said calmly. ''Have your attorney call me with any questions.''

''Mother, sit down and let the man finish,'' Jacob told her.

She rounded on her son, her face bright crimson. ''I know collusion when I hear it,'' she snapped. ''They won't get away with this.''

Eden stormed from the room, clutching the packet to her chest. Jacob rose as well, looking acutely embarrassed. ''I'm sorry.''

''You don't have anything to apologize for, Jacob,'' Hayley told him.

''Thanks. I'd better go see to her.''

There was a moment of silence as he left, closing the door with a soft snick.

''I was under the impression that the terms of your grandfather's will were general knowledge,'' Gavin said.

''I thought so, too,'' Hayley responded. ''Mom and Grandpa told us a long time ago how the estate would be handled. Marcus knew. I know he did.''

''I guess he forgot to mention it to Eden,'' Leigh said.

Gavin held her gaze. She felt a moment of vertigo as her stomach muscles contracted.

''According to Mr. Rosencroft, it was Dennison Hart's wish to keep Heartskeep intact within his family. He went to considerable lengths to set up trusts to ensure that the estate would be protected.''

''From Marcus?'' Hayley asked.

Gavin shifted in his chair. When he spoke, his tone was deceptively mild.

''From anyone who might seek to take it away. Ira said you'd understand your grandfather's misgivings.''

''Absolutely,'' Hayley agreed bitterly. ''What I've never understood is why Mom married Marcus in the first place. What happens if I decline to accept the estate?''

Leigh gasped. Even Bram looked startled.

''What are you saying?'' Leigh demanded.

Bram gripped Hayley by the shoulders, forcing her to look at him. ''Don't do this, Hayley. Not because of me.''

Leigh knew that Hayley's wealth and Bram's lack of money had been an issue for Bram from the start. Given her sister's nature, she should have expected something like this.

"That's not it, Bram. Honest. I *want* Leigh to have the house. I don't even like the place anymore." She shuddered. "And not just because of what happened." Hayley looked at Leigh. "It stopped being home for me the day Mom disappeared. I can't see myself ever living there again. Look, I'd hate to see it fall into any further disrepair, but if you refuse to take it on, that's probably exactly what will happen."

"But no pressure, right?" Leigh asked. "What makes you think I want that albatross?"

Gavin leaned back in his chair and regarded them. "Well, this is something Ira and Dennison didn't foresee. Are you sure about this, Hayley?"

"Positive."

"Leigh?" he asked.

"I...don't know. I never gave any thought to owning Heartskeep. Mom always said it would belong to Hayley one day. That was fine with me. I mean, what am I going to do with a place that size?"

"Well, for one thing," Hayley said, "since Eden already hired R. J. Monroe and his crew to repair the fire damage, I think we should have him tear down those walls upstairs and put the house back the way it was designed."

"Hold on a minute," Gavin interrupted. "Let me be sure I understand your position, Hayley. You definitely want to decline your inheritance?"

"As far as the house and grounds, absolutely. I lost any affinity for the place after being trapped inside Marcus's office area while the house was burning down around us."

Bram squeezed her fingers and Leigh shut her eyes,

thinking how close her sister had come to dying for the sins of their father.

''Leigh?'' Gavin asked.

She opened her eyes and looked at Hayley. ''You could have warned me you were going to do this,'' she chided. ''I don't want the place, either.''

''Then we'll give it to charity.''

''That would be fine with me, but Grandpa would be crushed if he knew.''

''He's dead. But you're right,'' Hayley agreed reluctantly. ''He loved Heartskeep.''

Leigh realized that Bram would never feel comfortable if Hayley accepted the house. More than likely, he'd never ask her to marry him. Her wealth was bad enough, but Bram would hate living at Heartskeep. He'd made no secret of his feelings where the estate was concerned.

''I'll tell you what,'' Leigh told her sister. ''I'll accept Heartskeep as long as I can hold it for *your* firstborn child.''

''Deal!'' Hayley turned to Bram in obvious relief. ''And while I love the fence and gate you made, I want those bars off our windows and our stone lions put back. Right, sis?''

''I'm having them repaired as we sit here,'' Bram told her.

''Lions?'' Gavin asked Leigh.

''Two big stone lions used to sit on brick columns where Marcus had Bram put the wrought-iron gate.''

''I remember now,'' Gavin said. ''You seem to have some definite ideas about what you want done with the estate, Hayley. Are you certain you don't want it? Nothing says you have to live there.''

''Good, because you couldn't pay me to live there again. I really don't want the estate, Gavin. I don't want the responsibility.''

''Leigh?''

"My mother loved Heartskeep as much as my grandfather did, so I'll take care of it for them."

"Thanks, sis."

Gavin frowned. "Then I'm afraid we're going to have to have you accept the property, Hayley, then sign it over to your sister. You'll get a terrific tax break, but she'll have to pay."

"Thanks a lot."

"I'll cover the taxes," Hayley promised.

"I'll have to draw up some new papers and get back to you on this."

"Great! I feel a million pounds lighter already," Hayley beamed.

Which explained why *she* felt a million pounds heavier, Leigh mused.

"Ah, sorry, but I'm afraid we aren't quite finished yet," Gavin told them.

"Marcus's will," Hayley said.

"That, too. We can dispense with your part of that pretty quickly. The will on file is dated nearly fifteen years ago. You were both mentioned by name," Gavin told them. "The language is a bit, uh, strong, but the gist is that you didn't need his money so you weren't to get a cent from his estate. He left everything he had to Eden Voxx."

Leigh sat back in relief.

"Good!" Hayley said. "That should make her happy."

"I gather that won't be a problem, then?" Gavin asked.

"Not with us," Hayley assured him, looking to Leigh for confirmation.

She nodded at both of them.

"Then we can dispense with that part of this meeting. If you have any questions after you've looked over his will, feel free to call me. Ira wanted to meet with you on another issue completely."

Gavin's expression turned grave. He laid his palms flat on the desk and made eye contact with them.

"You know that Marcus was in charge of caring for Heartskeep under Ira's supervision. What you may not know is that Ira was confined to a wheelchair for the past two and a half years. He didn't get around much before that, either."

"I know," Hayley told him. "And Marcus never bothered to take care of the grounds or the buildings."

"No," Gavin agreed, "He didn't. But he did bill the estate for hundreds of thousands of dollars in repairs that were never made."

"What?" Hayley demanded.

"Copies of the receipts are in your packets. Eden's doesn't contain this information. I was going to ask her to stay while I told you about this privately, first, but..." He shrugged.

"Marcus bilked the estate?" Hayley asked.

"Ira transferred several hundred thousand dollars into an account managed by Marcus shortly after your mother disappeared. He signed off on all the bills presented to him without sending anyone out to make sure the work was actually done. It wasn't until I happened to drive past the entrance to the estate one day that I realized something was wrong. We had just paid Marcus a fortune for a completely new driveway that had never been installed."

"You can say that again," Hayley told him with asperity.

He held up a sheaf of papers. "I suspect all of these bills are phony. Some of these companies don't exist except on paper."

Leigh looked at the photocopy in her folder and nodded. "Computer generated?"

"That's my guess. As near as I can tell without an audit,

your estate has been defrauded of over six hundred fifty thousand dollars.''

Hayley gaped at him. Bram, sitting silently beside her, covered her hand.

Gavin's eyes, which always seemed to see so much more than they should, pinned Leigh where she sat.

''You and I will need to work closely together. Will you be all right with that?''

Her heartbeat gave a little stutter. She lifted her chin and met his gaze. ''Of course. Will you?''

Chapter Three

Heartskeep rose defiantly against the sky. Leigh stared at the sprawling, once-elegant mansion and wondered what had become of the welcoming warmth the house had once projected. She suspected it had disappeared the same day as her mother.

Workmen were gutting the fire-damaged wing and all manner of trucks and equipment filled the turnaround out front. Leigh drove around to the back. She'd have to find R.J. As the supervisor, he needed to move repairs to the long, tree-shrouded driveway up on the list of priorities. The ruts had been bad enough before trucks had started lumbering over it. Now the ruts were beginning to resemble craters, making for a seriously bone-jarring ride.

R.J. was a couple years younger than Gavin, and was another of their neighbors' foster sons. Leigh vaguely remembered him as a quiet loner in his teens. Tall and dark haired like Gavin, he was leaner, but just as good-looking. He'd been orphaned young and, after being abused by a series of foster parents, had become a serious disciplinary problem. Fortunately for him, like Gavin, he'd ended up under the caring supervision of George and Emily Walken. The couple had accepted and encouraged his need to work with his hands. Leigh was glad Eden had hired his fledging firm to take on the renovations, even if she'd done so for expediency and not out of any altruistic desire to help a neighbor.

Parking behind the house, Leigh stepped from the car and paused to stare up at the house. The sinister feel was even stronger back here. The bars Bram had installed over the windows didn't improve things any. Leigh couldn't wait for him to take them all down. Her sister owed her big-time for taking on this albatross.

Gavin had spent more than an hour going over the details and the money with them yesterday. He'd kept the discussion on a professional level the entire time, but Leigh had been aware of him every minute.

The myriad fictitious bills showed all sorts of major repairs that hadn't been made—and most were desperately needed. Restoring the house inside and out was going to demand an enormous amount of time and money. Leigh didn't mind spending either one, but she had a degree in telecommunications and one in computer science. Neither one would do her much good out here in horse country, but she'd called this morning and turned down the exciting new job she'd been offered in Boston because she realized the renovations were going to require a lot of time and thought. Leigh needed to be here—at least part of the time, so what was going to happen to their Boston apartment? She couldn't see her sister moving back there without Bram any more than she could see Bram moving to an apartment in Boston.

Fretting, Leigh turned away from the house and headed for the peace of the garden maze. Gavin wasn't due to meet her here for another twenty minutes or so and she wanted that time alone to think. Since yesterday, she'd been telling Hayley and the Walkens that she wasn't the least bit concerned to find herself working so closely with Gavin. What had happened between them had been a long time ago and was unimportant now. She could deal with the situation like a mature adult.

An entire year, working closely with Gavin.

Why did he still have to look so incredibly good? Each time she met those penetrating eyes of his, her control slipped a notch and she had to struggle to surface from their compelling force. Flashbacks of that long-ago night kept her so on edge, it was hard to concentrate on anything else when she was around him. And what kept her awake late into the night was the certainty that Gavin hadn't forgotten a thing any more than she had. She was almost certain she'd seen more than a flicker of masculine approval when he'd first looked at her in his office.

Right. Thinking that Gavin still had the hots for her was certainly dealing with the situation like a mature adult.

Leigh stumbled over a vine that had inched its way onto the path. Yanked from her troubled thoughts, she gazed around in dismay. The gardens were an even bigger mess than the house.

At one time, there had been three distinct mazes. Her grandfather had kept them trimmed to waist height to show off the ornamental trees and topiary animals sprinkled about. Dead ends had culminated in large circles with inviting benches, shade and ornamental trees, and a profusion of flowers. The water fountain and underground sprinkler system had been carefully planned before their grandfather's death. Both had been installed the week her mother had disappeared.

The mazes had been a showplace, yet despite obnoxious bills to the contrary, no work had been done on them since the fountain was completed. The bushes that composed the walls now towered a good six feet or more. In several places, they'd overgrown the paths, uniting the mazes in a vast labyrinth. Most of the topiaries were unrecognizable, and the flowers were either gone or had been replaced by the roses Marcus had become so fond of tending.

Still, Leigh could almost sense her mother's presence here among her gardens, as she'd called the mazes. Leigh half expected to round a curve and see Amy Thomas in her wide-brimmed sun hat, tending some flowers. She'd be distraught if she could see their present condition. Hiring a landscaper had just moved to the top of Leigh's to-do list.

A squirrel suddenly skittered in front of her, racing away as if in mortal danger. Leigh realized she'd wandered down a dead-end trail by mistake. She turned to go back, when she heard the distinct crunch of footsteps approaching. A large shape abruptly blocked her path.

"Hello, Leigh."

For a minute, she couldn't place the vaguely familiar face. Then he smiled without humor.

"Nolan?"

Nolan Ducort III was the last person she had expected to see here, of all places. His blond good looks were dissipating right along with his hairline. His once-firm jaw had softened and rounded thanks to the thirty pounds or more he'd put on since she'd last seen him. Only his eyes were the same. Cold, and unnaturally blue thanks to contact lenses, they stared at her in a way that made her shiver despite the mid-June heat wave.

"Cat got your tongue?"

"You startled me," she said warily. She was suddenly conscious of how quiet the maze had become. "I'm... surprised to see you here."

He swaggered closer. Leigh took an involuntary step back. Instantly, she knew she'd made a mistake. His eyes glittered in triumph at the small show of weakness, and she found herself inside one of the dead-end circles.

"We have some unfinished business, you and I."

Her stomach twisted in sudden fear. Surely Nolan didn't mean to attack her. Not now. Not here in her own backyard.

She drew in a steadying breath, tossed her head and raised her chin as she'd seen Hayley do many times before when confronting an annoying person. Hayley was much better at handling the male of the species, but Leigh had learned a thing or two since her last meeting with Nolan.

Imitating her sister's best haughty glare, she forced herself to look him up and down coldly, taking extra seconds to stare at the paunch that had started to bulge above his belt buckle. Color swarmed up his neck.

Satisfied that the pounds he'd gained would slow him down once she got past him, Leigh managed a sneer. "Get lost, Nolan. Unless you'd like to start doing your *business* from the inside of a jail cell."

A flicker of surprise came and went. His features hardened. She had to work to keep her own expression from revealing her core of fear.

"We both know you aren't going to go to the cops or you'd have done it by now."

He was right, of course. They both knew what he'd tried to do that night, and they both knew there was no way to prove a thing.

"So, what *were* you doing at Saratoga the other day?"

The question came out of nowhere and made absolutely no sense.

"Saratoga?" There was a disturbing intensity behind his cold, penetrating stare. "I haven't been to Saratoga in years."

"Going to try and pretend it was Hayley?"

Leigh had no idea what he was talking about. She didn't care. All she wanted was for him to move away from the opening so she could escape.

"Go away, Nolan."

He tilted his head. A quiver skittered straight down her

spine at the fury in his steely blue eyes. Despite her intention not to show any fear, Leigh looked away.

"Now you've made me curious, Leigh," he said with chilling softness. "I wonder exactly what it is you're trying to hide?"

What was he talking about? She started to protest and stopped. Arguing was pointless. It didn't matter what he was talking about. Escape was all that mattered.

"Get lost, Nolan. I mean it. You don't have any business here."

"Now, that's where you're wrong," he said, sounding pleased. "We're doing business together right this very minute."

His evil smile sent her pulse racing.

"Didn't you know? I have an interest in R.J.'s construction company."

While his voice leered, his expression did not. Cold and calculating, he seemed intent on deliberately baiting her.

"I've got an interest in any number of local businesses," he continued when she remained silent. "In fact, it looks to me like you could use the services of my landscape company." He waved a flaccid hand toward the overgrown hedges.

"Not even if they are the only ones in town. I'm not afraid of you," she lied boldly. "I know exactly what you did."

His eyes gleamed, murderous shards of blue. Her fingernails bit into the palms of her hands.

"Why don't you call the cops then?" he demanded. "Let's see which one of us they believe."

"I know all about your family's political pull, Nolan. I don't care if your father and Chief Crossley are old friends. And I don't care how many other politicians he's bought. Do you really believe you're invincible? Even you must realize you can't buy your way out of everything."

Fury brought him a step closer. She held her ground by sheer force of will.

''Don't try to play games with me, Leigh. You're out of your league.''

''Get out of here.''

''We aren't finished yet. Don't think I forgot how you made me look like a fool seven years ago.''

''Oh, please. You didn't need any help from me.''

She hadn't meant to say it out loud and she knew immediately that she'd gone too far. Nolan reached for her. Even as she dodged away, Gavin's distinctive voice whipped through the clearing.

''I thought you understood what would happen if you ever touched her again, Ducort.''

Nolan pivoted in shock. ''Jarret?''

Leigh exhaled in relief. The cavalry had arrived.

''Maybe you need a reminder,'' Gavin added, his voice dangerously soft.

There was no swaggering bravado in the way he stepped forward. He wasn't as big as Nolan, yet he appeared larger and far more intimidating. He seemed to glide into the clearing, dominating the space with easy assurance. Faded jeans and an open-necked shirt accentuated his tough, lean build. His hands swung loose at his sides, yet his casual air was far more daunting than any cocky pose.

Nolan wasn't stupid. If it came to physical blows between the spoiled rich kid running to fat and the lean, once street-savvy bad boy of the county, there was little doubt of the outcome. Gavin would take him apart without even working up a sweat.

''I warned you once before. You should have listened. I never make idle threats, Ducort.''

Despite his casual tone, a lethal, raw energy flowed from Gavin. Nolan began backing away. He stopped when the back of his knees came up against the concrete bench that sat under the large maple tree.

Leigh was frightened by the leashed power she sensed so clearly in both men. Nolan's cheeks deepened to a dark cherry red. He shot her a look of pure malice.

"If your pet goon lays a hand on me, I'll sue you for every cent you inherited."

Despite her shock and fear, she wanted to laugh at his posturing. "Pet goon?"

"I think he means me," Gavin said without a trace of humor. "Since you plan to sue her, Ducort, I'll give you one of my cards. I'm also her attorney."

Gavin made no attempt to reach for his pocket. Nolan's gaze darted from one to the other. His anger was as tangible as the waiting silence that had settled over the clearing. He settled for glaring at Leigh.

"I don't know what your game is, bitch, but nobody screws with me."

"I can understand that," she muttered.

Raw fury started him in her direction. Gavin moved so fast Leigh didn't have time to do more than gasp. The lawyer vanished in one beat of her heart, replaced by the street warrior Gavin had once been. He grabbed Nolan by his tailored, white linen shirtfront and spun him to one side, shoving him hard against the prickly, overgrown hedge.

"That's going to cost you," he promised.

Nolan squealed. A shadow speared the entrance to the clearing. Bram Myers stood framed in the opening. He was dressed all in black, from his sleeveless T-shirt to a stained pair of jeans. He appeared completely relaxed as he stood there blocking the only exit. Leigh would have thought him totally unconcerned if she hadn't seen the expression in his midnight eyes.

"Problem, Gavin?" he asked lightly.

Gavin kept his gaze riveted on Nolan. He released the

shirt with deliberate slowness before stepping back. ''No problem. I was explaining some basic facts to Mr. Ducort.''

''I'll have you on charges for assault and battery,'' Nolan threatened. He straightened his shirt with unsteady fingers and shot Leigh a look that made her stomach contract.

''Now, what assault would that be?'' Bram asked quietly. ''You look pretty good for someone who's been battered.''

Nolan sent him a look of impotent rage. ''You'll pay,'' he sputtered. ''You'll all pay,''

''Ah. Now *that* sounded like a threat,'' Bram said.

''The only one who's going to do any paying around here is you, Ducort.''

As if he, too, worried Gavin might lose control, Bram stepped all the way into the circle. Leigh spoke quickly, hoping to diffuse some of the surging testosterone before someone got seriously hurt.

''Nolan was just leaving,'' she said. ''Weren't you, Nolan?''

''Then why don't I escort you to your car, Mr.…Ducort, was it?'' Bram said. ''I wouldn't want you to trip and fall or anything on your way out. I think you've overstayed your welcome at Heartskeep.''

For a moment, Leigh thought Nolan would explode from the fury so plainly visible on his ruddy face. Without a word, he pushed past both men and stormed down the path, never once looking back.

Bram and Gavin shared a silent exchange. Bram nodded and turned to follow Nolan. Gavin focused his attention on her. Leigh only hoped the quaking turning her muscles to jelly wasn't visible on the outside.

''Did he touch you?'' Gavin demanded.

''N-no.''

Gavin's unwavering scrutiny was chilling. This was a side of him she'd heard about but had never seen. Dark and intense, his anger was slow to fade. Where Nolan had blustered, Gavin projected a hard determination.

Leigh crossed her arms protectively over her stomach. Her knees felt absurdly weak and her stomach was queasy.

"Sit down," he ordered.

The hands that guided her onto the unyielding bench were surprisingly tender. She'd forgotten he had such large hands. They were warm, with the long tapered fingers of a musician. Those hands had once roused her body to incredible heights, but now they soothed, lightly stroking her shoulder. Amazingly, his touch helped to dissipate the chills lifting the hairs on her bare arms.

"I'm all right," she told him.

"I know you are."

The warmth in his tone sent her pulse leaping. She shook her head, telling herself she was imagining things. Gavin wasn't interested in her.

"Do you make a habit of rescuing women in distress?"

His gaze became shuttered. "Not generally, no."

"What did you mean when you said you warned him once before?"

His eyes went flat and hard. "Nothing you need to worry about."

Leigh shook her head. Her mind whirled, slotting the pieces together. The picture that formed shocked her.

"You went after him seven years ago, didn't you? Of course you did. That's why you had cuts and scrapes on your knuckles when they arrested you. That's why the police were so sure you were the one who hit poor Mr. Wickert."

He squeezed her shoulder. "Let it go, Leigh."

"But—"

"You didn't want to press charges against Nolan, remember? You wouldn't even let us report that you'd been drugged."

As if she could ever forget. Memories of that night and what might have happened without Gavin had haunted her for years.

"There was no point. His family has all sorts of influence in this county. You know the police wouldn't have believed us. They would have said you put the drug in my drink."

"I know," he said thoughtfully, releasing her to rub a hand across his chin. "I didn't realize you did."

"Of course I did! We couldn't prove anything. Nolan would have said he handed me the wrong glass, or that someone else had slipped the drug into my soft drink."

But she knew Nolan had deliberately handed her the drugged glass. There'd been something in his smirk, she'd seen it even then. She just hadn't understood.

Leigh knew she'd been lucky. If he'd been able to slip the drug into the beer she'd drunk first, things would have ended very differently that night.

Looking back, she'd take bets that he had asked her and not Hayley to go out with him because Hayley would have taken one look at that party scene and created such a fuss Nolan would have had to take her home. Leigh's stomach still churned at the memory of that awful party and Nolan's group of leering friends.

"You went after Nolan after the Walkens came to get me. You beat him up." She knew she was right.

"I wouldn't phrase it like that," Gavin said, his tone lightening as he rocked back on his heels. "Ducort and I exchanged a few words. One or two blows were traded for emphasis, that's all."

"But—"

His quiet humor faded. "Leigh, Ducort was dangerous then and he's dangerous now. He hides behind his family's money and position. You don't want any part of him."

"You've got that right."

"I'm glad we agree. So, you're going to take the appropriate legal steps to avoid being one of his victims again. I know a judge who'll issue you a temporary restraining order right away with my corroboration."

"Can't we just ignore him?"

Gavin touched her arm again. Her body hummed at the contact. Gavin withdrew his hand, as if he too had sensed the primal current.

"He'll be back, Leigh."

"That's crazy." And frightening.

"No. He's sly and he's rich, and he's used to getting his own way, but he isn't crazy. Keep that in mind. Ducort has investments in a number of local companies—construction, landscaping, real estate... What?"

Beneath that penetrating stare she squirmed. "Nothing."

Gavin's silence demanded an answer.

"He said he has some connection to R.J.'s company."

"I'll talk to R.J."

"Wait!" Leigh reached for him, but stopped just short of physical contact. "I don't want to cause any trouble for R.J."

"We won't."

"It's not R.J.'s fault Nolan is lower than slime."

"An apt description."

She dropped her hand. "A restraining order won't keep him away. You know that."

"Let me worry about that."

"You're a respected lawyer now. You can't just go after him and beat him up anymore."

Amusement softened his features. "Worried about me, or him?"

"Don't be a fool!" Leigh rose to her feet. Gavin didn't step back. The move put her tantalizingly close to him. Close enough to smell his aftershave. The unexpected distraction nearly made her forget what she was going to say.

"Nolan isn't worth the trouble he would cause."

The gray of his eyes turned to silver. Her heart began thumping in a ridiculous fashion. Gavin reached out and cupped her chin. The charge of invisible current was stronger this time and intensely sensual. She was filled with restless energy.

"He'll try to hurt you."

The smile started in his eyes and slowly spread to engulf his face. Her heart stuttered. In all the years she'd known him, she had never once seen Gavin smile like this.

"*Try* being the operative word," he said.

Immediately, she bristled at his complete assurance that he could handle the situation.

"Oh, for pity's sake. You just said Nolan's dangerous. You aren't invincible, you know."

"I'm crushed at your lack of faith." The smile dissolved, but the amusement lingered. "Ducort would try to hurt me if he thought he could, but I think he's just smart enough to know better than to try. He prefers easier prey, Leigh."

"Like me."

"You're the one who got away, remember?"

She trembled, suddenly cold all over. "*We're* the ones who got away."

He reached out as if to touch her, but Bram reappeared.

"Ducort took off down the driveway doing about sixty. With any luck, he'll break an axle on one of the ruts. I told R.J. to call the cops if he comes back."

"R.J. works for him," Leigh protested.

"No, he doesn't," Gavin said. "Ducort may have his loan, but R.J. works for himself." He looked back at Bram. "I'm going to take Leigh into town and initiate a temporary restraining order. It's going to make him mad. We'll need to keep a close eye on Leigh and Hayley."

Leigh inhaled sharply. Bram looked fierce.

"Hayley?"

"I wouldn't bet he can tell them apart—or would care even if he can," Gavin added.

"We should have taken him down," Bram said.

Ruefully, Gavin tipped his head. "Don't think I wasn't tempted. Unfortunately, as an officer of the court, I have to play by the rules."

"He won't," Bram stated.

"I know."

"I'm not under any such restrictions."

"Bram Myers, don't you dare get involved in this!" Leigh admonished. "Nolan has nothing to do with you."

"He does if he's threatening you and Hayley," Bram said. He looked at Gavin, who barely nodded.

Leigh realized that, once again, a conversation was taking place between the two men on a totally nonverbal level. Shaken to the core by the savagery of purpose she sensed in them, she leveled them with a glare.

"What is it with you two? Nothing like a woman in danger to create a bonding moment between two macho males, is that it?"

Bram looked startled. Gavin nearly smiled again.

"She's definitely related to her sister," Bram told him.

"Yes, I am."

Gavin's eyes sparked with humor. "That quiet-twin reputation is all relative, huh?"

Scared and furious, she strode past them and hurried down the path without responding. The men trailed closely behind.

"Interesting tattoo," Gavin said casually. Leigh knew he was referring to the colorful dragon wrapped around Bram's bared upper arm.

"Hayley seems to like it," Bram responded.

To add to her frustration, he sounded equally relaxed.

"I never got around to a tattoo. Never had the money as a kid, or the opportunity as an adult," Gavin told him.

Leigh wanted to scream at them both. Instead, she was relieved to find her sister and Emily pulling up out back. Tersely, she explained what had taken place.

"Why, that miserable, slimy, disgusting piece of pond scum. Someone should neuter him permanently," Hayley ranted.

"Ouch," Gavin said mildly. He raised his eyebrows at Bram.

"I live in fear." The larger man slid an arm around Hayley's shoulders.

"You'd better live in fear," Hayley warned him. "You retired your superhero costume, remember? Stay away from Nolan."

"As long as he stays away from you and Leigh, there's no problem."

"Leigh and I will drive into town and start the legal process now," Gavin announced. "I'll call Judge Armstrong's office from the car to give her a heads up."

NOLAN FUMED as he sped away from the estate. He wasn't afraid of some no-name punk just because he'd gone to law school. Who did Jarret think he was, messing with Nolan Ducort? This was twice now the bastard had stepped in where he didn't belong. He needed to be taught a lesson. A permanent lesson.

Nolan stood on his brakes to avoid hitting the horse trailer that suddenly filled the road ahead of him. He hated horses—loathed and feared the ugly beasts. It would have served the driver right if he'd plowed into the back of the lousy rig.

Anger pulsed through him with every breath. Damn horse people thought they owned the county. His fingers curled around the steering wheel. He thought how much more satisfying it would be to curl them around Jarret's throat. That bastard had gotten in his way for the last time.

Jarret had made him look like a fool in front of his friends seven years ago. Keith Earlwood and Martin Pepperton had been as eager for retribution as Nolan when they'd discovered Jarret had disappeared with their prize all those years ago. After a couple of joints and a few more beers, they'd decided to set Jarret up for a burglary rap that night. Everyone knew the police chief hated the punks the Walkens kept taking in.

It should have been easy. Who could have known old man Wickert would come home early and catch them sneaking around inside his house? Nolan had had no choice. He'd had to hit the old man a couple of times.

They'd all been scared. The remembered taste of fear was one he'd never forget. Especially after he'd learned the old man had gone and died. They hadn't even been able to plant the evidence on Jarret. Keith had been so scared he'd wet himself. They'd wasted hours getting him calmed down.

They'd had to convince him they'd had no choice, and the heart attack hadn't been their fault. The old man would have died pretty soon anyhow. Besides, a murder charge was even better than burglary. While Earlwood fretted, Martin had gone ahead and made the anonymous call about seeing Jarret's bike near the house.

Nolan hadn't expected Jarret to be waiting for him when he finally went home. The bastard had worked him over good. Nolan had barely been able to move for days after that, yet the only marks that had showed outside his clothing were the bruises he'd gotten on his knuckles when he'd hit the old man.

When the cops had pulled Jarret in, he'd told himself it was a small price to pay. Then that little bitch had surprised them all by coming forward to act as Jarret's alibi.

Nolan ground his teeth in remembered frustration. He owed them. Both of them. But first, he had to figure out what sort of game they were playing now. Obviously, Leigh had seen him in the barn with Martin. Why hadn't she pointed the finger at him? He'd set up a solid alibi immediately, expecting her to go straight to the cops. But she hadn't.

Martin's body hadn't even been discovered until some groom found the horse running free. Nolan had waited for the cops to show all weekend. The waiting had left him nervous and edgy. He'd been shocked when they'd finally arrived at his office yesterday afternoon. The dumb bastards hadn't even known he'd been at the track that morning. He couldn't believe they had only come to him for information on Martin's potential enemies—and his drug use.

Quick to seize the opening they'd provided, Nolan had told them everything he knew about both, with suitable sounds of regret. Let them chase down Martin's supplier and nail him for the murder. It was no skin off Nolan's nose. He'd even volunteered the information that he'd been there that morning with a group of business acquaintances, but he'd assured them he hadn't seen Martin there that day. He hadn't talked to his friend in several months. The cops had gone away satisfied, and in part, so was he.

Except that Leigh Thomas had seen him with the gun.

Nolan slowed his speed even further, no longer riding the trailer's bumper on the two-lane road. More than likely, she figured the cops wouldn't pay her much attention if she did tell them what she'd seen. Everyone knew what Police Chief Crossley thought about the Thomas twins, and cops stuck together. The Saratoga police wouldn't listen to her, either.

The important question was, what had Leigh been doing there? It couldn't be coincidence. Martin had been the only owner using that barn, so she must have gone there to see him. Why?

And how was Jarret involved?

Nolan's mind whirled with possibilities. Until a few minutes ago, he hadn't even been certain which twin he'd seen at Saratoga. He'd driven all the way out to Heartskeep on a phony pretext to talk with R.J. that morning, hoping one of the Thomas girls would show. It hadn't been easy to hang around until Leigh had arrived, but then his luck had changed. She'd conveniently wandered out back alone.

He had to admit, she was still a sexy-looking package. She still managed to project that innocent air that made a man itch to teach her a few things. But of far more interest was her business with Martin Pepperton. That was a puzzle he couldn't let go of. Obviously she didn't want the cops to know about her presence in the barn, so there had to be a way to use that to his advantage.

With both her parents dead now, the bitch had plenty of money. No wonder Jarret was sniffing around again.

Nolan's fingers tightened on the steering wheel as he thought about what he'd like to do to Gavin Jarret. He owed that bastard, and Jarret was going to get what was coming to him, no two ways about it. But first, Nolan knew he should try to figure out what sort of deal Martin had had going with Leigh Thomas.

Nolan reached for his cell phone. He wondered if Keith Earlwood was still hard-pressed for cash. The whiny little weasel had been a pain recently, expecting Nolan to bail him out of his newest financial hole. Maybe he could offer to help his old buddy out after all.

Chapter Four

Judge Ellen Armstrong proved to be a stern-faced woman whose demeanor concealed a compassionate side. Watching Gavin in his professional capacity was an eye-opening experience for Leigh. The bad boy of the county had come a long way in seven years. It was obvious the judge liked and respected Gavin.

Still, it was a relief to finally put the ordeal and the courthouse behind her. According to the judge, Nolan would be informed that a hearing was scheduled. Gavin was right, Nolan wasn't going to take the news kindly.

"You did very well in there," Gavin told her as he waited for her to slide back inside his dusty blue sedan.

"Funny, I was thinking the same thing about you."

Gavin's lips turned up as he closed the door and came around the car, sliding into the driver's seat with that careless air of assurance she'd always admired in him. He gripped the wheel and she thought again that he should have been a musician. She could picture him running those fascinating fingers over an ivory keyboard with the same sensitivity he'd displayed running them over her skin.

She really had to stop thinking about things like that. What was wrong with her?

"Are you okay?" he asked as he turned the key in the ignition.

Leigh hoped her fair skin wasn't giving her thoughts away. She'd insisted on changing into a dress before going to the courthouse with him. Now she smoothed down the skirt to give her fingers something to do.

"I'm fine. It's just been a long day. And we never did get around to discussing the problem with the estate."

"Would you like to stop at The Inn for something to eat before we head back?"

There went her pulse rate again. Sternly, she told it to calm down. They knew each other in the biblical sense, but they had never been on a date, and this invitation didn't qualify, either. Did it?

"I missed lunch and I figure we can talk about the situation over a meal. Then we'll run back out to the house for a quick look around before it gets dark. What do you think?"

"All right."

Of course it wasn't a date. It was a business meeting. She had to keep that in mind. Gavin had never been interested in her on a personal level. She wasn't even sure he could tell her apart from her sister.

So what if he was wildly attractive? She knew dozens of attractive men. She'd even dated a few. She was his client. They'd been thrown together by chance.

Again.

She met his gaze and her stomach fluttered. Did he look at all his clients that way? She was imagining things. Yet his satisfied expression when she agreed was disturbingly masculine.

The Inn, they discovered, had been hosting a private party all afternoon. The dining room wasn't available yet to the public. One glance inside the darkly paneled bar revealed that it was already filled to capacity. The Inn was famous for its food, and most of the local people ate there on a regular basis. She wasn't surprised or concerned by the crowd, but as Gavin stood there, something cold lifted the hairs at the back of her neck. Even as she ran a hand over her nape, she realized they were being watched.

Leigh scanned every face. Most of them were familiar. More than a few were people she knew by name. The unpleasant feeling persisted even though no one seemed to be looking at them in particular.

"How do you feel about Italian food?" Gavin asked.

She jerked her face to his. He seemed unaffected by the dread pressing down on her.

"I love Italian food," she said quickly.

"There's a new place in town I think you might like, as long as you don't mind backtracking."

"I don't mind." Anything to get them away from here.

As they doubled back toward town, Leigh tried not to let Gavin catch her watching the road behind them.

"Is something wrong, Leigh?"

Yes. Her nerves were racing along at a good clip and she couldn't seem to steady them. "I'm a little edgy, I guess."

"Does being with me bother you?"

"Of course not!"

He frowned. "Look, I don't want you scared to death of Ducort, I just want you to be careful."

"That's me. Careful."

She debated telling him about the crawly feeling she'd gotten at The Inn's bar, but she didn't want him thinking she jumped at shadows. Bad enough that he thought she was scared of Nolan.

Okay, she was, but she wished he didn't know that she was. Gavin was confusing her. If only she understood men better—but she'd never been very good when it came to relationships.

The aroma that greeted them as soon as they opened the door of the Italian restaurant restored her mood and reminded her that she hadn't had lunch, either. Leigh figured she'd have to add an hour of exercise to work off anything she ate here, but she suspected it would be well worth every calorie.

Though the restaurant was small and new, everyone inside seemed to know Gavin by name.

"I eat out a lot," he explained wryly.

"I gathered."

Their hope for a real conversation was dashed by a boisterous party of teenagers that was seated nearby shortly after they were served.

"Sorry," Gavin said.

"Don't be, this is fabulous pasta."

"The food is good. Mario and Kiki just opened this place. I think they're going to do well."

"Definitely."

The girls seated nearest them were chattering on about a singer who featured heavily in their fantasies. Their male companions were busy pointing out all his faults. Leigh wondered what Gavin would say if he knew he was the one who had figured most often in her fantasies at that age.

"What are you thinking?" he asked.

Startled, she searched for a safe answer. "That I'm glad I'm not that young anymore."

His expression became somber and remote. "Amen."

"Don't," she said sharply.

"Don't what?"

Embarrassed, she gazed quickly down at her plate. "Nothing. Sorry."

"Okay, now I'm intrigued. What did I do that you wanted me to stop?"

Darn it, she always managed to say or do the wrong thing around men she was attracted to. And no matter how much she wanted to deny the truth, she was attracted to Gavin.

"Leigh?"

She shrugged. "For a minute, you had that remote look again."

"Remote?"

When would she learn not to speak her mind? He wasn't going to let the subject go. The darn man was nothing if not tenacious.

"When you worked at the gas station I always thought you had old eyes," she told him, wishing she could just shut up. "You always seemed to be watching everyone while daring the world to see the real you."

Gavin put down his fork.

"I'm sorry," she said quickly. "I shouldn't have said that. Why can't I learn to keep quiet?"

His hand reached out and covered hers before she could withdraw it from the table. There was an immediate connection that infused her with warmth.

"Honesty is nothing to apologize for," he said softly. "I don't know about the old-eyes part, but the rest of your assessment isn't far from the truth. I was pretty unreachable after my parents and my older brother died. I resented everyone I came in contact with. It seems stupid now, but I was angry with my family for dying and leaving me alone—as if it had been their choice."

He released her hand and looked away, but not before she saw the sadness, and the raw core of his vulnerability.

"How did they die?" Gavin had never spoken about his family to anyone as far as she knew. She hadn't even known he'd had an older brother.

"The usual. A car crash. I was thirteen."

"I'm sorry."

"So was I. It's a bad age to lose your family—not that there's a good age."

He rubbed his jaw and picked up his fork again, but made no attempt to use it.

"Most people threw in the towel after dealing with me

for a while. Looking back, I don't blame them. I was sullen, quick to anger and good with my fists. I did what I wanted and resented anyone who tried to tell me what I could and couldn't do."

"A tough guy, huh?"

He didn't smile back.

"I had to be tough. I was a loner. Loners are often viewed as prey. I had to prove otherwise, so I did. I'm not sure why Emily and George took me on, but they were the best thing that could have happened to me. They're special people."

"Yes," she agreed softly. And she understood his anger better than he knew.

"I felt wild and angry after my mother disappeared, too," she admitted. Only, she hadn't picked fights. She'd picked a dangerous man to go out with instead. "Emily and George were there for Hayley and me as well."

Leigh had never felt the pull of his eyes more keenly than she did right then. They shared a moment of unspoken understanding before he released her gaze to resume eating. The silence that fell between them was comfortable this time.

Leigh caught two of the young females at the next table sneaking glances at Gavin and whispering. He might not be a rock star, but their appreciation of him as a male was evident.

"What's the smile for?" Gavin asked.

"Don't look now, but you've picked up a couple of new admirers."

"Are you trying to make me blush?"

"Could I?" The idea intrigued her.

"If anyone could, it would be you."

Humor lurked in his expression. Impishly, she grinned. "You can't fool me. You must be used to feminine attention. Half the girls in town were fascinated by you, even in your wild days.''

He laid his fork across his mostly empty plate. ''Okay. Now you've embarrassed me.''

''Ha. You didn't really think all those girls needed to stop by for gas every day?''

His lips quirked. ''Now that you mention it, I did notice a lot of gas tanks being topped off back then. I just didn't realize it was my looks drawing them in.''

''Now who's teasing?''

''Only a little.'' His expression turned serious. ''I wish I could say I noticed you in particular, Leigh, but—''

''I never was much for flirting,'' she said quickly. ''And I've never liked being part of a crowd. Besides, I was a little young for you to have noticed.''

''Yes,'' he said sadly, ''you were.''

And she knew they were both remembering the night she hadn't been too young for making wild abandoned love on the side of the road.

''If the police had known I seduced a minor that night they would have kept me in jail.''

''You knew?''

He shook his head. ''Not until Emily told me later. She said you and Hayley skipped kindergarten and started first grade a year ahead of the other children your age because you were so intelligent.''

''Not really. It's just that my mother tutored us from an early age,'' Leigh explained. She didn't add that being a year younger than all their classmates had been a social challenge. They'd gone to great pains to conceal their true age in high school. And that led her thoughts right back to the night she and Gavin had made love. It was a memory she still couldn't face, so she was extremely grateful for the waiter's timely interruption.

They decided against any of the temptingly fabulous desserts he suggested and were soon back in Gavin's car, heading for Heartskeep.

"I just remembered something," she said. "Didn't you used to smoke?"

Gavin nodded. "It got to be too expensive. Besides, I decided the habit didn't go with my new image."

"Good."

"I thought you'd approve."

Leigh settled back. They drove several miles in comfortable silence.

"I tried to call you after you saved my butt that day," Gavin said without warning.

Leigh shook her head. She didn't want to talk about those events. She didn't even want to think about them. But his words had created a question that demanded an answer.

"To apologize?"

"No," he said, to her intense relief. "Although I probably would have gotten around to it. Actually, I was steamed by what you'd said to me outside the police station."

She'd told him to grow up, she recalled, mortified.

"At the same time, I couldn't believe you came down to the police station all by yourself and faced down that blustering fool of a police chief."

Leigh stared at his profile. She wished she still had her long hair to play with. She needed something to do with her hands. They were clenched together tightly in her lap.

"You humbled me that morning, Leigh. I didn't like the feeling. And I resented being indebted to you."

"You preferred being a noble martyr?"

He sent her a sharp look and nearly veered off the road. Then he laughed. The deep, rumbly sound was so unexpected it immediately eased the pressure in her chest.

"You do have the most uncanny way of seeing to the

heart of things, don't you? Do you know I became a lawyer because of you?''

''What?''

''It's true. What you said that day nibbled away at me. I'd been going to college with no real goal in mind. Heck, I never expected to graduate from high school let alone go on and get a degree, so I didn't have much of a sense of purpose. I only went because Emily and George expected me to go.''

She could understand that. They had offered him stability and a home when he was in desperate need of both. He would have wanted to please them if he could.

''When George told me Marcus had driven you and your sister to school early, I decided I might as well go back early too. With Mr. Wickert dead, I didn't have a job to go to anymore. And since I had nothing else to do once I got there, I met with an adviser. She had me take one of those aptitude tests. I've got to tell you, when lawyer showed up on the results, I had a good laugh. But I kept thinking what an interesting irony it would be. Two classes later, I was hooked.''

For once, she didn't know what to say.

Gavin lowered his voice. ''This is going to sound like some corny pickup line, but I never forgot you, Leigh.''

Her lungs forgot how to breathe.

''You changed my life in more ways than you'll ever know.''

She didn't want to hear this. She didn't want to think about that night, but she didn't know how to change the direction this conversation had taken.

''You thought I was Hayley,'' she whispered. And that still had the power to hurt.

''Actually, I had no idea who you were at first. George and Emily often mentioned you, of course, but I'm afraid I always linked you and your sister in my mind as 'the twins.' You were alone that night. In the dark, with your hair all piled on top of your head, you looked bold and sexy as all get out. And a whole lot older than seventeen."

Leigh felt a heated blush crawl up her neck. Gavin smiled at her gently. "It was an older crowd, remember? I wasn't expecting to see someone like you there."

A little girl who'd been playing dress up with the adults.

"And while it pains me to admit it," he continued, "the truth is, I wasn't paying a whole lot of attention to your face. The outfit you were wearing was...well, I still remember how you looked."

Like a woman who knew the score instead of a scared kid.

"And how brazenly I acted," she said in remembered shame.

His gaze swung to her face. "That was the drug, Leigh. If I'd known—"

"You wouldn't have touched me with a ten-foot pole. I know." Oncoming headlights suddenly blinded her. "Gavin! Look out!"

A bright red pickup truck with dark, tinted windows barreled around a sharp bend in the road. Without warning, it crossed the center line and came straight at them. Gavin wrenched the steering wheel hard right. At the last possible second, the truck veered away and sped off. Gavin brought the car to a jolting stop on the side of the road amid a cloud of dust.

"Are you all right?" he demanded. His knuckles were white where they clenched the steering wheel.

Quaking all over, Leigh managed to nod.

"Did you get a look at the driver?"

She shook her head. All she'd seen was that bright red hood bearing down on them.

"He must have been drunk."

Slowly, Gavin released his grip on the steering wheel. There wasn't another car in sight on the two-lane road.

"Maybe."

Like an avalanche, fear tumbled inside her. His tone was all wrong. "You don't think—"

"That it was Ducort?" His features were darkly forbidding. "I don't know. But I intend to find out."

She reached for his arm. His skin was reassuringly warm beneath her cold fingers. "How?"

Gavin covered her trembling hand with his. "It's okay. I won't go over to his place to wait for him this time. The bar association frowns on lawyers taking the law into their own hands. I have a few sources I can call. I'll see if I can find out what vehicles he owns or has access to."

"And if it was him?"

"We'll deal with the situation appropriately then. It will be okay."

Leigh was only partly appeased. Her heart was still racing when they turned up the rutted lane to Heartskeep. The work crew was long gone, but Gavin drove around back anyhow. Bram's truck was no longer parked there. Leigh remembered that he and Hayley had plans for the evening. The only car sitting out back was a rather battered old station wagon that she didn't recognize.

Before Gavin could bring the car to a stop, the rear door to the house flew open. Mrs. Norwhich raced outside, her expression terrified.

Gavin was out of the car before Leigh could find the release for her seat belt. The older woman ran to him, her features distorted by fear as she cast a glance over her shoulder.

"Someone's in the house! I was just getting the last of my stuff when I heard a noise in the kitchen. Someone closed the pantry door! They're still in there!"

"Stay here with Leigh," Gavin told the distraught woman.

"Gavin, no!"

Gavin ignored Leigh's cry and entered the kitchen. The room was large and spacious. Two of the walls were mostly windows. Ahead and to his left were two closed doors that immediately drew his attention. He headed for the nearest one.

"That's the laundry room."

He whirled to find Leigh at his back. Mrs. Norwhich hovered behind her.

"Wait outside."

"No!"

Arguing wasn't going to get him anywhere. He could see that in the way she held her head. Instead, he pointed at the closed door next to the laundry.

"That the pantry?"

"No. That's a bathroom. The pantry is in the middle over there. Gavin, what if he's armed?"

"Then he'd better be ready to commit murder."

Gavin flung open the door. "Empty," he announced.

"It can't be. I saw that door closing!" Mrs. Norwhich protested.

Gavin didn't doubt her. Her distress was obvious. The door next to the pantry was a closet filled with cleaning equipment. No one hid in there, either. The bathroom and laundry room proved equally empty.

"Gavin, you can't search the whole house," Leigh protested. "Do you have any idea how big this place is? Most of the bedrooms share adjoining bathrooms. If someone is in here, they could elude you indefinitely."

"Telephone?"

"On the wall over there," she replied, pointing. "But the police won't come all the way out here."

"They'll come," he stated flatly.

"Fine. By the time they do, whoever it is will be long gone."

"We'll report the break-in anyhow."

She shook her head as he reached for the telephone. The prowler couldn't have been Nolan. Not if he was the one who'd run them off the road. He couldn't have doubled back fast enough to beat them here.

Two officers did respond, and surprisingly fast considering how far Heartskeep was from town. The officers kept them waiting in the kitchen while they searched through the house.

"Front door's unlocked," the spokesman said. "He probably went out that way, but the doors to your attic and basement are locked. You folks have the key?"

Mrs. Norwhich shook her head. "My passkey doesn't work on those doors."

"No one could have used those doors. Grandpa always kept them locked. You need an old-fashioned skeleton key to open them," Leigh told them.

"We can break down the doors if you want," the officer told them.

"No. You're probably right. He must have gone out the front door."

Gavin tended to agree, and Mrs. Norwhich nodded fervent agreement.

"What's in the basement?" the second officer asked.

"The furnace," Leigh told him. "It's the only thing down there. And Grandpa used the attic for storage. It's full of old furniture and that sort of thing."

"All right then, do you want to have a look around the house to see if anything's missing?"

"I'm not sure I'd know. I haven't actually lived here for several years," Leigh told him.

"Don't look at me," Mrs. Norwhich protested when they turned to her. "I only do the cooking and the laundry. I tend to this area of the house. The missus hired someone else to clean the rest.''

Since neither Leigh nor Mrs. Norwhich knew the contents of the house well enough to ascertain if anything had been taken, the officers claimed there wasn't much they could do except file a report. Frustrated, Gavin listened to their advice about getting the alarm system reactivated. He made a mental note to see that the job was given priority in the morning.

''I've got one more thing to add to your report,'' he told them. ''Leigh and I were run off the road on our way here from town tonight.''

Seeing he'd captured their attention, Gavin gave them what information he could on the make and model of the truck, and the precise location of the incident.

''You two are having quite a night, aren't you? Okay. We'll put out a watch for the vehicle, but if the driver was some drunk, he's probably home in bed by now, sleeping it off.''

Gavin thought about telling them about his earlier scene with Ducort, but decided he'd do a little checking on his own, first.

After the officers left, he turned to Leigh. ''Going to say I told you so?''

''You mean because the police aren't going to do anything? Why bother? I'm surprised they actually responded. Between my mother's disappearance and Marcus's murder, the local arm of the law isn't too happy with anyone here at Heartskeep.''

Mrs. Norwhich shook her frizzy white head. ''That's a fine thing. Wasn't your fault, what happened to the mister.''

''Thanks, Mrs. Norwhich. I'm not sure Chief Crossley would agree with you.''

''Man's a windbag. All puff, no stuffin'. If you won't be needing me anymore tonight, I'll be getting back to town.''

"I'm sorry you had such a scare."

"Why don't you let me carry your belongings out to your car for you," Gavin offered.

"I'll just let you do that," she agreed readily.

They watched the sturdy woman drive away a few minutes later.

"She's a little odd, but I think she means well," Leigh said. "I hope we don't lose her, too."

"I don't think you will. She appears the self-reliant sort, despite being spooked. I suspect she'll hang in for the long haul. Besides, we're paying her for not working. She should look at this as a bonus vacation. The police were right about one thing, though, we need to get the security system up and running again."

"No argument here."

"I'd like to take a quick look around the house, Leigh."

She tensed. "What if someone is still inside? It'll be dark soon and I think R.J. has the power turned off."

"We'll make it quick. Like the cops said, it isn't likely anyone hung around."

"At least we know it wasn't Nolan—not if he's the one who ran us off the road. He can't be in two places at once."

"I never said Ducort was connected to either incident," he corrected. "But I'd give a lot to know whether he has an airtight alibi for his time tonight. Either way, I'd really like to understand the layout of Heartskeep. I've never been inside the estate before."

"All right. I'll give you the grand tour. There are eleven designated bedrooms, if you include my grandfather's suite as one room."

"Eleven? Was Heartskeep used as an inn?"

"No. My great, great grandfather, Woodrow Hart, had nine children and a staff of eight when he built the original Heartskeep."

"Wow. So this isn't the original structure?"

"More or less. I think part of the main house was destroyed and rebuilt at some point but I'm not sure when. Grandpa had all sorts of files on the history of Heartskeep and the Hart family, but we probably lost most of them in the fire," Leigh said regretfully.

The dining and living rooms were so impressive that Gavin forgot about the number of bedrooms. He stared at the massive stone fireplace that took up most of one wall and jutted several feet into the dining room. Built-in shelves stood on either side.

"Quite a fireplace."

"You ought to see it lit."

He could imagine. Another curved fireplace of matching stone filled the far corner of the living room. That fireplace backed to the grand staircase.

The sheer, towering height of the two rooms, open to enormous skylights overhead, made them unique. The vast living room was open on two sides, set off from the halls by marble pillars.

"They hold up the balcony that surrounds both rooms," Leigh told him.

She seemed skittish around him. Not that he blamed her. She was as aware as he was that there was an attraction building between them. The truth was, he hadn't been able to stop thinking about her since he'd seen her again at her father's funeral. She'd looked exactly as he'd remembered.

"All these years Hayley and I thought the railings and the overhang were nothing more than architectural design," Leigh said, "but according to Emily Walken, the balcony used to be completely open to the second floor. A person used to be able to leave their bedroom, walk over to the balcony, step down and watch whatever was happening below. Emily said Grandpa had the balcony walled off when we came here to live. He was afraid we'd fall or something."

Gavin stared up at the polished wood railings overhead. The area beyond them lay in deep shadow despite the setting sun overhead. Troubled, he let Leigh guide him down the hall. There were two bedrooms, two bathrooms, Dennison's office and an inviting room that Leigh called the library, all on the undamaged side of the house.

''Mostly we used the library as our living room,'' Leigh confided.

Gavin could understand why. The library and Dennison's office were the only cozy rooms he'd seen.

''Massive foyer,'' he said, gazing around. A grand piano sat tucked partially under the staircase. ''Not too many people keep a baby grand piano in their front hall.''

Striding over, he ran his fingers across the yellowed ivory keys. The notes were startlingly loud, disturbing the ominous silence of the house.

''Eden must have had it moved here. It used to sit in the living room.''

''Do you play?''

''Not really. Mom did. She used to play a lot. Hayley and Grandpa and I would sit and listen or sing along while she played.''

He liked that image, but not the look of wistful sadness that crossed her features.

''Seems like a lifetime ago,'' Leigh added. ''Hayley and I took lessons when we were kids, but we hated to practice. Eventually, we gave up. Now I wish we'd continued.''

The ballroom, parlor and what had once been her father's offices were roped off on the damaged side of the house. The odor of scorched wood still lingered heavily in the still air. The blackened walls made it easy to picture Hayley's terror when she and Bram were trapped inside the office area while the arsonist calmly set fire to the place.

''What's beyond the ballroom?''

''Another spare bedroom and the room Mrs. Norwhich

is using. Mrs. Walsh and Kathy, the previous housekeeper and her daughter, used to live in those rooms.''

Gavin nodded, familiar with the names from her grandfather's will.

''You sure this place wasn't used as an inn?'' he teased to ease the growing tension between them.

''Not to my knowledge. We'd better hurry if you want to see upstairs. The light's fading fast.''

She was right, and this was not a house he wanted to be caught inside in the dark.

Gavin followed her up the sweeping staircase and tried not to notice the slight sway of her hips or the graceful length of leg displayed below the hem of her dress. He told himself to stop fantasizing. Leigh was a client. She couldn't be anything more, despite the attraction he was feeling.

''Grandpa's rooms were over the parlor and ballroom. They were pretty well destroyed in the fire. I always loved his suite as a kid,'' she said over her shoulder. ''Grandpa kept all sorts of treats for us in a small, golden treasure chest.'' She stopped at the top of the stairs. ''I guess it was destroyed along with everything else.''

''I'm sorry.''

''Me too. I'm thinking I may convert that area into a gym, or maybe a large playroom for children.''

Unfortunately, it was all too easy to picture Leigh's children filling that playroom. Gavin found the image of her holding a tiny infant unsettling. Maybe because she could so easily have had *his* infant after their one night together.

He'd sweated out those weeks after making love to her until Emily had assured him Leigh wasn't pregnant. Oddly enough, his relief had been tempered by a strange sense of loss.

He'd never taken sex lightly after that night, nor had he ever forgotten to use protection again. He wondered what

Leigh would say if she understood how much that evening had changed his life.

"A gym or a playroom would be good for resale value, don't you think?" Leigh was saying. Her voice faltered as she stared up at him.

Those innocent blue eyes stirred memories he was certain she'd prefer he didn't have. Desire slammed into him, unbidden. She lowered her lashes. Her breathing quickened. The hand that gestured toward the opposite hall had a decided tremor. He resisted the impulse to stroke the soft skin of her lightly flushed cheek. Instead, he hooked his thumb over his belt and tried not to remember how soft she was all over.

"I thought you were going to keep Heartskeep for Hayley's children," he managed to say calmly.

"I am. I just thought I should keep all my options open. You never know what might happen."

Yeah. He might just give in to one of the crazy impulses pounding away inside him right now. Gavin was embarrassed to realize he was becoming aroused.

"Why not save the estate for your own children?"

He heard the delicate catch of her breath. Were her thoughts running parallel with his again?

"I...it should go to my sister's oldest child."

She wouldn't look at him. A restlessness gripped him as he studied her profile. Leigh had changed very little in the past seven years. She was definitely a woman now, but there was still an aura of innocence about her.

Leigh gestured toward the roped-off hall where fire damage had opened one wall to expose the gutted interior to view. The heat and intensity of the fire were almost secondary to the damage done by the smoke and the water used to put out the blaze.

"The bedroom Jacob uses is on the other side of

Grandpa's suite. I don't know if that room was damaged or not. We'll have to go around the back way to see."

Gavin followed her pointing hand down the corridor. Like the rest of the house, the walls up here were covered by rich, dark wood paneling. Despite the large picture window at their back, there would be little outside light to brighten either hall. Once the sun set, these walls would resemble tunnels—dark and suffocating.

His body tensed. He found himself moving closer to her side as if preparing to defend her from some unseen danger.

Leigh looked up at him with a questioning expression. Her voice dropped to little more than a whisper.

"You feel it too, don't you?"

"Feel what?" But he knew exactly what she meant.

"There's an evil feeling to this house now."

She was right. There was a brooding quality up here that hadn't been as noticeable downstairs. Gavin recalled the prickly nervousness he'd experienced when he'd looked up at the balcony. The sensation was back. He didn't like it one bit.

"It didn't used to be this way," she added.

Gavin shook his head. He was irritated by his own reaction. He wasn't generally given to such a fanciful imagination.

"How do you get onto the balconies?"

"You don't. I told you, Grandpa had that area walled up."

"He must have left some sort of access, if only to clean the dust."

Her thoughtful frown probably matched his own.

"I hadn't thought about that. There aren't any doors to it that I know of."

"What about those?" He pointed at a set of doors on the other side of the staircase.

"Linen closets."

Gavin walked around and opened the nearest one. The closet contained shelves on either side. The shelves were filled with an assortment of linens. "Big closet."

"It's a big house. Gavin, we're going to lose the light up here any minute now. I think the rest of your tour had better wait for tomorrow. At the risk of sounding like a coward, I'd like to leave now."

Anxiety threaded her voice. He didn't blame her. There *was* a bad feeling to this house, imagined or not.

"You're right. We'll come back tomorrow."

She turned quickly and started down the stairs. As he followed, he was almost positive he'd heard the sound of a door closing softly near the back of the long dark hall.

Chapter Five

Leigh awoke feeling tired and edgy. The dreams that had plagued her sleep were evaporating like so much mist, leaving behind only traces to cling to. Somehow, she was certain they were important traces. Her mother had been trying to warn her about something, but that something was gone no matter how hard she tried to remember.

Naturally, Gavin had visited her sleeping mind, since he seemed to be there constantly when she was awake. In her dreams, Gavin made love to her again, but not like the flash-fire explosion they'd once shared. There had been a huge difference. Only, she couldn't remember what that difference had been. Those particular wisps of memory were playing havoc with her emotions this morning.

"Stop it!" she told herself sternly. "You are too old to start fantasizing over Gavin Jarret again!" But she couldn't face her reflection in the bathroom mirror.

The Walken house was so quiet she thought everyone had left for the day, but she found Hayley and Bram sitting at the kitchen table when she finally made it downstairs.

"The Walkens had a meeting this morning."

"What about Nan?" Leigh asked, looking around for the friendly but authoritative cook-housekeeper.

Bram grinned knowingly. "You're safe," he told her. "You won't be forced to eat breakfast this morning. Nan went shopping. Oh, and Gavin called for you a few minutes ago,'' Bram added. ''He wants you to meet him at Heartskeep around noon.''

Hayley frowned. ''Are you okay with this, Leigh? I feel sort of guilty dumping everything on you this way.''

''As well you should,'' Leigh told her pertly. ''It's fine. I wouldn't have chosen to own the estate, but that's okay. I want to talk with R.J. about tearing down the walls upstairs and restoring the house to its original condition. Emily said she had some old photographs around someplace that she could show me.''

''I wonder if any of Grandpa's files survived. You might ask R.J. Bram has to run into town for a few minutes this morning, so we could drop you off over there since you turned in the rental car you got at the airport. We'll have to make a trip to our Boston apartment to pick up your car one of these days. We need to check on our mail anyhow. Bram's going to finish removing the grates from the rest of the windows.''

''And I need to know what you want done with the old stone lions,'' Bram added. ''I can remove the front gate—''

''Don't you dare! That thing is a masterpiece,'' Leigh told him.

''That's what I said,'' Hayley added smugly.

Bram looked embarrassed.

''What about putting the lions on either side of the front porch?'' Leigh suggested.

''Not a bad idea,'' Bram said. ''Since R.J. has to replace part of that area anyhow, I bet he could make a few changes to accommodate them.''

''Like what?''

Bram grabbed a napkin and began to sketch. ''If the steps were wider and swept out like this…''

''I like it!'' Leigh told him when she saw what he was

suggesting. "The lions would fit on either side on the ends."

"Too much like a library?" he asked.

"I don't think so."

"Me neither. Let's go talk to R.J.," Hayley enthused.

"Why don't you let Leigh have some breakfast first."

"Thanks, but I never eat breakfast," she told him. "Let me grab my purse."

Even the sunny new day didn't diminish the house's brooding appearance, Leigh discovered. R.J. and his crew were sweating heavily as they ripped away at the fire damage. R.J. stopped to mop his face, coming over to talk with them when Bram called to him.

R.J. studied Bram's crude drawing and nodded. "We can do that. In fact, if you want to spend the extra money, we could replace this entire front porch with stone and bricks to give you a more uniform look."

Everyone looked at Leigh. "Sounds good to me."

"I'll work you up a price then."

"Do you need anything in town?" Bram asked.

R.J. and Leigh shook their heads.

"Okay. Hayley and I will be back shortly."

"Let's have a look at these walls you want removed," R.J. said to Leigh.

Despite the noise from his crew and the bright sunlight streaming in through the large window on the second floor, a sense of wrongness lingered upstairs. R.J. tapped the walls for several minutes.

"Feels like wood panels over wallboard. Taking them down won't be a problem, but you'll probably have to replace all the carpeting underneath."

"I was going to do that anyway."

"Okay. I'll need to inspect the balconies and the support structure, but I don't see a problem."

"Thanks, R.J. Oh!" Leigh gaped as an enormous black

dog came bounding up the main staircase. It gave a shake before trotting over to them as if it owned the place.

"Lucky, sit!"

The ferocious-looking animal immediately dropped to its haunches and looked at R.J. with such wistful canine adoration Leigh was tempted to laugh.

"Sorry," R.J. apologized. "He's supposed to stay outside, but he only obeys when he's in the mood. Good boy, Lucky."

The stubby little tail wagged wildly as the animal rose and leaned against R.J.'s legs.

"I hope it's okay to bring him along. He gets bored if I leave him at home, and when he's bored, he has a tendency to eat things—like couches or other furniture."

"Ah. Well as long as he confines his taste to furniture and not people… What breed is he?"

"Only his parents know for sure. The vet said he's part standard poodle with some Great Dane, and a few other genes thrown into the mix. Whatever his heritage, he's a character."

A little nervously, Leigh held out her hand and let Lucky sniff for a second before timidly stroking his broad head. A long wet tongue swiped at her hand in response.

"Why, you big fraud. You're a lover, aren't you?"

"You've got his number." R.J. ruffled Lucky's fur and the dog grinned up at him. "He's a pussycat at heart. All size and no threat to anything more dangerous than a recliner."

"Where'd you get him, R.J.?"

"In an abandoned well on a job site I was working. The cover had rotted away and Lucky must have fallen in. The vet thought he'd been stuck in there for several days. He had two broken legs and some pretty bad lacerations, but he was alive and happy to be rescued. No one came forward to claim him, so I paid the vet bill and we've been buddies ever since, right, Lucky?''

The dog woofed happily at the sound of his name while the stubby tail wagged agreement. But when R.J. called him to leave, Lucky sat down next to Leigh with the air of one who had no intention of going anywhere.

''It's okay, R.J. Lucky can stay with me if he wants.''

The truth was, she was happy to have the dog's company. She didn't like being alone in the house even if it was filled with workers. Lucky followed her back downstairs and into her grandfather's office. Thumbing through her grandfather's Rolodex, she found a business card for the landscaper who had put in the fountain and the sprinkler system. He answered her call personally, and offered to stop by and give her an estimate within the hour since it was on his way to another appointment.

Relieved, Leigh hung up and smiled at Lucky. ''Come on, fella, let's stretch our legs.''

Her grandfather's desk used to be neat and orderly, but now it was a jumbled mess. Leigh had to hunt through the messy drawers to find a pad of paper and a working pen, but as soon as she did, she began going from room to room, making notes of what needed work or replacing.

She was surveying the living room when the prickly sensation of being watched gradually demanded her attention. Lucky lifted his head alertly, as if he was studying the balcony. His very stillness was scary. She tried to determine where he was looking.

Leigh could hear workers talking to each other above the loud radio station they were playing, but there was no one in view. Yet the sensation intensified. Someone *was* watching her. Lucky whined softly. He moved to stand against her legs. Laying her hand on his head, she scanned both rooms closely.

The overhead skylights filled the rooms with sunlight,

yet somehow the balconies still lay mostly in shadows due to the darkly paneled walls that encased them. Was there a way to access that area? Could someone be standing in one of those shadows, watching her? The shadows appeared deeper near the corner where the two rooms met. Was it her imagination, or had there been the slightest of movements in the darkness up there?

Lucky growled low in his massive chest. The hairs on the back of her neck lifted. In the front hall, the main door opened.

"Leigh?"

"Gavin!" She turned and ran toward him, but Lucky beat her there. "Lucky, no!"

Gavin braced himself as the animal leaped. Staggering back under the animal's weight, he ruffled the dog's fur, even as he pushed him down.

"Hey there, Lucky, how ya doin', fella?"

Leigh came to a halt. "You know Lucky?"

"Sure. R.J. and I play on the same softball team."

"You play softball?" The image was so unexpected she shook her head.

"Some of my teammates might argue that point, but *you* shouldn't look so surprised. You haven't even seen me play."

"No. I mean, I…well…I just never thought…"

"I was a team player?" he provided wryly, stroking the big dog's head affectionately. "People do change, you know, Leigh. What are you doing?"

"I think someone's in the house again."

"Several someones from the sound of all that noise." Then he seemed to recognize her tension. "What's wrong?"

Leigh lowered her voice, even though no one could hear much over the hammering and the country-western song blaring away.

"You were right. There must be a way onto the balconies. I think someone is up there right now."

His features tightened as his gaze lifted. "Where?"

"I'm not sure, but I think something moved in the shadows between the two rooms. Lucky was looking up there and growling right before you came in."

"Lucky's been known to growl at leaves, but let's have a look."

Anxiously, she followed him back into the living room. The area near the corner no longer looked as dark as it had, and the sense of menace was gone.

"I think they're gone."

As if in full agreement, Lucky ambled over to the nearest love seat. After sizing it up, he gave a surprisingly graceful leap and settled himself across it with a loud doggy sigh of satisfaction.

"At least he isn't eating it," Leigh said.

Gavin's lips quirked in amusement. "There is that. Wait here."

"Where are you going?"

Gavin didn't answer. He strode back out the front door. Lucky raised his head, but decided action on his part wasn't called for and he settled back down.

"Some protector you are," she told the contented animal. "R.J. was right. You're a pussycat at heart."

Gavin returned with R.J. and a large extension ladder.

"You aren't going to climb up there, are you?" she demanded.

"It's too high to jump."

"That isn't funny. You're crazy. He's crazy," she told the dog. Lucky sighed and went back to studying the insides of his eyelids. Gavin had stripped off his suit coat and tie outside, but he still wore dress slacks and a white shirt.

"You're going to ruin those pants," she warned as the

men propped the long ladder against the balcony railing near a marble support column.

"They'll dry-clean."

"Leigh has a point," R.J. told him. "You aren't dressed for this. I'll go up and take a look around. I'm used to ladders, not desk chairs."

"I may not be part monkey like you, Monroe, but I think I can manage to climb a ladder," Gavin retorted.

Leigh held her breath as he mounted the rungs quickly while R.J. braced the ladder for him. The balcony was a good fourteen to twenty feet above them. If he fell, Gavin would break his fool neck.

He didn't fall. He paused to survey the balcony before he swung a leg over the railing with a lot more grace than she could have managed.

"Be careful," R.J. cautioned. "I haven't checked the soundness of the flooring up there."

Gavin stamped his foot. "Feels solid to me. There's dust around the edges of the carpeting, but this has been vacuumed in the not so distant past. That means there must be a way in and out. But, if someone was up here, they're gone now."

He moved away from the railing.

"Can you still see me?"

"Yes," she called out nervously.

He moved deeper into the shadows.

"That white shirt's pretty easy to spot," R.J. added. "No. Now you're out of sight."

"But you aren't," he said. "Whisper something."

"What?"

"Whisper something."

"What do you want me to whisper?" Leigh asked very softly.

"The acoustics are something else. I think I could hear a pin drop on the carpeting down there."

"The paneling may be acting like a funnel," R.J. told him.

"Gavin? What are you doing?" Leigh asked.

"Looking for a door."

"I'm coming up," R.J. called out to him. "Hold the ladder for me, Leigh."

Before she could protest, he scaled the ladder with a speedy nimbleness that made her blink. Lucky raised his head to watch. Seconds later, R.J. also disappeared from view.

Leigh fretted, unable to hear even their footsteps. The idea that someone had been able to stand there all these years and watch everything that happened down here was disconcerting. The men reappeared several minutes later, arguing. She gripped the ladder as R.J. swung back onto it and started down. He in turn held it for Gavin.

"There has to be a door," Gavin grumbled. "Even an expert isn't going to climb that high carrying a vacuum cleaner."

"I agree, but it's well concealed. I'll go up later with a light and have a look around," R.J. told him. "I figure the door has to be built into one of the wood panels, but I need light to spot the seam and I don't want to turn on the main power until we finish gutting the place."

"Can't we use your generator?"

"Yeah, but I'll have to rig something up first."

They all turned as the front door opened again and Hayley and Bram walked in. The two of them stopped at the sight of the men pulling down the extension ladder.

"What's going on?" Hayley asked.

"They were checking out the balconies."

"Leigh thought someone was up there," Gavin added.

"How would they get there?" Bram asked.

"That's what we're trying to figure out."

Hayley interrupted, looking over her shoulder out the

open door. "There's a van that says Franklin Nurseries pulling up outside. So is a large flatbed trailer with a big container on back."

"Gotta go," R.J. said.

Lucky uncurled himself from the couch, gave a shake of his massive body and jumped down to greet the newcomers.

"Ohmygod! What is that?" Hayley demanded.

"Meet Lucky," Leigh told her sister. "He belongs to R.J."

"What is he, part bear?"

"Could be, but don't worry. His taste runs to furniture—or so I've been told. Listen, I wasn't expecting Gavin to get here so early. Would you do me a favor and show Mr. Franklin what needs to be done out back while I talk to Gavin for a minute?"

"Sure."

"Come on, Lucky," Bram said.

The dog followed them outside and she turned to Gavin. "You said you wouldn't get here until noon."

"Mrs. Carbecelli decided not to change her will after all. How sure are you that someone was up there?"

"I'm not sure of anything. I couldn't see anyone, but I felt like I was being watched. Then the dog started growling. Did you find anything?"

He fished in his pocket and held up a gum wrapper.

"That could have been there forever."

"I don't think so. You can still smell the spearmint on the wrapper. Know anyone who favors spearmint gum?"

Leigh shook her head.

"Last night when we were leaving, I thought I heard a door close up there."

"Why didn't you say something?"

"Because I thought it more prudent to get you away from here at the time. Let's finish that tour we started."

"What about Mr. Franklin?"

"Hayley can handle him, can't she?"

Of course she could, but Leigh's nerves were jumping.

"Obviously, you and Hayley didn't know about the balcony access," Gavin said. "Who do you think did besides your mother and grandfather?"

"I don't know. Maybe Mrs. Walsh and Kathy."

"We definitely need to have a talk with them. What about Eden and Jacob?"

"I don't know about Eden, but I don't see why Jacob would know when we didn't."

"Have you talked to either of them since that meeting at my office?"

"No. Why? Do you think it was one of them up there?" She didn't like thinking of Eden standing there spying on her.

"Anything's possible," he said as he started up the main staircase. "What about Jacob's father? Does he have any contact with the family?"

Leigh hesitated, debating how to answer the question.

"It's a simple question, Leigh. Yes, no, or I don't know."

She paused at the top of the stairs and looked around. There was no one in sight. "Actually, it isn't that simple. Hayley asked Jacob about his father once. Jacob said he died when Jacob was a baby."

"But?"

"His father isn't dead. I'm not sure if he knows that or not. The only reason I know is because there was a disturbance in the front hall one day. I was about twelve, I think. Eden and my grandfather were arguing with a man I'd never seen before. Eden was shouting that he'd signed away his rights to Jacob before the boy was born and she didn't owe him anything. My grandfather told him if he didn't want to go back to prison he should stay away from everyone connected to Heartskeep.''

Gavin frowned thoughtfully and she wished she hadn't said anything.

''I shouldn't have told you. I never even told Hayley.''

He laid a hand on her arm. ''I won't repeat it, Leigh. I'm trying to get a feel for anyone who might be connected to Heartskeep.''

''You don't have to worry about Jacob's father. The first year we started college I overheard Eden telling Marcus that Jacob's father was back in prison where he belonged. She said he'd be an old man before they let him out again this time.''

''Interesting.''

Feeling guilty for revealing something so private, she sought for a change of topic. ''Gavin, what are we doing up here?''

''I want to have another look at that linen closet.''

''You think the entrance is through the closet?''

''Seems like the perfect spot to hide an entrance to me. What kid's going to pay attention to a linen closet?''

The idea sent her heart pounding. She'd seen Kathy go in and out of the two side-by-side closets on numerous occasions and never gave it a thought. He opened the first door, which was lined with shelves full of linens. The door next to it held cleaning supplies and paper products.

''Did your grandfather own stock in the toilet-paper industry?''

''We do have something like thirteen bathrooms in this house,'' she reminded him.

''See, I told you it was a ready-made inn.'' He poked past the vacuum cleaner, mops, pails, plungers and related items. Near the back, a small cart, similar to those used in most hotels, blocked the back wall. Gavin shoved it to one side, tossing her a look with raised eyebrows.

''So we grew up in a hotel,'' Leigh said. ''Sue me.''

''I'd rather kiss you.''

Her heart gave a funny little flip, but he didn't even look at her. His attention seemed focused on the back wall and she decided she must have heard him wrong. How could he say something so outrageous and then act as if nothing out of the ordinary had happened?

''Bingo.''

''What did you say?''

He turned around to face her. ''I said, bingo.''

''No, I mean before that.''

Everything changed. She felt it in every fiber of her body. He regarded her steadily while her pulse jumped crazily.

''Surely you aren't surprised I'd like to kiss you?''

Suddenly, the closet felt a whole lot smaller. Her mind went blank and her lungs forgot to inhale.

''You had the softest lips I've ever tasted.''

''How can you say that?'' There was nothing soft about his lips. She remembered them being bold and firm—like the rest of him.

''Because it's true.''

''I'm sure you've tasted plenty for comparison.''

Flecks of amusement sparked in his eyes.

''Jealous?''

''Hardly.''

She took an uncertain step back and bumped into the vacuum cleaner.

Gavin told himself not to be a fool. So what if thinking about her was keeping him up half the night? He was not going to act on the attraction, even though she stared at him with such guileless yearning that his body hardened in instant arousal.

His hand reached out to lift her chin before he could stop

himself. Her lips quivered in silent invitation. He ran his thumb over her bottom lip and they parted.

Slowly, deliberately, he lowered his face and covered those lips with his own, even as he told himself not to be so stupid.

He meant to keep it simple—a chaste kiss. Something to take the edge off the tension that had been building inside him since the moment he saw her again. But his body filled with hunger the moment he tasted her.

Her eyes closed and she leaned into him, sliding her hands around his neck to draw him closer. Need coiled inside him. He felt the press of her breasts against his shirt, desire in the dart of her tongue as she opened her mouth and invited him in. The kiss deepened, turning hot and hungry as his resolve melted away.

Someone called her name in the distance. His mouth located the sensitive spot below her ear and he was rewarded with a mew of pleasure that blocked the sound completely as she kissed him back with greedy fervor.

"Gavin? Leigh?"

Her fingers fumbled at the buttons of his shirt.

"Leigh? Where are you?"

Hayley's voice shattered the powerful urgency hammering inside him. Gavin pulled his mouth from hers and raised his head. They were necking inside a linen closet. Workmen were only a few yards away. A radio belted out a song of longing. Gavin shared the sentiment.

"Leigh? Are you up here?"

Her expression of dazed desire made it almost impossible not to ignore everything else and take what they both wanted so badly.

"She probably can't hear me over this racket," Hayley called to someone. "I'll be right down. Let me check her room."

Gavin released her. He watched as awareness replaced

the mist of desire that glazed her eyes. Leigh dropped her arms with a stunned expression. She tried to step away and tripped over the vacuum cleaner. Mops and brooms clattered to the floor.

He reached for her as she flailed to keep from falling. He caught her against his chest, all too aware of the firm yet soft skin beneath his fingers. She was shaking. Wide-eyed, she stared at him in confusion.

"Easy," he said gently.

The door at her back had been ajar. Hayley flung it wide open. Backlit against the large picture window, she took in the scene and her lips parted in shock.

"What are you doing in there?"

Gavin maintained his grip on Leigh's upper arms to keep her turned away from her sister until she could regain her composure.

"Trying to keep your sister from falling all over everything," he told Hayley, surprised when his voice came out sounding relaxed.

He felt Leigh inhale. She tugged free of his grip.

"I'm not the one who backed up without warning," she retorted. Quickly, she twisted away, bending over to retrieve the fallen items. Her face was a becoming shade of pink, but Gavin had to hand it to her for such a clever, rapid comeback. With any luck, her sister would put the high color down to annoyance and embarrassment rather than a passionate embrace.

"But what are you doing in here?" Hayley asked as she bent to help.

"Looking for a way onto the balconies," he inserted smoothly.

"In a linen closet?"

"Can you think of a better place to hide the entrance?" Leigh fired back, to his amusement.

"No. I must admit I never would have thought to look

in here. Smart thinking, but can it wait? Mr. Franklin has to leave to get to his next appointment."

"Go ahead, Leigh," Gavin told her. "I'll straighten up the mess."

For the first time, she met his gaze directly. "I'll be right back," she said firmly.

"Take your time, I'm not going anywhere."

"Then wait right here."

Her hair was mussed and her eyes glittered brightly. Gavin had the strongest urge to smile.

"Permission to use the nearest bathroom?" he teased.

"Just stay off that balcony until I get back."

Hayley followed the exchange with a puzzled expression.

Leigh stepped into the hall beside her. Maybe to someone who didn't know them they were identical, but now that he knew them, Gavin would never mistake Hayley for Leigh. They shared the same heart-shaped face and creamy smooth skin. Their golden-brown hair was worn in the same style, but those were the exterior trappings. Their slight build gave the mistaken impression of fragility, but a smart man could read the inner core of strength under those womanly shapes. Hayley was assertive. Leigh's approach was softer—until she got riled. Gavin wouldn't mind provoking that part of her on occasion. He enjoyed watching the flash in her eyes when she was annoyed with him—like now.

He found himself watching the swing of her hips beneath the stretchy material of her pink shorts. She rounded the corner to start down the steps and caught him staring. The color in her cheeks deepened. Gavin winked at her. Hayley eyed them with a look of speculation.

Gavin made a mental note not to let Hayley catch him alone. He headed for the bathroom with the taste and scent of Leigh clinging to his still-hard body.

Chapter Six

"What's going on?" Hayley demanded as Leigh closed the door behind the landscaper.

Leigh didn't pretend to misunderstand, but she did try to stall the inevitable. "Gavin may have found a way onto the balcony."

"Tell me you aren't still hung up on him."

"Don't be silly."

Hayley shut her eyes and opened them again. "I shouldn't have dumped the estate on you."

"Of course not, but what has that got to do with anything?"

"You were locking lips with him in a linen closet! Have you forgotten how badly he hurt you the last time?"

"Hold it right there. Gavin did nothing to hurt me."

"Come on, Leigh. I was there. You had a crush on that guy the size of California, remember?"

"What I remember is that Gavin saved me from being raped, beat the heck out of Nolan for drugging me..."

"He did?"

"Yes, and he was willing to face murder charges rather than ruin my prissy reputation. He even pestered Emily for weeks until he was sure I wasn't pregnant. She told me so. And now, in his capacity as our lawyer, he's trying to do his best for both of us. I'm not seventeen anymore and I'm not naive, Hayley. And if I want to kiss Gavin that's my business.''

About to respond, Hayley's gaze flashed to something over her shoulder. Leigh twisted to find Gavin halfway down the stairs.

How much had he heard?

Though she felt her face flame, she refused to look away from his enigmatic expression. ''Being the older twin gave Hayley a mother complex,'' she told him.

''Darn right it did,'' Hayley agreed.

The front door opened and Bram strolled inside.

''I'm warning you,'' Hayley continued, pointing a finger at Gavin. ''You'll answer to me if you hurt my sister.''

''Hayley, shut up. I am perfectly capable of running my own life.''

Bram studied the scene and looked at Gavin. ''What's going on?'' he asked as Gavin descended the rest of the way.

''Nothing,'' Leigh said sharply.

''I can handle this,'' Hayley told him at the same time.

''If you want any privacy around here, I'd skip the linen closet, if I were you,'' Gavin advised deadpan.

Bram relaxed. ''I'll keep that in mind.''

Even Hayley seemed to relax, and Bram's cell phone rang before anyone could say anything further.

''Hello?'' As he listened, pain creased his features and he swore softly. ''Okay, slow down. No, you did the right thing. There's nothing else you can do. Look, I'll leave right now. Are you okay? You're sure? Yeah, okay. Call the others. I'm on my way.''

Hayley reached for his arm. ''Is it your dad?''

''Yeah. My brother found him on the floor this morning. He's in a coma. I have to leave.''

''Is there time to stop by the Walken estate so I can get a few things?''

"Hayley, you don't need—"

"Yes," she said firmly, gazing up at him. "I do."

Bram pulled her into his arms. Closing his eyes, he held her close for a minute. The simple action seemed intensely private. Leigh took an involuntary step toward Gavin, relieved when his hand came to rest on her shoulder. She was pretty sure the couple had forgotten anyone else was standing there.

"This isn't how I wanted you to meet my family," Bram said with his eyes closed against the top of Hayley's head.

She pulled back and scolded him with a dry expression. "Don't even go there. You think my way was better? Being chased by a killer, watching you nearly get shot, oh, and by the way, meet my sister?"

Bram managed a wry twist of his lips and kissed her forehead. "I could be there several days."

"It will take me two minutes to pack a bag."

His eyes lightened. "You can have five."

Hayley broke free of his arms and turned. "Leigh?"

"Go," she said. "I'll be fine. I'm sorry about your dad, Bram. I hope he'll be okay."

"So do I."

Minutes later, Leigh stood on the porch and watched them leave, with a host of mixed emotions. Bram's family lived in Murrett Township, a tiny place up in the hills about an hour's drive north of Stony Ridge. If Marcus hadn't hired Bram to construct the fence and the gate out in front of Heartskeep, it was highly unlikely that Hayley and Bram would have ever met.

"Is Bram the reason Hayley didn't want the estate?" Gavin asked.

"Partly. She's wildly in love with him and Bram's got a fierce pride. But I think the truth is, Heartskeep isn't our home anymore. The heart of Heartskeep died with Grandpa. And that wasn't a pun."

"I know," he agreed softly. "Leigh—"

A woman's shrill scream pierced the air, audible even over the din coming from the workmen. Gavin bounded off the porch. He was sprinting around the side of the house before Leigh's stunned brain had finished assimilating the unexpected sound.

As she raced after him, Leigh wondered, what now? She jerked to a stop abreast of the side door and stared at quite a scene. Eden was shrieking and clawing at Gavin in an effort to take back a large kitchen knife. Lucky stood several feet away, baring his teeth and growling low in his throat.

"Eden, stop!" Leigh yelled. "He's going to attack!"

Eden swung toward her, her features puckered in fury. Then she saw the dog and froze.

"Lucky. Come here, boy. It's okay. Come here, fella," Leigh coaxed.

The animal never took his eyes from the pair.

Footsteps pounded up beside her. "Lucky!" R.J. called. "Come here!"

Others ran up behind him. They also came to a halt as they saw what was happening.

"Lucky!"

The dog stopped growling at the sound of R.J.'s voice, but he still didn't take his eyes off Eden and Gavin.

"Good boy, Lucky. Come on, boy," R.J. encouraged more softly.

With obvious reluctance, the massive dog turned to look back over his shoulder.

"That's the boy. Come here, Lucky."

For a long, silent moment, no one moved. Then Lucky trotted over to R.J. Leigh released the breath she'd been holding.

"Does that horrible beast belong to you?" Eden demanded.

Lucky swung his head back and barked sharply. Eden stopped moving again.

"Yes, ma'am, he does," R.J. said quietly. He took a firm hold of the dog's collar, stroking the silky head.

"Get him out of here! Do you hear me?"

"Half the town can hear you, Eden," Leigh said as the dog began to growl again. "You're upsetting him. Calm down."

"He was digging in the garden!"

"And you were chasing him with a knife," Gavin announced tightly.

Leigh gasped. She sensed R.J. stiffening at her side. Lucky bristled, growling low in his throat.

"I saw him run in there," Eden said, her voice ragged with emotion. "I knew what he was going to do."

"Make sure he isn't hurt, R.J.," Gavin said. "I think I got to the knife before she got to him, but I'm not sure."

"He was digging in the garden!" Eden screamed again.

Lucky suddenly lunged in her direction. Fortunately, R.J. had a firm grasp on his collar. Still, it took most of his strength to hold the dog back.

"Don't say another word," Gavin warned Eden. "Not another sound if you don't want that dog to maul you."

"Let's get Lucky in the house, R.J.," Leigh said.

Maneuvering one hundred-plus pounds of dog that didn't want to be maneuvered was no simple task. Leigh was reminded of the handlers who put racehorses into a starting gate. There were definite similarities. She opened the door and R.J. managed to get the animal into the kitchen. R.J.'s crew was already heading back around the house.

"What did you think you were doing?" Leigh demanded of the woman as she shut the door behind the animal.

"He was digging in the rose garden," Eden wailed.

"So what? Most of the roses were destroyed anyhow."

"But that's...where Marcus died!"

Shocked, Leigh gaped at her. Eden was actually trembling. Her face had gone pasty white except for two spots of bright color high on her cheeks. It had never occurred to Leigh that Eden might actually have loved Marcus. She and Hayley had often speculated on Eden's relationship with Marcus, but the pair of them were so emotionally cold that it had seemed professionally platonic.

When Marcus had filed for divorce from their mother and had married Eden more than two years after Amy Thomas had disappeared, Leigh had been shocked and angry at first. But she'd concluded that Marcus had married Eden for the sake of convenience. He no longer had to wait for her to drive to work every day, plus he had someone to run the house for him.

Leigh had never considered the reason Eden had married Marcus. Love had simply never entered the equation in her mind. Obviously, it should have done. Leigh had never seen Eden so distraught.

"I won't have that horrible beast digging up the garden. I won't have it, I tell you!"

"All right, Eden," Leigh said gently.

"Take it easy," Gavin told her.

Eden pulled free of the restraining hand he'd laid on her arm and fled to her car. Leigh exchanged a troubled look with Gavin before calling to Eden to wait. The woman was far too upset to be driving a car. But Eden had already climbed behind the wheel and started the engine.

"Let her go," Gavin advised.

They watched as she peeled down the driveway. Leigh shoved a hand through her hair. "I didn't even know she was on the grounds."

"Neither did I," he said thoughtfully.

"We should see if she hurt Lucky."

"He isn't hurt," R.J. told them when they went inside. He was obviously still shaken by the situation. "I've never seen Lucky act like that before. I'm really sorry. I'll keep him home from now on.''

''Don't you dare,'' Leigh said, stroking the animal's fur.

''I might growl myself if some woman chased me with a knife,'' Gavin pointed out.

''Gavin's right. Lucky was just warning Eden that he was prepared to defend himself. She was the one acting like a wild animal. Lucky's a gentleman. Aren't you, boy?''

The dog gave her face a swipe with his tongue.

R.J. wasn't appeased. ''I'll cover any damage he may have caused out there.''

''Please. There is nothing he could hurt in that overgrown jungle. Trust me. He can dig all the holes he wants right now. I just hired someone to fix the landscaping.''

R.J. ran a distracted hand through his hair. ''It's strange. I've never known him to dig in the dirt. I've got several acres out where I live, and he's never put so much as a hole anywhere. I don't understand what got into him.''

''Maybe he was chasing gophers,'' Gavin suggested.

''R.J., it doesn't matter, it's fine. Honest. Eden was…'' Leigh looked to Gavin for help.

''Overreacting,'' he supplied.

''I was going to say deranged, but overreacting works, too. Please don't punish Lucky because of her. I don't even know what she was doing here today. I thought she already took her belongings from the house.''

''We need to change the locks,'' Gavin said. ''We don't know who has keys to this place and I don't think we want people coming and going at will until the estate is inventoried.''

''But her belongings—''

''We'll see she gets them back, but we should be monitoring what goes in and out of the house from now on. Know any local locksmiths, R.J.?''

''Actually, I do. Want me to give her a call?''

"A woman, huh? Interesting choice of profession. Leigh?"

"I...okay. If you think it's necessary."

"I do. We can't bring the security people out here to reinstall the alarm system until R.J. gets the outer walls, doors and windows completed."

"Give me another couple of days," he told them. "I'm having some delivery problems. In the meantime, I'll secure the site so no one can get inside the house once we're finished for the night."

"Do it," Gavin told him. "Once he's back, I'm going to ask Bram to get started on a gate for that back entrance, if that's okay with you, Leigh."

"All right. R.J.? You'll keep bringing Lucky, won't you?"

He nodded, though he still looked concerned. "I'll try to keep a closer watch on him."

"It's okay. Really. I don't even care if he eats a sofa. He's a good boy, aren't you, Lucky?"

The dog woofed agreement.

"I'll call about the locks, then get back to work," R.J. said, reaching for his cell phone. "Come on, Lucky. Let's see if you can stay out of trouble for the rest of the afternoon."

"I still want to finish having a look around upstairs," Gavin told Leigh as the dog trotted after R.J.

"You want to check out the balcony?"

"Later. Now that I know where the entrance is, that can wait. I want to check out the rest of the room. Where are you going?" he asked when she started toward the front of the house. "Aren't the back stairs closer?"

Leigh hesitated.

"Something wrong with the back stairs?"

She shrugged, but if she'd hoped to convey nonchalance, she failed.

"We seldom used them, so I don't think about them."

Gavin knew a half truth when he heard one. "Why didn't you use them?"

"We just don't."

He waited.

"If you must know, they come out close to Marcus's room."

Something cold began to crawl through his mind. Gavin stopped her when she started walking toward the back staircase.

"Leigh, did Marcus ever—"

"No," she said quickly. "He never laid a hand on either of us, but I was always afraid of him anyhow. I guess that sounds silly, especially now that he's dead."

"No. Not silly at all."

She looked away. The vulnerability he'd glimpsed in her expression was haunting. How could a father not love someone as lovable as Leigh?

She hurried up the back steps, not quite running, but not walking at her usual pace, either. Gavin followed more slowly as he thought about all the ways a parent could abuse a child.

Leigh paused on the landing to wait for him. The staircase had been narrow and steep and dark, but the landing, and especially the hall, was disturbingly dark in both directions. He could understand why a pair of little girls wouldn't want to use these stairs. Not for the first time, he became conscious of the brooding quality that hung over the house. The lingering scent of wood smoke only added unnecessary atmosphere to the mix.

Heartskeep was no place he would want to call home.

"I was just thinking," Leigh said. "It must have been Eden on the balcony watching me earlier."

Gavin nodded. "I wonder if she was here last night."

"We didn't see her car."

"We weren't looking for it. She could have put it in the garage."

"Or parked out near the old barns where Bram's been working. You don't really think she's stealing things, do you?"

"Someone has been, Leigh. There's a lot of money unaccounted for."

"But that was Marcus. Wasn't it?"

"Maybe. I've got people looking into his finances right now."

"Why didn't Mr. Rosencroft pay the firms listed on the bogus bills directly?"

"Marcus was a physician and your father. Ira had no reason to distrust him. Marcus lived here at the estate, and it was becoming increasingly difficult for Ira to get around. In retrospect, Ira's decision to create an account for household expenses was a bad idea, but at the time it made sense. Want to bet Eden was given access to that account after she and Marcus were married?"

Her eyes widened. Gavin stepped into the hall. Thanks to the paneling and lack of windows here, the corridor appeared far narrower than it actually was. He no longer questioned Leigh's dislike of the back staircase. Gavin wanted them both out of this hall.

"Which room belonged to Marcus?"

Leigh pointed left. The closed door faced the hall. She approached it tentatively, twisting the knob as if she expected to find it locked. The door swung open.

"Would you believe I've never been in here before?"

"Never?"

Leigh shook her head. Her hand automatically sought a light switch. Nothing happened when she flipped it because R.J. still had the main power switched off. Leigh offered him a sheepish smile. Gavin walked over and pulled back the heavy damask drapes covering the windows. The room was instantly flooded by what he suspected was unaccustomed daylight.

The spacious room was comfortable despite the clutter of heavy, dark furniture. Flocked green wallpaper covered the walls. Not to Gavin's taste, but at least it was a change from dark brown paneling.

A worn green recliner sat against one wall facing a wide bookcase with a television perched on top. The shelves held books dealing with roses and gardening for the most part, but there were also medical books and professional magazines.

"Not much for light reading, was he?"

Leigh didn't answer. Gavin didn't think she'd even heard him. She wandered around the room, silently inspecting. A heavy sleigh bed sat at the far end. There was a matching nightstand and a dresser. There was also a rolltop desk and even a small refrigerator tucked beside it.

"Looks like he spent a lot of time in here," Gavin said.

"Marcus wasn't much for socializing," she told him.

He watched her move around, lightly skimming her fingers across the surface of the nightstand. Idly, she opened a dresser drawer.

"That's odd. It's empty."

Gavin moved to her side. They quickly discovered that all the drawers were empty. So was the desk. Gavin began to swear as he opened the closet. Heavy cedar paneling lined the large space but the closet was empty. Even the hangers were gone.

"Now we know what Eden was doing here," Leigh said.

"We should have changed the locks sooner."

"According to his will, she did inherit his entire estate. But why would she leave his books and the television?"

"She probably didn't have time to get them. She'll be back. She doesn't want to leave anything for us to find."

Leigh tossed her head. "That implies there was something in here for us to find."

"Maybe there was. She was thorough, wasn't she?" Gavin's scowl deepened. "I've got more than a few questions for Eden. Where's her room?"

"At the other end of the hall."

As he left the bedroom, he glanced in the direction of the construction area that had been roped off.

"What about that door?" he asked, pointing down the hall.

"That's the spare bedroom I told you Jacob uses when he stays here. It's one of the few rooms that has a private bathroom."

The room was bright, almost cheerful. The walls had been painted a light blue-gray, and while the furniture was similar to the heavy dark pieces in Marcus's room, there was less of it, so the room appeared larger and more airy than the corner room had been. The dresser drawers were just as empty, however.

"At least Jacob left the hangers."

"You don't think Jacob had anything to do with the missing money. How could he?"

Gavin could think of a few ways, but there was no point mentioning them now. He knew he should have anticipated this and taken steps sooner. He'd known someone was stealing from the estate.

"It's probably pointless, but let's go have a look at Eden's bedroom."

The four-poster bed, like the rest of the furniture in her room, was white and undeniably feminine. The walls were papered in a delicate print of yellow and blue flowers.

"Not what I expected," he muttered. The more massive furniture he'd seen in the other rooms seemed more suited to her taste.

"This used to be my mother's room," Leigh explained. "Eden took it over after she married Marcus."

No need to ask if Leigh resented that action. The lack of emotion in her words was self-explanatory. Like the other two rooms they'd investigated, the drawers and cedar-lined closet were empty.

"Are all the closets lined with cedar?"

"All the bedroom ones are. What do we do now?"

Gavin hesitated. "Let me see the rest of the upstairs, then we'll decide what action to take."

"You mean, like legal action? Gavin, I don't think I want to go there. At least not over clothing and personal items."

"Let's argue about that later."

"Fine. Hayley's room is down here on the right."

As they started down the other dark hallway Gavin paused at a door on his right and turned the handle, surprised to find it locked. "The attic, right?"

"Right."

"You've been up there?"

She gave a tiny shudder. "Once, when I was little. I'm not real fond of attics and basements."

"How come?"

Leigh eyed him strangely. "That's where the bogeyman lives."

She said it with a straight face, otherwise he might have been tempted to tease her.

"Did you believe that when you were growing up?"

Her eyes slid away from his.

"It's just an attic, Gavin. Hot, stuffy, filled with dust and cobwebs. Like I told the police the other night, Grandpa stored old furniture and stuff up there."

"Might be worth exploring when we get hold of the keys. Remind me to have R.J.'s locksmith unlock these doors. Some of that 'old stuff' they stored up there may be valuable antiques by now."

"Be my guest. You can let me know what you find."

She walked down the hall and opened the door to Hayley's room. The room was a jumble of color and femininity. Posters decorated the light blue walls. The furniture was of dark cherry and scattered with signs of occupancy. Gavin could easily see Hayley in this room as a teenager.

"Closet?" he asked, indicating a door to the right.

"No, the other door is the closet. That's the connecting bathroom. My room's on the other side."

"Okay to take a look?"

"Sure."

But she looked away again, obviously a little uncomfortable at the idea. The bathroom was clean and neat, retaining several light, feminine scents. The furniture in the room beyond was identical to Hayley's, but that was where the sameness ended. The two rooms were very different, reflecting the very individual personalities of the two women. He would have known this was Leigh's room without being told.

No teenage posters hung from the walls in here. Leigh wouldn't have wasted time dreaming of unattainable rock stars. Two soft watercolors graced the cream-colored walls. Several photographs sat on her dresser. He lifted one and studied it. Leigh and Hayley were about twelve in the picture, standing with a lovely woman who could only be their mother.

"You look like your mother," he said, picking up another picture of the girls with their grandfather. The three were carving pumpkins and laughing together.

"We were ten," Leigh told him. "Grandpa was telling us about a Halloween party where everything went wrong. He was a marvelous storyteller."

"You miss him."

"Every day," she agreed. "Don't you miss your family?"

Reluctantly, he summoned up a memory of his mother and father and his older brother. "I don't think about them much."

"Why not?"

He considered that. "I was angry for a long time."

Leigh nodded in understanding.

"My brother was an athlete who never did anything wrong. Good grades, tons of friends, helpful around the house. I was the one always getting into some sort of trouble. I got good grades when I bothered, but school bored me, so I was usually in danger of failing because I ignored things like homework.

"My folks had gone to Bryce's high-school football game that afternoon. I was supposed to stay home and work on a book report that was due. Instead, I went out with some friends who came by. My dad was stopped at a traffic light when a speeding truck lost control. The truck was carrying a load of bricks. They crushed their car like a toy."

"You saw it happen?"

He nodded. "I was on my way home."

"I am so sorry, Gavin."

He covered the hand she placed on his arm. Her fingers felt fragile, almost delicate under his palm. He brushed at the silvery thread of her tears with the back of his finger.

"Don't cry. It was a long time ago."

"Maybe so, but that isn't something you ever forget."

"No," he agreed. "I'll never forget."

And the pain would never heal completely. If he'd been a better person, he'd have been there with them that day. If he'd obeyed them, he wouldn't have to live with the memories.

"They'd be very proud of you," she said quietly, brushing at more tears.

"Think so?" He shook his head and tried for a smile. It failed, but she squeezed his fingers. "Maybe they would at that."

Stepping back, he looked around the room seeking a new focus. His gaze fell on her bookcase, filled to overflowing with brightly colored paperbacks. The topics ranged from classics to mysteries, romance, biographies, and even some old science-fiction titles.

"Eclectic taste," he said, relieved to see she was under control again.

"I like to read."

"Me, too. No rock stars or movie idols on your walls?"

"Mooning over the unattainable always seemed foolish to me."

It was what he'd expected, yet according to Hayley, Leigh had had a crush on him the size of California. That wasn't something he wanted to think about right now, either. Not when she was standing so close, looking so vulnerable.

Gavin headed for the door. "There's just one more room on this corridor, right?" he asked briskly.

Leigh nodded. He suspected she was relieved as well. He wondered why he'd told her what had happened to his family when he'd never told anyone else.

"This was my mother's room when she was a girl, but it's been a guest bedroom ever since I can remember."

Gavin gave the room a cursory look and stepped back out into the hall. Across from them, R.J.'s men were hard at work, tearing apart the remains of her grandfather's suite.

"Are you hungry?" he asked. "It's after four already and I didn't get lunch again. What do you say we go into town and grab an early dinner?"

Leigh hesitated. "I, uh, need to check with Emily."

"No problem. I'll let R.J. know we're leaving and have him lock up. I can meet you at the Walken estate."

"You don't need to buy me dinner, Gavin," she said, stalling.

"Actually, I do." He found himself strangely reluctant to let her go. "We need to discuss how we're going to proceed."

"With Eden?"

"And the missing money, and a new security system, and a few dozen other items." Like the way she'd crept under his skin, keeping him hovering on the ragged edge of desire without doing a single thing beyond looking at him. Lots of women had looked at him over the years, but only Leigh had disturbed him like this.

"Oh."

Tension crackled between them. R.J.'s crew ceased to exist. Even the noise of their radio faded away. Leigh slid her gaze from his. She tossed back her hair and stared fixedly at the top button on his shirt. He allowed himself a brief second to imagine her reaching out and undoing that button.

The tip of her tongue flashed across her lips. The impact was as strong as it was heady. He knew exactly how sweet she tasted and he suddenly wanted another taste badly.

He couldn't remember the last time a woman had left him feeling uncertain.

"You don't have to worry, you know. I don't plan to jump your bones as soon as I get you alone."

As expected, up came that pointed chin. A spark ignited the blue of her eyes.

"You certainly won't."

"No, but it will give you something to worry about while you drive to the Walkens' and work on an excuse for not having dinner with me again."

Chapter Seven

Leigh was craftier than Gavin had expected. As he sat across from her at the Walkens' dinner table, he was reassured by the knowledge that she wasn't immune to the electricity between them. Otherwise, she wouldn't have arranged for them to be eating here with his foster parents instead of going out to eat like he'd planned.

She didn't have to worry, though. If Leigh had been any other woman, he knew exactly how he'd handle this unfortunate craving he'd developed where she was concerned.

But Leigh wasn't any other woman. Not only did they have a past, she presented an ethical dilemma for him. Getting personally involved with a female client was a short road to disaster. He'd already violated his own rules by initiating that kiss, and yet he kept thinking how much he wanted to do it all over again.

Gavin groaned. Three pairs of eyes swung in his direction.

"What's wrong?" Emily asked in concern.

Embarrassed, he said the first thing that came to mind. "Bit my tongue."

Emily and George commiserated, but he'd swear Leigh saw right through the fib. Her gaze slid from his and her color brightened. She was twenty-four. He could attest to the fact that she'd had at least one lover—not that he was particularly proud of that performance—yet Leigh somehow projected a beguiling aura of untouched innocence.

You had a crush on that guy the size of California.

Hayley's words still haunted him. Was it possible Leigh still felt that way despite what had happened between them?

He watched her take a sip of water. She was careful not to look at him. A simmering swirl of anticipation built inside him. He was almost certain she wasn't trying to provoke him, yet he found himself seriously tempted to test her control right along with his own.

''Have you heard any unofficial scuttlebutt on the Pepperton murder?'' George asked.

Leigh turned to him with a puzzled expression. ''What Pepperton murder?''

''You haven't been keeping up with the news lately, dear,'' Emily told her. ''Martin Pepperton was trampled to death by one of his racehorses.''

Leigh's features paled.

''No, that's what they thought at first,'' George corrected. ''Well, I guess, the horse did actually trample him to death, but only after he was shot.''

Leigh looked to Gavin for confirmation. He knew she was remembering the party seven years ago. Martin Pepperton had been the host.

''The police think there was some sort of a fight inside the horse's stall,'' Gavin told her. ''The horse caused so much external damage trying to get away that no one realized Pepperton had been shot until they ran an autopsy.''

Emily set down her coffee cup. ''What took them so long? Don't they perform autopsies right away?''

''Normally,'' Gavin agreed. ''Only they were backed up because the chief medical examiner and his aide were involved in that nasty car wreck out on the interstate last Friday. When the autopsy finally did get performed, there was a major screwup. The report never got to where it was supposed to go. Someone will probably lose their job over it, but the bottom line is that the investigators didn't realize he'd been shot until the other day."

"Good grief."

"What happened to the horse?" Leigh asked.

Gavin wasn't the least bit surprised that Leigh's immediate thought had been for the more valuable animal.

"That was my first question, too," he admitted. "Wyatt told me it was returned to the Pepperton stables."

"Who's Wyatt?"

"Wyatt Crossley," he supplied. "You probably wouldn't know him."

"He's Chief Crossley's nephew," George explained. "He moved here from Connecticut, I think it was, wasn't it, dear?"

"I believe so."

"I've run into him a few times around town. Seems like a nice young man."

Leigh pursed her lips. "A police officer?"

"Afraid so, dear," Emily confirmed, "but he's not at all like his uncle."

"Uh-huh."

"Emily's right," Gavin told her. "Wyatt's actually a good guy. I know you aren't fond of our local officials..."

"Neither were you once, as I recall."

His lips curved. "I got over it."

"By joining the team?" she mocked with raised eyebrows.

"Hey, I'm just a lawyer, remember?"

"Do the police have any suspects?" Emily intervened in an effort to play peacemaker.

"Not really," he told her. "The Saratoga police are trying to locate anyone who was at the track that morning but you can imagine their frustration. With all the time that's elapsed, even if someone did see something useful, their memories are apt to be faulty at best by now.''

And privately, Gavin didn't figure too many people were going to mourn Martin Pepperton. He still suspected Pepperton was the one who had supplied Ducort with the date-rape drug all those years ago.

''I've heard rumors that it was a drug buy gone bad,'' George said.

Gavin shrugged. He watched Leigh tense and knew exactly what she was thinking.

''It's common knowledge that Pepperton was a substance abuser,'' George continued. ''His mood swings were becoming legendary right along with his wild parties.''

''I don't think you can blame his moods entirely on drugs, dear. If you'll recall, the Peppertons all have quick tempers,'' Emily put in. ''Bram was married to Martin's cousin several years ago. Remember how one of them accosted him at the hospital right after his wife died? He acted as if her death was Bram's fault somehow.'' She pursed her lips. ''And to change the subject entirely, Leigh tells us Eden has been cleaning out everything she can from the house.''

Leigh fiddled with her coffee cup.

''I've already started legal action on behalf of the estate,'' Gavin said, ''but it's probably too late to recover most of what she's removed.''

''That's okay,'' Leigh interjected. ''Hayley and I don't want anything that belonged to Marcus. And I think Eden genuinely cared for him. You saw how upset she was this afternoon. As far as I'm concerned, she's welcome to whatever she took.''

''Including the missing six hundred fifty thousand?'' Gavin asked.

George whistled in surprise. ''That much?''

''At least. I have auditors coming in to work on the situation. Leigh and I will sit down and go over everything once they finish. I'm afraid Ira hadn't been on top of things for a number of years.''

George rubbed the side of his nose. ''You don't suspect him of stealing from the estate, do you?''

''To tell you the honest truth, I don't know. I don't want to believe there was any collusion, but the situation's a mess. A lot of money is gone. Frankly, his records are a disaster. I've spent months trying to go through everything. The first thing I did after Ira died was to let Corrine go and hire a receptionist with paralegal training.''

''You let Corrine go?'' Emily chided. ''She's worked for Ira forever.''

''I know,'' he said, his expression grim. ''That was part of the problem.''

''Emily,'' George said in a warning tone. Emily immediately subsided, but her brow stayed furrowed.

''The office was more than she could handle, Emily. She told me she'd only stayed this long because Ira asked her to. She wanted to spend more time with her grandchildren.''

Tiredly, Gavin rubbed his jaw. Corrine Simpson was nearly Ira's age. She'd told Gavin flat out that she'd wanted to leave, but Ira had been her husband's best friend and she hadn't wanted to leave him in the lurch. She'd have done him a bigger favor if she'd gone.

''I'm sorry, Gavin. Of course you need to do what's best. I didn't mean to question you.''

''No problem,'' he assured Emily. ''Do either of you know who actually managed Heartskeep after Amy Thomas disappeared? Do you know if Marcus saw to the day-to-day household needs or did Eden take over right away?''

''Marcus didn't confide in us,'' George told him flatly.

''The people you ought to ask are Livia and Kathy

Walsh,'' Emily said. ''They knew more about what went on there than anyone else.''

''Until Eden chased them away,'' Leigh put in sadly.

''I hired an investigator to locate them. He traced Livia Walsh this morning.''

''You didn't tell me that,'' Leigh said.

''I planned to tell you over dinner. She purchased a house outside Saratoga Springs right after leaving Heartskeep. I thought maybe you'd like to drive up there with me tomorrow. If she agrees to see us, I'm sure she'll be more forthcoming with you there than if she talks with me alone.''

''I'd like to see her again,'' Leigh agreed. ''I feel guilty that I didn't stay in touch after we moved to Boston.''

''I'm sure she understood,'' Emily told her.

''Maybe, but Hayley and I should have made more of an effort. What time do you want to go?'' Leigh asked.

''My last appointment is at one. Would three o'clock be too late?''

''Not at all. That will leave me free to help you organize your fund-raiser in the morning, Emily.''

''Wonderful. The garden club can use all the help we can get.''

''I'll give Mrs. Walsh a call tomorrow then,'' Gavin said.

Driving up there would give him several hours with Leigh. He'd keep everything on a businesslike footing if it killed him. And remembering that kiss, he thought it just might.

When he finally rose to leave some time later, he turned to Leigh. ''Walk me out?''

''Did you forget the way?''

Amused, he watched her cheeks turn pink when she remembered they weren't alone.

''See how she treats me?'' he complained. ''No respect for her own lawyer.''

"I didn't realize you were asking as my lawyer," Leigh said tartly.

"Did you think I was expecting a good-night kiss?"

The pink brightened. "Hardly."

"Too bad," he said with a theatrical sigh.

Her cheeks turned cherry red. "Stop that."

George and Emily watched the exchange with interest. Gavin tried for a woebegone expression. "Shot down again. 'Night, George, Emily. Thanks again for dinner."

"Good night, Gavin," Emily replied. The bridge of her nose was pleated despite her smile and he realized she was worried. He should have remembered how easily she'd always been able to read him.

"Drive safely," George told him.

"Always. Coming?" he asked Leigh. "After all, you wouldn't want me to walk out there alone in the dark and get attacked by the bogeyman."

"I'm sure the bogeyman wouldn't waste his time."

"Ouch." But he winked at the Walkens to ease their concern as she rose to accompany him.

He waited until they were at the front door before saying anything more. "Do I make you nervous?" he asked Leigh.

Up came her chin. "Of course not."

"Good. Then if you don't want George coming after me with a shotgun, it would be nice if you'd stop acting so jumpy around me."

Startled, her lips parted in protest. "I'm not acting jumpy."

They stepped onto the front porch. Deliberately, he closed the door behind them.

"You don't think so?"

"Of course not."

"Then why are you trembling?"

He'd forgotten to turn on the porch light. There wasn't enough of a moon to let him see her expression clearly.

"I'm not trembling."

He traced her jaw with the back of his finger. She inhaled sharply.

"What are you doing, Gavin?"

"Darned if I know." He dropped his hands to his side. "I have a rule. I never get personally involved with a client."

Was that a flash of hurt in her expression?

"Very wise."

"Yeah. So why do I suddenly resent the heck out of that rule?"

"You never were one to follow rules—even your own."

She was right. There was something special about Leigh. He'd known it seven years ago when he'd first seen her standing under a tree looking sexier than any pinup.

"Why did you ask me to come out here with you?"

His mind went blank. She tilted her head in question.

"You must have wanted something."

"I want a lot of things," he told her honestly.

"Is that why you kissed me in the closet?"

"That was a mistake. You're my client."

"And kissing a client is a bad thing," she said in a flat voice.

Gavin ran a hand through his hair in frustration. The last thing he wanted to do was hurt her again. "I'm not expressing myself very well here, but you can understand why we need to keep things on a professional level. If the situation was different..."

"Then what? Kissing me would be okay? Do I have a say in this?"

He shook his head. She was hurt and angry and spoiling for a fight. "You don't want to provoke an argument with me, Leigh," he said gently.

She raised her chin and even in the dark he could see the glitter of challenge in her eyes. "Why not?"

"Because I'm a lawyer. You wouldn't win."

"What an egotistical stateme—"

"Did you really have a crush on me the size of California?"

"Of course not!"

He stared at her in silent challenge. She didn't look away, even though it was obvious that she was embarrassed. After a second, her tension eased and she swung her head in a purely feminine gesture.

"It was more like Nebraska."

The unexpected words took a minute to sink in. A smile started inside him, spreading until he could feel it in every pore. She was incredible. Utterly unpredictable and as open and honest as she was lovely. His body hardened in desire.

"You'd better go back inside and I'd better leave."

Neither of them moved.

"You're turning into a major temptation, Leigh."

"Am I supposed to be flattered?"

"Well, my ego would probably appreciate it."

"Your ego doesn't need any help from me. Why did you ask me to walk out here with you?"

"I wanted to apologize for stepping over the line this afternoon and assure you that it won't happen again."

"Gee, thanks. But, this isn't going to magically go away, you know. There's a chemical reaction taking place between us."

"I know all about pheromones, Leigh, and I know we can ignore them."

"What if we don't want to ignore them?"

His pulse leaped. "Didn't anyone ever tell you that sometimes honesty isn't the best policy?"

"Why not?"

Any number of responses came to mind. None of them made it to his lips. She stood there looking up at him and he could feel his resolve trickling away. "This is a bad idea."

"What is?"

"If you don't go inside right this minute, I'm going to kiss you again," he warned.

A quiver seemed to run straight down her body.

"Not if you don't stop talking."

Gavin stopped talking.

Leigh melted against him. Her body was coiled so tight in anticipation, she felt as if she could explode right there. Instead, it was the kiss that exploded in a bubble of excitement too raw to be contained. Need was a living thing inside her, pulsing without restraint.

Her lips parted, inviting him to explore. There was nothing tentative in the way his mouth took possession of hers. He held her firmly, one large, warm hand sliding beneath her hair to cup the back of her head. He held her there in place as he kissed her with shocking thoroughness.

Leigh could feel the throbbing hardness of him against her thigh. She opened her mouth and kissed him back, craving more. Much more.

It had been like this in her dreams, but the reality was so much better. She pressed against him, moving in restless excitement that sent her senses soaring, taking her higher and higher.

The porch light suddenly winked on overhead.

They sprang apart as if scalded by the brightness. Her breath shuddered out of her as her heart continued its uneven thud against her rib cage. Leigh was aware of her body in a womanly way she had never known. The unfamiliar sense of feminine power was exhilarating.

"I think someone's trying to tell us something."

The deep timbre of his husky voice was thick, the words not quite steady. But at least he had a voice. She couldn't seem to find hers.

"Are you all right?"

Leigh managed a nod.

"Do I owe you another apology?"

She glared at him. "Do I look like I'm waiting for one?"

"You look..."

His gaze swept her, as intimate as a caress.

"...like a fantasy," he said on a ragged note. "I'll see you tomorrow at three."

She didn't move as he spun abruptly and left the porch. She remained standing there long after his taillights disappeared down the driveway.

Baiting him had been stupid. He was right. A relationship between them was foolish and impossible. Yet she was still crazy about Gavin Jarret.

What was she supposed to do now?

"THERE'S A SLIGHT HITCH in our plans," Gavin said when Leigh was ushered into his office at seven minutes past three the next day.

"A hitch. Is that like a hiccup?"

"Same thing."

She loved the way his eyes softened until the rest of his face followed suit. She'd decided to take her cues from Gavin. If he wanted to act like nothing out of the ordinary had happened last night, she would be casual as well, no matter what it cost her.

There was definitely masculine approval in the gaze he sent sweeping over her. She was glad she'd left the garden club meeting early enough to shower and change clothes before driving into town.

"What's the hitch?"

"I've tried to reach Mrs. Walsh, but she's not answering her telephone. We can drive up there and see if we can catch her anyhow, or we can wait and try again tomorrow."

"Since I promised to help Emily again tomorrow, I think

we should go ahead. Mrs. Walsh may be out shopping or something.''

''That was my thinking, too.''

Gavin shed his suit coat and tie as he led her out to his car. Leigh was disappointed, but not surprised, when he made no effort to touch her and kept the conversation businesslike.

''I've been looking over those bogus bills Marcus submitted. I'm pretty sure they were all computer generated. Was he good with computers?''

''I don't know. He and Eden had one in their office.''

''What about a scanner?''

''I don't remember seeing one, but Grandpa had one in his office. Everyone in the house had access to it.''

''Okay. Who among the household members had good computer skills?''

''Jacob and I have the most knowledge.''

''Jacob?'' he asked sharply.

''Oh, please. Not you, too. I know why Bram doesn't like him, but you have no reason to dislike Jacob. Besides, he wouldn't have had access to the household account and Marcus didn't like him.''

''Why not?''

''Marcus didn't like anyone.''

''No, but Eden was his mother.''

''You really do sound like Bram. What is it about Jacob you guys don't like? Generally speaking, everyone likes Jacob.''

Gavin slanted her a wry look. ''I don't know Jacob well enough to like or dislike him. I'm trying to look at all the angles here. Jacob could have shown his mother how to use the computer and scanner so she could create the bills.''

''Or she may have known how to do it without his help. So could Marcus. There's no way to tell, Gavin. Maybe

Mrs. Walsh will know. Or more likely, Kathy would. She's the one who used to clean their offices.''

''My detective still doesn't have an address for Kathy, but he's working on it. She may have gotten married and moved away.''

''You know, it's funny. They seemed so much a part of our lives growing up, but I don't even know if Kathy had boyfriends when she worked for us. Why don't we simply ask Mrs. Walsh how to find her?''

''I plan to.''

LIVIA WALSH LIVED in a house so far outside Saratoga Springs that Gavin expressed surprise that it was still in the same county. The one-story ranch-style house was part of a cluster of brick homes built in the 1950s. Neat, well-manicured lawns were shaded by large trees and mature shrubs. The neighborhood had a quiet, prosperous, settled look.

''Looks like we made the trip for nothing,'' he told Leigh as they started down the street. ''She must be out of town.''

Leigh saw what he meant. A couple of newspapers sat in the driveway of an otherwise pristine yard. The mailbox number matched the one his investigator had given him.

''Something's wrong,'' she said in concern. ''Mrs. Walsh would never go away without stopping the newspaper. She'd at least arrange for someone to pick them up. She was compulsively organized, Gavin.''

''Maybe something came up unexpectedly.''

''All the more reason she'd have someone watch the house and take in her papers.''

Leigh got out of the car as soon as he came to a stop and hurried over to the mailbox. She could see the drapes and shades were all drawn to cover the windows. It felt wrong and the mailbox confirmed her fears.

"There's three days' worth of mail in here," Leigh told him. "Something's wrong."

Gavin spotted a woman watching them from the window of the house next door. "Let's go see what her neighbors know. Maybe one of them has a key."

The woman who answered the door looked to be in her mid-thirties. She wasn't hostile, but she wasn't the trusting sort, either. Watching Leigh paw through her neighbor's mail probably hadn't helped instill a sense of confidence in them. Gavin identified himself and handed her a business card when she reluctantly cracked open her screen door.

"I don't know where Mrs. Walsh is," the woman told them. "I admit, I did begin to worry when I saw she hadn't picked up her papers. She usually asks Jane, across the street, to take them in if she's going away for a few days."

Leigh shot him an 'I told you so' look.

"Does she go away a lot?" Gavin asked.

"Not really, no."

"Does Jane have a key to the house?"

"I don't think so. You'll have to ask her. She's at work right now."

"Would you have a work number where I could reach her?"

"I'm afraid not. Do you think something's happened to Mrs. Walsh?" The woman stepped out onto her porch, brushing at her untidy hair. "She's a lovely person. I'd hate to think she might be lying inside hurt or injured. Maybe we should call the police."

"We may have to," he agreed. "Let me go back over and have a look around first."

"I could call her, see if she answers her phone."

"I already tried that. Come on, Leigh."

"We should break a window or something," Leigh said as they walked away. "The woman's right. She could be lying in there hurt."

"Take it easy. We'll try the doors and windows first. One of them might be unlocked."

While the neighbor stood on her porch watching nervously, they determined the front door was locked with an impressive dead bolt. Gavin couldn't see in through the windows because of the heavy drapes, but he tested each window as they walked around the house. Near the back, he got lucky. One window slid upward with a little coaxing.

He boosted himself up. "Mrs. Walsh?"

Pushing aside the drape, he peered inside and swore. Instantly he dropped back down to the ground.

"What is it?" Leigh demanded. "What did you see? What are you doing?" she added as Gavin pulled out his cell phone.

"Calling the police."

"Is she dead?"

"I don't know, but either your housekeeper likes retirement so much she gave up all cleaning, or her house has been ransacked."

"We should go in there! She could be hurt!"

Gavin shook his head as his call was answered by an emergency operator.

Despite her agitation, Leigh agreed to wait for the police to arrive. When two officers did arrive, the neighbor joined them and watched while Gavin showed them his identification and explained the situation. The neighbor added that she, too, was worried.

After ordering them to wait in the driveway away from the house, the younger officer climbed through the same window Gavin had used. A moment later, he stuck his head back out, said something to his companion, and disappeared from view again. The second officer hurried to the back of the house.

Gavin rested his hand lightly on Leigh's arm. Her body pulsed with tension as they waited in silence for the police to reappear. When they did, both men came from the back of the house.

"Sir, the house was ransacked, but there is no evidence to suggest that Mrs. Walsh was inside at the time."

Gavin felt some of the tension leave Leigh.

"There's no sign of a struggle. The back door's unlocked so it's probably just a random break-in."

"We didn't make it all the way around the house," Gavin told him.

The neighbor spoke up, obviously distraught. "I should have taken in her papers when I saw them lying there. It's just an open invitation for thieves."

"Yes, ma'am," the officer agreed.

"What about her car?" Leigh demanded.

That sent the officers around to the detached garage where they found the door unlocked and the car gone.

"It can't be happening again," Leigh whispered.

"What can't?" Gavin asked.

Leigh peered up at him with stricken eyes. "My mother simply vanished, and now Mrs. Walsh has disappeared."

Gavin shook his head. "This isn't like what happened to your mother, Leigh," he told her firmly.

"How do you know that? No one knows what happened to my mother."

"This is different," he assured her.

"Is it?"

Gavin wrapped an arm around her shoulders. He could feel small tremors in her slight frame as she stared at the garage. He wished he could think of something more comforting to say. After a minute, she leaned against him, but remained tense until the officers returned and reported that her car was also missing.

"But there's no sign of violence or a struggle," the older officer was quick to point out. "We'll secure the house and start an investigation, but odds are Mrs. Walsh will turn up."

"You have my number," Gavin said. "Make sure someone gives me a call when you do locate Mrs. Walsh."

"Yes, sir."

In the end, there was nothing they could do but leave.

"We don't even know how to find Kathy to tell her that her mother's missing," Leigh muttered, staring back at the house as Gavin drove away.

"But we did learn that Kathy has a boyfriend."

The neighbor, whose name had proved to be Dee Millhouse, had offered that information.

"But she didn't know where to find Kathy or her boyfriend."

"No, but she did notice he drove a car with license plates that weren't issued here in New York."

"How is that going to help? She didn't even know which state they were from. And where are you going? You should have turned back there."

"There's a good pasta place downtown."

"You want to eat? Now?"

"You can sit there and wring your hands if you want," he told her with deliberate calm, "but it isn't going to help you or Mrs. Walsh."

Her head jerked up.

"More than likely, the neighbor was right. Mrs. Walsh probably went somewhere with her daughter and they were gone longer than they expected. Or it's possible that her other neighbor, Jane, forget to take in her mail and papers, and some kid passing by saw the newspapers, found the open window like we did and tore the place apart looking for cash."

"But I heard those officers say the television and VCR hadn't been touched."

"Not every thief wants to lug a television around with him. It's difficult to explain away if you're seen."

He kept his eyes on the road, but was aware that she tilted her head to one side as she regarded him.

"That sounds like the voice of experience talking."

His lips curved with humor. "Nope, but I knew a few guys who knew a few guys."

"Uh-huh."

Leigh fell silent. Gavin cast a quick look in her direction and was relieved to see normal color returning to her face. Her mother's disappearance obviously haunted her the same way the death of his family had haunted him. Watching them die had been horrific, but he wasn't sure how he would have dealt with the situation if he'd never known what had happened to them. At least he'd had bodies to bury.

"I'm sorry," she said as he found a parking space close to the restaurant. "I know you're probably right."

"You don't have anything to be sorry about. You care and that's a good thing. My guess is that Mrs. Walsh will turn up in a few days with a perfectly logical explanation for her absence."

"I hope you're right."

"Lawyers are supposed to be right. That's why we get the big bucks. Come on. I think you'll enjoy this place."

"Is food all you think about?"

He gave her a long, slow look. A pulse jumped in her throat. "Food is definitely not the only thing I think about."

The restaurant was crowded, but Leigh agreed that she didn't mind a wait. She wasn't the least bit hungry and Gavin's sudden mood switch wasn't helping. What was she supposed to think when he was all business one minute and flirtatious the next?

"You okay?"

She managed a nod.

"Saratoga Springs is a pretty town, isn't it?" Gavin asked as they stood in the restaurant's foyer waiting along with several other couples. "I haven't been here in a number of years, but I used to hang out some at Lake Lonely in my wilder days. The name appealed to me."

When he smiled at her like that, it was hard to concentrate on anything else. "Do you miss them?"

"My wilder days? No, I can't say that I do."

Leigh knew Gavin was trying to keep her from dwelling on Mrs. Walsh's disappearance, and she did her best to go along with him as they waited. When they were finally led to their table, Leigh noticed a man in his fifties, dining alone. He stared hard at Leigh, then abruptly smiled as if in recognition, the way a casual acquaintance might do. Leigh inclined her head politely while she wracked her brain for some idea as to who he was. His round, friendly face and the steel-gray mustache rang no bells whatsoever with her. Gavin didn't seem to notice the exchange, so she didn't say anything, but she was aware of the man's gaze as she studied the menu, and wondered if he was someone who knew her sister. They were often mistaken for one another.

"I need to use the men's room and check my messages," Gavin told her after they placed their orders. "I'll be right back."

Leigh nodded. The restaurant bustled with noise and people, but she barely noticed. She was still thinking about Mrs. Walsh. Even though Gavin was probably right and there was a simple explanation for what had happened to Mrs. Walsh, Leigh couldn't help feeling worried. Lost in thought, she was startled when the man she'd noticed earlier suddenly appeared beside her table.

"Hello, again. Matt Klineman," he said. "We met the other day."

She stared at his weather-seamed face with absolutely no recognition. ''I'm afraid—''

''Don't worry about it. I'm not great with names and faces, either, but a lovely lady like yourself is hard to forget. I don't mean to interrupt, but I wondered if you'd pass along a message to your friend, the vet, for me.''

Leigh shook her head. ''I'm sorry. I think you have me confused with someone else.''

For a moment he look baffled. Then his drooping eyes lit in understanding. ''Ah, you'd rather your vet friend doesn't know you were here with this friend, huh? I understand. I'll give the vet a call later then. You don't have to worry. He won't hear about your date from me.''

''No, wait. You're mistaken. I don't have a friend who's a vet. Maybe you met my sister.''

He eyed her with obvious skepticism. ''No problem, missy. Sorry to have bothered you.''

Leigh watched him amble away. Normally, she wouldn't have thought twice about such an event. She would have pulled out the picture she carried that proved she was a twin. But she let him go because this was different. Leigh was fairly certain Hayley didn't have any friends who were vets, yet the man seemed so convinced that she was feeling distinctly uneasy.

She drummed her fingers against the tablecloth before reaching for her cell phone. She hated people who used cell phones in restaurants so she peered around for a place to go as the waitress arrived with their drinks.

''Where is the ladies' room?''

''Back there,'' the woman said, pointing in the direction Gavin had taken.

''Thank you. I didn't want you to think we were running off, but I need to make a quick phone call.''

The woman smiled. ''No problem. I'll have your salads out in a moment.''

"Thank you."

Leigh stopped in the alcove short of the rest rooms and punched the button that would connect her to her sister's cell phone.

"Hayley? It's Leigh," she said when her sister answered. "Did I call at a bad time?"

"Nope. We're leaving the hospital right now, but I forgot to charge my phone, so if I cut off suddenly, it's because the battery died."

"How's Bram's father?"

"Conscious, thank heavens. Apparently, he had a severe reaction to one of his medications. He should make a full recovery, according to his doctor. Bram wants to introduce me to him tomorrow after they move him out of intensive care. If everything looks good, we'll head back to Heartskeep after that. Is everything okay there?"

"Not exactly. Mrs. Walsh is missing and I need to know if you have a friend who's a vet."

"What do you mean, Mrs. Walsh is missing?"

A familiar, prickly feeling lifted the hairs at the back of her neck. Her gaze swept the restaurant, searching faces while she sketched in what had happened. There was no sign of the man who'd approached her, yet the feeling that she was being watched persisted. Hayley was speaking when the phone went dead.

"Nuts." Leigh clicked off her phone and looked up to see Gavin standing there, watching her.

"Was that Hayley?"

"Yes."

Across the room, the waitress was setting salads on their table.

"Is everything all right with Bram's father?" he asked.

"Yes. I'll explain at the table."

Leigh scanned the room as they walked back together. No one appeared to be paying any special attention to her, but more than one pair of female eyes was busy checking out Gavin. She knew all too well how appealing his air of confidence could be. They weren't the watchers that concerned her.

When they reached the table, she leaned close to Gavin and told him about the man who'd approached her. "He must have thought I was Hayley. He thought I was pretending not to have met him because I was two-timing this vet person with you," she concluded.

Gavin sat back, looking more relaxed. "I wouldn't worry about it too much if I were you. He obviously made a mistake."

"I know, but I'm sure Hayley doesn't know any vets."

"Ask her when she calls you back," he advised. "As long as no vet comes looking to challenge me while I'm having dinner with my biggest client, I'd say there's nothing to worry about."

There he went again, running hot and cold. Biggest client indeed. She was tempted to tell him it wasn't going to work. They were both guilty of sending mixed signals, but she was tired of games. They needed to find out whether this attraction was simply sex, or something more.

Simple.

Ha.

Nothing about Gavin would ever be simple.

He picked up his fork and his lips curved. "Maybe you and Hayley have a double."

"You don't think two of us are enough?"

"Actually," he said, looking her straight in the eyes, "I think the world could use a lot more people like you and Hayley."

Chapter Eight

Afterward, Leigh couldn't have said if the meal was good or not. She ate automatically, caught up in thoughts of starting a relationship with Gavin. She could see where a casual affair would present all sorts of problems, but they couldn't keep ignoring the situation.

They were waiting for the waitress to return with his change when that prickly feeling at the back of her neck intensified. For a while, it had gone away. Now it was back with a vengeance. Her gaze slipped over the people sitting around them.

"Something wrong?" Gavin asked.

About to deny the charge, she found herself nodding instead.

"We're being watched," she told him.

His nod was so slight she might have imagined it. "I didn't realize you'd spotted him. Let's go."

"Spotted who? What about your change?"

"Forget it."

Gavin rose. Leigh did the same. The restaurant was even more crowded now than it had been earlier. A line of people waited to be seated. Gavin hustled her past everyone.

"Stay close," he said softly against her hair.

As if she had a choice. He had a grip on her arm that practically pinned her against his side. He hurried them to the door. Once there, he paused an instant to rake the busy street with an alert gaze. Again, the terse nod.

"Go."

Leigh went. She all but ran to keep up with his longer stride, but she didn't complain. His urgency fed her own.

"When we reach the car, get inside and fasten your seat belt," he ordered. "Stay low."

"Who did you see?"

He didn't answer.

Her pulse leaped. "Nolan?"

"No."

Even before they reached his car, she heard the door locks thunk as he pressed his key chain to undo them. Gavin didn't waste time holding the door open as usual. He went immediately around the car and slipped behind the wheel.

"Who did you see?" she demanded again as he started the engine.

"Keith Earlwood."

It took her a minute to make the connection. A tall skinny youth with a serious overbite, he'd been one of Nolan's friends. The one with the open leer and the irritating laugh. Her stomach crawled.

"Where was he?"

"Across the street while we were eating. I lost track of him when we stood up."

"The whole time? He was across the street the whole time?"

"I didn't see him arrive."

"Don't split hairs. Why didn't you say something?"

Gavin pulled out into traffic. "He has as much right to be in Saratoga Springs as we do."

"Then why are we running away?"

"Because he may not be here alone."

Her stomach lurched, heavy with the undigested pasta. "We filled out papers to keep Nolan away."

Gavin shot a quick glance her way. His expression was wry. "You knew he wasn't going to pay attention to a piece of paper."

"Then why did we bother?"

"So we'd have legal grounds to take action against him when he makes his move."

There was an almost feral satisfaction in his tone.

Slowly, Leigh shook her head. "You picked the wrong form of law, you know. You should have been a prosecuting attorney." Anything else was far too tame for a hunter like Gavin.

"Think so?" he asked with a thread of humor.

She knew so. She could practically see the waiting intensity humming inside him. He wasn't concerned. She'd bet money Gavin was looking forward to another opportunity to pound Nolan into the ground.

He drove, giving equal concentration to his mirrors. Leigh had to resist an urge to turn around and keep watch behind them.

"Got him," he said abruptly.

"He's following us?"

"Someone is. Dark green sedan."

"You're enjoying this, aren't you?"

He flashed her a look.

"You will remember that you're a lawyer now, not a street tough anymore. Won't you?"

His lips curved. "Don't worry."

"Yeah, right. What are you going to do?"

"Take him on a little tour of the area."

That sounded foreboding.

"We could call the police."

He turned down a side street. "And tell them what? He hasn't done anything illegal that I know about."

"Yet," she muttered.

Gavin's lips twitched. "Stop fretting. I want to be sure he's alone first. Then we'll have a little conversation with him. Sit back and let me handle it."

Leigh didn't like the sound of that at all. As Gavin took a series of side streets, several signs indicated they were heading toward the racetrack. It would be closed to the public at this hour since the horse-racing season didn't start there until some time in July.

Her frown deepened as they bypassed the road that led to the track. Leigh had no idea what he was doing, but obviously Gavin had a destination in mind. She stared out her side mirror and fretted.

Gavin made several more turns until a dark green car was the only vehicle left behind them. It dropped back when the driver became aware that he was now clearly visible. At least it wasn't a red truck like the one that had run them off the road the other night.

She hated remembering the way Keith Earlwood and Martin Pepperton had leered at her all those years ago. She'd often wondered exactly what would have happened if Gavin hadn't come along when he did. Of the three men, Keith had seemed the least threatening at the time. He was certainly no match for Gavin.

She realized Gavin had circled around to the back side of the park. Stable roofs could be glimpsed through the treetops. As he turned onto an empty stretch of road that eventually led to a fenced gate, he sped up.

"Brace yourself."

That was the only warning she got. He threw the car in reverse and backed down a rutted side road she hadn't even noticed. The car jolted to a halt, pitching her against the seat belt. Trees and shrubs lined either side of the road. Seconds later, the green car rolled past.

"Gotcha," he said with a satisfied grin.

Gavin pulled across the road, effectively blocking the street. The other driver hadn't yet realized his mistake. He stopped his car in the middle of the road a few yards ahead of them, but well short of the gate. He appeared to be talking on a cell phone.

"Stay in the car and stay down," Gavin ordered. He stepped out, ignoring her protest. Opening the rear door, he pulled an aluminum baseball bat from the floor of his car. Leigh gasped.

Earlwood still hadn't seen the trap. Gavin watched him put down his phone and reached for the gearshift. Gavin flung open the driver's-side door.

"Get out of the car, Keith," he ordered.

Earlwood's lanky form had filled in some over the years, but Gavin figured he had a least twenty pounds on the other man. Earlwood started like a rabbit, gaping up in shock. His eyes grew almost comically wide at the sight of the baseball bat in Gavin's hand.

"What are you going to do?" Fear made his voice shrill.

"We're going to have a little chat."

Earlwood cringed back against his seat. "You can't hit me! You're a lawyer!"

Gavin bared his teeth in a smile meant to intimidate. "Is that what Ducort told you? Put the car in park right now unless you want to see how shatterproof your windshield is."

"I'll have you arrested," Keith sputtered.

"Hard to do if you can't talk."

Gavin stepped back and tapped the bat against his open palm. He knew exactly how menacing the action appeared, but it was the fastest way to get cooperation from someone like Earlwood.

"You're bluffing."

Gavin lowered his voice to a gravelly purr. "Let's find out. Shall we?"

"All right, all right!" Earlwood put the car in Park.

Once in a while, it helped to have a bad-boy reputation, Gavin decided. Too bad Leigh wasn't as easily intimidated. He heard her get out of the car. He should have known she wouldn't stay put. Later, he'd chew her out for not following a simple order. Right now, he couldn't afford to spare her a glance. He kept his attention on Earlwood.

"Aren't you a little old to still be running Ducort's errands, Keith?"

"I don't know what you're talking about."

His gaze shifted nervously toward Leigh. Her appearance seemed to boost a return of his confidence. He managed a sneer.

"You're all talk, Jarret. You aren't going to do anything with her here."

"On the contrary," Leigh said pleasantly. "I just came to watch him work. I don't like you, either."

Darting a glance in her direction, Gavin managed to swallow his surprise. She'd picked up his softball. Now she tossed it lightly in her hand. Her expression was unexpectedly hard and cold as she regarded Earlwood.

The woman amazed him. He couldn't tell if she was serious or just trying to back his play, but the ball, he decided, was a nice touch.

"I don't like being spied on," she told the confused man darkly.

Gavin realized he needed to get control before the situation spiraled out of hand. "Neither do I, Keith, so why don't you tell us what's going on. What does your old pal want you to do?"

"Nothing!" He looked around wildly. Seeing no help in sight, he managed a shrug. "Nolan just asked me to keep an eye on the two of you, that's all."

"And you still do whatever Ducort tells you to do."

Gavin shook his head. "Not smart, Keith. Not smart at all. Why does Ducort want you to follow us?"

"I don't know. It's the truth! Look, I've had a few setbacks at work recently. The economy, you know? Like everyone else, I need a little cash infusion for my dry cleaning businesses. Nolan offered to make me an interest-free loan if I'd follow the two of you around for a couple of days. I'm just supposed to call and tell him what you're up to, that's all."

His Adam's apple slid up and down his long neck, but for all his nervousness, Gavin sensed Earlwood was telling the truth. The economy was tough, especially for the small businessman, and Ducort made a habit of gobbling up businesses in trouble.

Keith looked to Leigh for support. "It's the truth, honest. I don't need any trouble."

"Then you ought to get yourself a new set of friends," Leigh told him coldly.

Seeing no support there, he turned back to Gavin. "I swear I don't know any more than what I've told you, man. Nolan was real upset when I told him that the two of you came here to the track after dinner."

Gavin gazed around the still-empty stretch of road. They were pushing their luck. Any moment now someone could come along and interrupt.

"Why did that upset him, Keith?"

"Beats me. He wanted me to climb the fence and find out where you went. Do you believe it? I told him no way." Earlwood spread his hands. "I'm not climbing any fences and getting myself arrested for trespassing just to follow you around."

"What were you supposed to do if we split up?" Leigh asked.

The question caught him off guard, but Gavin realized it was one he should have asked himself.

"I was supposed to stay with you," Earlwood told her.

The admission infuriated Gavin, particularly when Keith continued with a sly expression.

"Nolan's always had a thing for you and your sister. He's a little crazy if you ask me."

"No one's asking you," Gavin told him gruffly. He needed to leave before he gave in to the temptation to forget he was an officer of the court. Reaching past Earlwood, he grabbed the man's car keys from the ignition.

"Hey! What are you doing?"

Gavin walked to the side of the road and tossed them into the woods. Earlwood's face pinched in fury. He took a couple of steps forward and stopped.

Gavin started back toward him. He skittered back several steps.

"You don't want to follow us anymore," he told the man. "I'd hate to have to have another conversation to make you understand that I'm real serious about that."

"If you need a loan," Leigh put in, "try a bank next time."

"Okay, okay, I'm out of it. But I'd watch my back if I were you," he warned. "Nolan has hated your guts for years, Jarret. And he's been acting real weird since Martin got killed."

Gavin stopped moving. "What do you know about Pepperton's death, Keith?"

"Nothing! Hey, man, I don't know a thing. I haven't seen Martin in months. That's the God's honest truth! We don't exactly move in the same circles anymore, you know?"

That protest rang true as well. Ducort might have gotten Keith to help him with something, but Gavin couldn't see them sharing confidences. He reached inside the car and retrieved Keith's cell phone.

"Hey, what are you doing? Wait! I need that!"

He flipped it over and tore off the battery. ''Just a suggestion, Keith. It might be a good idea for you to disappear for a couple of days. I don't think Ducort's going to like you a whole lot right now, either. Nice chatting with you.''

He slid the battery into a pocket and tossed the disabled cell phone to the man. ''Get in the car, Leigh.''

For once she obeyed. Earlwood shot him a look of pure malice before hurrying to the side of the road to retrieve his keys.

''Save the lectures,'' Leigh said as he climbed in beside her. She chucked the softball over the seat and clicked her seat belt into place. He did the same with the bat and his belt. Putting the car in gear, he turned it around in a spray of gravel.

''I don't take orders from anyone,'' she told him. ''And in case it slipped your mind, *you* work for *me*.''

''You're even more formidable than your sister when you get riled.''

''Thank you.''

''It was still a stupid thing to do,'' he told her, pulling out into traffic.

''I'm glad we agree. It would have been a little awkward if racetrack security had shown up to ask us what we were doing there.''

''I've no doubt you'd have come up with an explanation.''

''Somehow, I don't think they'd have bought the idea of a pickup softball game,'' she said wryly.

He found himself wanting to smile despite the annoyance lingering in his mind. When he glanced over at her, he realized she was shaking. Her words had been sheer bravado.

He covered her hand with his own. She jumped at the contact, another indication of just how tense she really was.

"A man could do a lot worse than have a woman like you to cover his back."

Her lips parted soundlessly. He released her to steer around a delivery van.

"I find it interesting that Ducort has been acting strange since Pepperton's death, don't you?"

"I wonder how Keith could tell," she muttered.

"Good point."

"You were right about Nolan."

"Yeah. Looks like he and I need to have another talk after all."

"Don't!" She grabbed for his arm, her fingers cool against the warmth of his skin. "Please, Gavin. Let the police take care of Nolan."

"I'd love to, but unfortunately, they can't do anything until he does, and I don't intend to give him the opportunity." The thought of Nolan anywhere near her was untenable.

"While I appreciate the sentiment, I'm not going to let you do anything foolish to protect me."

"Worried about me?"

"Yes. I don't want to have to break in a new lawyer."

A grin edged up the corners of his mouth, but the thought of Ducort coming after her made him swallow the smile. "We need to see about getting you some professional protection."

"You mean a bodyguard? Absolutely not."

"You just had a glimpse of how dangerous Ducort can be, Leigh. Even Earlwood's nervous about him."

"I don't see you hiring a bodyguard."

"Ducort doesn't want me."

"I wouldn't be too sure of that, especially after today."

"You're the one he's been targeting."

"Maybe I can borrow R.J.'s dog. His size alone would scare most people."

Gavin considered that. ''Maybe you should.''

''I was kidding.''

''I'm not.''

She subsided against the seat and closed her eyes. ''What are you going to do with that battery you took from Keith?''

''Put it in his mailbox later tonight, why?''

''Because it occurred to me that if he goes to the police, your having the battery would support whatever story he tells them.''

''Earlwood won't go to the police.''

She opened her eyes and turned toward him. ''How do you know that?''

''He doesn't want to look like a fool, Leigh. I won't be surprised if he really does take his family on an unplanned vacation tonight. He's starting to wonder if Ducort had anything to do with Pepperton's death. And he's going to start wondering if he may be next.''

''You're guessing.''

''Nope. I'm making an educated assumption based on what I know about the three of them. I find it interesting that Ducort was upset because we're here in Saratoga Springs.''

''You don't really think Nolan shot Martin, do you?''

''Anyone will kill if the provocation is strong enough.''

''Okay, but even if he did, why would he care that we're here? We aren't detectives. We aren't even asking questions about him.''

''Does he know that? Didn't you say the man who approached you in the restaurant wanted you to give some vet a message?''

''Yes.''

''What if the man has some sort of connection to the racetrack?''

''So what?''

"So, humor me a minute, I'm thinking out loud. Let's say Ducort has a guilty conscience. Earlwood tells him you talked to some guy from the track. Then we drive straight over there after dinner. If Ducort does have a guilty conscience, he's going to be feeling more than a little paranoid. Why do you think Ducort ordered Keith to climb the fence and follow us?"

His cell phone chimed before he could finish his train of thought. Gavin reached for it automatically.

"Jarret."

"Gavin? It's R.J. Do you know where Leigh is?"

"With me. What's wrong?"

Leigh straightened in her seat.

"I found something at the house. I think the two of you had better get over here."

"We're driving back from Saratoga Springs," Gavin told him. "You want to give me a clue here?"

"Not over the phone. You need to see this for yourself. I'll wait for you at Heartskeep."

R.J. hung up. Gavin clicked off with a frown. "R.J. wants us to meet him at Heartskeep. He says he found something we need to see."

"What?"

"He wouldn't say."

DUSK CAST pale gray shadows over the imposing structure as they pulled up in front of Heartskeep. Gavin had only seen the house in the daytime with all the workmen bustling about. Now the house had a ghostly, deserted sort of look. R.J.'s truck was the only vehicle sitting out front.

Lucky woofed a greeting from inside as they mounted the front steps. R.J. opened the front door before they reached it.

"You made good time. Sorry to be so enigmatic on the

phone, but I didn't want to be overheard,'' he said. ''I had a small accident.''

Gavin looked him up and down. ''Where are you hurt?''

''I'm not. The accident was to one of the undamaged walls upstairs. I put a hole through it.''

''Don't worry about that,'' Leigh said in obvious relief. ''I'm sure you can repair—''

''I can repair the damage okay, that isn't why I called. It's what I found on the other side of the hole that I thought you'd want to see.'' An almost mischievous grin appeared, giving him a boyish look.

''What's going on, R.J.?'' Gavin demanded, his concern giving way to annoyance.

R.J.'s engaging grin didn't fade. Unrepentantly, he turned to Leigh. ''Does this place have a lot of secret passages and hidden rooms scattered around?''

For a moment, she thought she had misheard. ''What are you talking about?''

R.J. could barely contain his excitement. ''Come with me.''

Lucky streaked ahead as he led them inside and started up the front staircase.

''I always double-check a work site before I leave for the day. Today I went through the whole house as soon as the crew left. The locksmith came out and changed all the locks, so I wanted to be sure no one was still lurking inside.''

''Did you check the balconies?'' Gavin asked.

''Yep. You were right about an entrance through the linen closet. The door's a little tricky, but it's there. Anyhow, one of my guys had left some tools sitting out. I was ticked when I picked up the hammer and I wasn't watching what I was doing. I bumped a loose board. I tried to grab for it before it fell and took down a whole pile of other stuff. In the process, the hammer I was holding went right through the wood paneling.''

He moved the sawhorse and tape that had blocked off the left-wing corridor. A gaping hole in one wall served as an impromptu entrance to her grandfather's suite now. The entire front portion of the room had been reduced to cross beams without flooring.

''Technically, you two shouldn't be in here, so be careful. Don't touch anything, and watch where you put your feet. There isn't a lot of solid flooring left.''

He led them through the hole into what had been her grandfather's bathroom. The plumbing was gone, along with the walls that would have separated it from the suite.

''We finished ripping out everything forward of this point,'' R.J. told them. ''The flooring that's left is perfectly stable, but be careful where you walk.''

Though the fire damage had been removed, the odor of charred wood still lingered in the muggy air of the room. R.J. turned their attention to the undamaged wall. A small hole sat in the middle of the paneling.

''Run your hand down that board,'' he told Gavin.

Leigh watched closely as Gavin did what R.J. instructed. He looked up with a startled expression.

''Press it,'' R.J. told him.

There was a barely discernible sound. One entire section of wall abruptly sank back several inches as if on springs. It slid back to reveal a hidden entrance to a small room.

Leigh gasped.

''Ingenious design,'' R.J. said eagerly. ''You can see this was installed when the house itself was built. Wasn't Heartskeep built in the early 1900s? Whoever designed this was a master craftsman. Your grandfather must have kept all the moving parts well lubricated. Did I mention the room's even wired for electricity? Unfortunately, I've still got the power turned off in this section, but I turned it back on in the rest of the house.''

R.J. clicked on a powerful flashlight. The windowless room came fully into view. The walls were unfinished and the floor was bare wood. An old card table held a dust-covered computer, monitor, keyboard, mouse and printer. A squat metal file cabinet sat on the floor beside the table, and a folding chair and a floor lamp completed the amenities.

''I never knew this was here,'' Leigh breathed.

''Didn't think so. Before you go in there, notice that my footprints are the only ones in the room,'' R.J. pointed out. ''I'd guess not too many people knew about this room's existence. It looks to me like nothing has been disturbed in here in a long time.''

''Seven years,'' Leigh murmured. ''That's how long it's been since my grandfather died.''

Gavin stepped inside. He ran his finger through the layer of dust, dirt and soot that covered the keyboard.

''There's more,'' R.J. told them excitedly.

He threw the beam of light on the far wall. The outline of another door was starkly evident.

''It operates exactly the same way, and it's just as invisible from the other side. I'd love to meet the guy who designed this room,'' R.J. enthused.

''This isn't like the hidden room Hayley told me about, that the firemen found off Marcus's office, is it?'' Leigh asked.

''Not even close,'' R.J. assured her. ''That was new construction, a simple push door. This is way different. I've never seen anything like this.''

''Where does the door lead?'' Gavin asked. He stepped forward to examine the mechanism more closely. R.J.'s footprints indicated he'd already checked out the other opening.

"There's a bedroom closet on the other side," he told Gavin.

"Jacob's room," Leigh reminded him.

Gavin found the second switch and opened the panel. He ducked to avoid the clothes pole and empty hangers that spanned the length of the closet, and stepped through. Beyond the open closet door they could see the bedroom.

"Close the panel from the inside, R.J. Let me see if I can open it from the closet side," Gavin requested.

Leigh joined him.

"Didn't you tell me all the closets in the house are lined with cedar paneling?"

"Yes," she breathed. "You think there're more of these rooms?"

"We won't know until we look."

Once closed, the entrance was invisible. The cedar paneling fit flush, making it appear to be a simple seam. Gavin ran his hands over the boards.

"I found the trip switch. It's easy once you know what to feel for. Why don't you give it a try?"

Eagerly, she traded places. She ran her fingers down the wood until she felt a slight depression. As she pushed firmly, the door slid back without a sound.

R.J. was still grinning. "What do you think?"

"I think," Gavin said seriously, "we ought to keep this little secret to ourselves for now."

R.J.'s grin melted away. The boyish look vanished. "What's wrong?"

Instead of answering, Gavin looked at Leigh. "If your grandfather hid this computer before he died, there may have been a good reason."

Leigh's eyes widened.

"I may be overreacting, but I don't think we want anyone to know what we've found until we can check it out. We'd better take the computer out of here."

"It may not run," R.J. pointed out. "I'd try to blow off the dust before you turn it on or you could have another fire on your hands."

"Good point."

"I've got a dolly in my truck," R.J. told him. "Do you want to move the filing cabinet too?"

"Where are we going to put them?" Leigh asked.

"The library?"

Leigh looked at R.J., suddenly feeling nervous. "Are you sure there's no one in the house besides us?"

Gavin tensed.

R.J. frowned. "Reasonably sure. In a place this size, it's hard to be positive, but Lucky hasn't raised an alarm."

"Would he? I mean, if it was someone he knew?"

"What are you thinking, Leigh?"

She shook her head at Gavin, unable to put her unease into words. "I think…" She shrugged helplessly. "I'm just nervous."

Gavin ran a hand through his hair. "Can you block the hole so your men won't notice it?"

"Sure. I'll rig something up," R.J. promised.

"Jam the opening from the inside as well," Gavin suggested. "We'll still have access through the bedroom, but none of your men can stumble onto this by accident the way you did."

"You two want to tell me what's going on?"

"I only wish we knew."

Chapter Nine

They decided to leave the file cabinet where it was until morning. Night wrapped the estate in a blanket so dark not even stars lit the sky. As Gavin loaded the computer in the trunk of his car, he caught Leigh staring up at the house.

''What?''

With a barely perceptible shudder, she turned away. R.J.'s taillights disappeared down the driveway.

''My imagination likes overtime,'' she told him.

''Your imagination isn't the only one,'' he agreed. ''This place is downright creepy in the dark.'' Hidden eyes seemed to watch them from behind the drapes. ''Let's get the computer over to the Walkens' and—''

''We can't take it there.''

''Why not?''

''The Jenkinses were coming for dinner tonight. You know what a gossip Mrs. Jenkins is. The entire county will know about the computer five minutes after she sees us bring it into the house. Can't we take it somewhere else? What about your place?''

Until that moment, Gavin had never thought twice about the shabby apartment he rented over the dry-cleaning shop in town. Cheap, furnished and convenient had been his only requirements when he moved back to help Ira. While the

Walkens had urged him to stay with them, he'd wanted the privacy and convenience of his own place in town.

"Is that a problem, Gavin?"

"Not if it doesn't bother you. I'd suggest taking the computer to my office, but that would require some explanations in the morning."

"Why would it bother me to go to your place? I don't even know where your place is."

"In town over the dry cleaners."

"One of Keith's shops?"

Gavin returned her stare. "I never thought about that. I suppose it must be."

"Keith doesn't own the building, does he?"

"Not to my knowledge. I rented the place through the real-estate company in town. Earlwood's family was into dry cleaning and the stock market, not real estate."

"Then he'd have no reason to know you live there."

"Probably not. Their main facility is outside of town."

"Then it should be safe enough. It just seems sort of an odd coincidence—you living above one of Keith's shops."

"I know what you're saying, but not really. There aren't many places for rent in a town the size of Stony Ridge."

"True."

He started down the rutted driveway, suddenly anxious to be away from the spooky old estate. They were totally isolated out here. Between the day's events and the atmosphere surrounding Heartskeep, he was feeling uncomfortably vulnerable this far from other people.

"Maybe my place isn't such a good idea after all."

"You don't think Nolan will come looking for you, do you?"

"No," he said thoughtfully. "Face-to-face confrontation's not his style unless the person is smaller than him, but I wish I knew what he thought we might learn at the racetrack. It strikes me as odd that Earlwood, Pepperton and Ducort maintained a relationship over the years."

"Why wouldn't they?"

"They never really had all that much in common. Martin Pepperton was part of the racing set. His family's wealth and position in the community set him apart from everyone else at school. I always wondered why he was there in the first place. His family's the private-school type."

"Maybe he got kicked out of private school."

"Possible. I know Ducort was. He used to brag about it. He was always looking for an angle. I can see him staying in touch with Pepperton because of his connections, but Earlwood puzzles me. I always thought he was just one of those fringe types that like to hang with the rich and famous because of their clout. That sort tends to drift away after a while. He didn't have the money or the charm to keep up with the other two. It seems odd that he's still running Ducort's errands after all this time."

"He said Nolan was going to loan him some money," she pointed out.

"I know. It just doesn't feel right somehow."

They fell silent for several minutes before Leigh spoke again.

"Not to change the subject, Gavin, but this computer R.J. found isn't going to help us figure out what happened to the money missing from my grandfather's estate, you know."

"I know. But he must have had some reason for hiding it away like he did."

"Maybe. Or maybe it's broken and he put it in there to get it out of the way," she said, sounding troubled.

"Think that's likely?"

"I don't know," she admitted. "I've been wondering if we took the wrong thing out of that room. Maybe it was the filing cabinet, not the computer, that he was hiding."

"You could be right, but moving the computer was easier than moving the files tonight. If the computer works, maybe we can learn something from it. You did say your grandfather had an extensive history on Heartskeep."

"He did, but most of that was on paper. I don't know how much is apt to be in the computer. Do you think there are more hidden rooms? When I think of all the time I wasted being afraid of the attic I feel stupid. People could have been spying on me from the balcony or hiding in rooms I didn't even know existed."

"What made you afraid of the attic?"

"I don't know, really. I guess because it was always kept locked. Secrets are always scary, don't you think?"

"And you did say it was the perfect place for the bogeyman to hide."

She couldn't smile despite his gentle teasing. "I always thought so," she said seriously. "But all this time he could have been hiding in my bedroom closet instead. Sort of gives me the willies."

"You're leaping to conclusions, you know. There's nothing to say every closet in the house has a hidden room. In fact, I'd think it's pretty unlikely. The room off your grandfather's suite wasn't even attached to a closet on his side."

"Actually, I think it might have been at one time. Grandpa's suite used to be two separate bedrooms. He had it remodeled right before we came there to live."

Gavin pondered that as he reached the outskirts of Stony Ridge. The downtown area was so quiet, it resembled a ghost town. And in light of their current discussion, that was a particularly disturbing thought.

He drove around to the back of the shopping center where he usually parked, but as his headlights swept the lot, he glimpsed something moving just beyond their range. More a flicker than anything concrete, but enough to send up an alarm.

Beyond the parking area the ground gave way to a steep, overgrown hillside. The spot was frequented by foxes and other wildlife. And possibly someone with a gun and a grudge?

Braking, he put the car in Reverse. "Get down."

"What's wrong?"

Even as she asked, Leigh sank low in her seat. He glanced over at her.

"Something moved near the edge of the hill. It may have been the wind, but we aren't going to take any chances. One confrontation a day is my limit."

"There isn't any wind."

"Yeah. I know."

He pulled onto the street. There were plenty of open parking spaces across from them. The stores were dark and empty at this hour, but an occasional car did drive past and there were lights in most of the apartments nesting over the old storefronts. If someone lurked behind his building, they could stay there all night. Gavin had no intention of tempting fate. Not with Leigh at his side.

"Do you think Keith called Nolan?" Leigh asked, sitting up.

"As soon as he got to a phone," Gavin responded dryly. He made a U-turn and parked. He turned off the engine, but sat there without pulling his keys from the ignition.

"Should we go inside?" she asked.

"No. I think I should drive you back to the Walken estate."

"I knew you were going to say that! Forget it, Gavin. We're here now and I want to see the inside of your apartment."

His lips twitched. "There isn't much to see. I don't spend much time there, Leigh. It's just a place to stay while I'm working in town."

"You talk like you aren't planning to stick around."

"I probably won't. Ira needed help about the same time I decided I wasn't going to be happy if I stayed at the large firm where I was working." As he spoke, his gaze raked the street. "A friend and I have been talking about setting up a practice in New York City."

She followed his gaze with an unhappy frown. "What are you looking for?"

"Trouble."

Gavin muttered an oath as he spotted a familiar green car parked a short distance behind them. "And darned if I didn't find it."

"Keith's car," Leigh whispered.

"I should have thrown his keys farther."

Lots farther. He hadn't expected this. Keith didn't strike him as the sort to retaliate unless he was goaded into it. On the other hand, an ambush with one or two "friends" was exactly Ducort's style.

"I don't suppose you'd wait in the car while I have a look around?" he asked.

"Good guess."

Taking Leigh inside was out of the question now. The only smart thing to do—

"Gavin! There's someone inside the dry-cleaning store!"

His gaze flew to the shop under his apartment. She was right. Someone was moving around inside in the dark. Even as they watched, the shadowy shape vanished from sight.

"Not exactly subtle, is he?"

"We should call the police," Leigh said.

"It's Earlwood's store. He has every right to be inside if he wants to be."

"But he's waiting for you to come home."

"We don't know that. He could have another reason for being there, although I admit, none comes to mind."

"After what happened earlier—"

"You mean when *we* accosted *him*?" Gavin pointed out.

Exasperated, Leigh glared at him. "Well, what are we going to do?"

"The more I think about it, the more I like your first idea." He picked up his cell phone. As soon as the police dispatcher answered, he identified himself. "I want to report a possible prowler inside the We Clean Dry Cleaners on Roster Avenue."

Leigh grinned in approval. They both looked toward the building.

A giant fireball suddenly exploded inside the shop. The blast rocked the street, shattering windows.

"Send the fire department!" Gavin yelled to the dispatcher. "The store just exploded!" He dropped the phone and reached for the door handle. "Stay here!"

Keith Earlwood—if the figure had been him—was still inside the building. Gavin sprinted across the street, wondering what had caused such a blast. No actual cleaning was done inside the building, so there shouldn't have been any flammable chemicals to cause an explosion like that.

Earlwood must be torching the place.

Most of the plate-glass window had fallen, spewing glass across the sidewalk, but several huge shards still rocked in the casing. He hoped Earlwood had escaped, but he would have had to have gone out the back. Gavin started to change direction when he realized something was moving inside the burning store.

He swore as a figure wreathed in flames staggered toward the front door.

Gavin got there first, but the door was locked. Every window along the block had blown out except the one over the door. Fate, or the wall inside, had sheltered it from the concussion. Frantically, he looked around for something to use to break the glass. Leigh ran over with his baseball bat in her hand.

Saving his admiration for later, Gavin took the bat and swung. The window had been reinforced with safety glass, but it gave with a satisfying crunch when he struck it a couple of times. Heat and smoke rushed out at him. Dropping the bat, he reached inside and fumbled for the dead bolt.

The figure collapsed to the floor, writhing as flames engulfed him. Grabbing the cloth that formed part of the front-window display, Gavin and Leigh used the fabric to smother the flames. Embers flew in all directions. Flames roared in his ears. The figure stopped moving. Gavin hoped he'd only passed out, but Earlwood was horribly burned.

"We have to get him out!" Leigh said, choking on the thick smoke.

Together, they got him onto the sidewalk. A passing motorist stopped. He ran over holding a small fire extinguisher.

A second explosion rocked the building. As the concussion whipped at them, the building seemed to swell with flames while the empty street began to fill with people.

Screaming sirens announced the arrival of the local police and the fire department. Gavin pulled Leigh aside to let the emergency medical technicians take over. He knew there wasn't much they could do for the victim. It would be a miracle if Earlwood survived.

Firefighters waved them back and set to work. Gavin found himself holding Leigh tightly when another blast shook the neighborhood.

"What's happening?" she asked.

"I don't know."

Wyatt Crossley appeared out of the sea of faces. Gavin noted that his friend wasn't dressed in his police uniform, but that didn't make him seem any less official. Wyatt strode forward commandingly. He started to say something, looked hard at the two of them, then quickly motioned to someone else. "We need an EMT over here now."

Gavin looked at Leigh. Blood ran down her arm.

"You're hurt!" he exclaimed.

"No, I'm not."

"You're the one who's hurt, Gavin," Wyatt told him. "Your hand is bleeding all over her."

A gash across his palm was bleeding freely. "I must have cut myself when I unlocked the door."

"You're burned, too," Leigh said in concern.

Small, angry blisters were forming on the back of his hand. "Thanks. I didn't feel a thing until you pointed them out." But they made up for it now.

"You sure you're all right?"

Leigh nodded as Wyatt addressed the question to her.

"I'm fine. He's the one who played hero."

"I didn't go in there alone," he pointed out.

As a paramedic tended to his hands, Wyatt asked the inevitable question. "What happened?"

"I'm guessing, Keith Earlwood was trying to torch the place when something went wrong."

Leigh inhaled sharply. "He was trying to kill you?"

"Why would he want to do that?" Wyatt demanded.

"She only means because I live over the shop. If I'd been in my apartment, I could have been killed," Gavin told him without looking at Leigh. "It's no secret Earlwood needed money, Wyatt. A lot of stupid people figure insurance is one way to collect."

"You think the victim is Keith Earlwood?"

"Yeah, I do." Gavin pointed down the street. "I noticed his car parked on the other side of that fire engine. Leigh and I were on our way up to my place when she spotted someone moving around inside the store. I called 911. I was talking to the dispatcher when the place literally blew up."

Satisfied, Wyatt nodded. "I'm Wyatt Crossley, by the way," he said to Leigh. "You must be Leigh Thomas."

"Sorry. I wasn't thinking about introductions."

Leigh inclined her head as the fire chief approached Wyatt. "Clear this street now! We've got a gas line involved. The whole block could go."

Wyatt hurried off, shouting terse directions to the uniformed officers milling around.

"Thanks," Gavin told the man who'd bandaged his hand and put salve on his burns. To Leigh he said, "Let's see if we can get my car out and get away from here."

Immediately, they saw that wasn't going to happen. Between fire trucks and police cars, they had no hope of working Gavin's car free.

"Now what?"

"Leigh? Is that you?"

Jacob Voxx appeared out of the crowd that was being ordered back.

"Jacob! What are you doing here?"

"I was driving through town when I got stopped by the fire. Hey, are you okay? You two look like you were *in* the fire. You weren't, were you?"

"Gavin and I helped pull a man out of the building."

Jacob took in the bandaged hand and the blood on her blouse and shook his head. "What is it with you and your sister and fire?"

"Folks, you need to clear this street now!" a young police officer ordered.

"Do you two need a ride?" Jacob asked. "My car's over there."

Leigh looked at Gavin. His first instinct was to say no, but that would mean calling George or someone else to come and get them.

"Thanks," Gavin said. "That would be great."

"Where to?"

"The Walken estate," he told the younger man.

"You aren't wearing your sling anymore," Leigh said. "Is your arm feeling better?"

"Yeah. It's still sore as can be, but it's healing. You've got a couple of nasty burns there, Gavin. They must hurt like the devil. Who did you pull out of the building?"

"We think it was Keith Earlwood," Gavin told him honestly. "He was badly burned."

"Someone said a gas line exploded."

"That's what we heard, too," Gavin agreed. Privately, he wondered just how much help the gas line had had. He eyed the low-slung sports car Jacob led them to in surprise. "Nice car."

"Thanks. It cost me a small fortune, but I got a good deal on it from a guy I know. He got one speeding ticket too many and lost his license. Basically all I had to do was take over his payments. It's a tight fit in back, Leigh, but I've driven with three people before."

"That's okay, Jacob. I'll manage."

"Just push all that stuff on the seat onto the floor," Jacob said.

Gavin noticed one of the items was a package of chewing gum. It was fruit flavored rather than spearmint, but he eyed Jacob with new speculation.

"What do you do for a living, Jacob?" he asked as Jacob pulled away from the curb.

"I'm in the computer field."

"Big field. Could you narrow that down some?"

Jacob flashed him a grin. "I'm a programmer for the most part, but I've done some networking stuff as well. I've got a great job with a company called Via-Tek. It's based in New York City, but I do a lot of work from home. Really, all I need is a computer and a modem and I can work just about anywhere."

"Must be nice."

"Yeah. The pay's great and the perks are even better."

"How's your mother doing?" Leigh asked.

"I'm not sure. I haven't talked with her in a couple of days. I'm sorry about the way she behaved at your office the other day, Gavin. Mom's been pretty upset since Marcus died. She'd sort of gotten used to playing lady of the manor, I'm afraid." He glanced apologetically at Leigh in his rearview mirror.

"You don't need to apologize for her, Jacob," she told him.

"I know. Part of the problem was that she'd just discovered Marcus had drained their accounts."

"What?"

Jacob jerked when Gavin barked the question at him.

"Uh, yeah. He didn't leave her any money. You'd think being a doctor and all he'd have plenty stashed away, but it turns out he was close to broke."

"Is she okay?" Leigh asked. "Does she need money?"

Gavin frowned, but Jacob was shaking his head.

"No, but thanks. Mom will be fine. She's a survivor, you know. She's been setting aside her own money for years. I guess she thought she'd be rich after Marcus died. His empty bank account came as a real shock. Still, that's no excuse for the way she behaved. She's always been a little high-strung," he told Gavin.

"You're sure Marcus was broke?" Gavin asked. He shot a look over his shoulder at Leigh. She shook her head, looking puzzled.

"That's what Mom said."

"That doesn't make any sense," Leigh said. "He may not have been the best doctor in the world, but he had plenty of patients and he didn't have many expenses. It didn't cost him anything to live at Heartskeep. What did he do with all his money?"

Jacob shrugged. "Beats me. Maybe he lost it betting on

horses. I don't know. I just know, according to my mother, there isn't any money."

Which partially explained why Eden had been taking what she could get from Heartskeep after his death.

"Did Marcus have a gambling problem?" Gavin asked as they pulled up to the Walken estate.

"Not that I knew about. I think Mom would have said something if that had been the case."

Gavin frowned as he reached for the door handle and stepped from the car. "Thanks for the lift, Jacob," he said as he helped Leigh out of the backseat.

"Glad I could help."

"You'll stay in touch?" she asked him.

"Count on it."

"Where are you staying?" Gavin asked.

"With a friend tonight, but I'm going back to my place in New York in the morning. I've got a meeting in the city tomorrow afternoon."

"Well, be careful," Leigh told him.

"You, too. I'm not the one rushing into burning buildings. 'Night, guys."

Based on the car parked in front of the Walkens' house, they still had company.

"Let's go in through the back," Gavin suggested.

"Good idea," Leigh agreed. "What do you think happened to all the money, Gavin?"

"That is a good question."

Nan wasn't in the kitchen, so they hurried up the back stairs.

Leigh stopped when they reached the hall. "I just realized you lost everything you owned in that fire."

"There wasn't all that much. Some clothing and a few books." He shrugged. "The only thing I regret is the picture of my family, but there's probably another copy in storage somewhere."

"In storage?"

"My grandparents died when I was in high school. George had their estate boxed up and put in storage for me."

"You've never looked at any of it?"

He shrugged. "My grandparents and I weren't exactly close. They were rigid disciplinarians. You can imagine how well we got along when I was sent to live with them after my aunt and uncle gave up. To their credit, my grandparents made an effort to stay in touch after I was placed in foster homes, but I'd given them such a hard time after my folks died that we never did find a way to communicate after they sent me away."

She rested a hand on his arm. "I'm sorry, Gavin."

"So am I. About a lot of things." He looked down to where her hand rested against his skin. She didn't move it away.

"If you're referring to what happened between us, there's no need for you to be sorry."

"Isn't there?"

She withdrew her hand. "Not unless you enjoy feeling like a martyr."

He blinked in surprise. "I didn't see that one coming."

"Do I really seem that fragile and traumatized to you?"

"Why do I get the feeling this is a trick question?"

Her eyes narrowed in warning.

"Okay. Truce," he said. "I'll accept that your fragile exterior hides a core of solid steel, if you'll accept that I'll always feel a little guilt for treating you like..."

"An easy conquest?"

"Close enough."

She could imagine the word he'd been thinking. She also knew that if they were ever going to move past their history, she was going to have to make him see it was unimportant to them now.

"You know what I think, Gavin? I think you're the one who was traumatized that night."

He rubbed his jaw and stared at her thoughtfully. "You could be right. It was certainly a turning point in my life."

Inwardly, she sighed in relief. "Mine, too, but I like to think there's a reason for the things that happen. We learn from them and move on."

There was a wry twist to his lips. "Do I detect a note of censure there?"

She shrugged lightly. "If the censure fits..."

He smiled with his eyes and his expression softened. "Which room are you using?"

"Over there," she said, pointing. "Hayley and Bram are across the hall."

"Then I'll use the room next to theirs."

She searched his features, looking past the smoke that stained his skin, but unable to tell what he was thinking. Maybe it was time to take another page from her sister's book and be a little more assertive.

"You could share my room."

He stilled. The air around them felt charged and her heart began to pound heavily.

Very gently, he reached out to trace a path down her cheek with his finger. "I would like nothing better than to share your room..."

He drew it across her lips.

"...your bed..."

Lightly swept it down the side of her throat to her collarbone.

"...your body."

Stopped at the juncture of her V-necked blouse.

Her breasts seemed to swell. A fluttery feeling started low in her belly, sending ripples of hot desire through every nerve ending.

"But—"

"No!" she protested. "No buts. I hate that word!"

His features softened in regret. "So do I," he said softly. "More so at this moment than I ever have."

He didn't want her.

"I've already compromised my principles enough where you're concerned."

She was determined not to let him see how those words hurt. She resented the gentle kindness in his eyes. She didn't want kindness from Gavin. She wanted—

"Tonight, neither one of us is thinking straight. I know I'm not. And to be honest," he added with a rueful smile, "I'm too wiped out to…well, be of use to you or anyone else. Get some sleep, Leigh. We've got a lot of decisions to make in the morning."

He kissed the top of her head before she could respond and turned away. Rooted to the spot, she watched him enter the room beyond Hayley's without looking back. He closed the door with a finality that was devastating.

He didn't want her.

When was she going to accept that she was nothing like her sister? Emulating Hayley never had worked for her. How was it she kept forgetting that lesson?

She heard footsteps coming up the back stairs and spun around as a figure came into sight.

"Leigh!" George said in surprise. "Nan thought she heard someone up here." He took in her smoke-stained features and his expression turned to immediate concern. "What happened? Are you all right?"

"I'm fine," she said quickly as he crossed to her.

She told him about the explosions and fire and Jacob driving them home.

"And while I'm okay, you might want to check on Gavin. Besides getting cut and burned in the rescue, he lost everything in his apartment."

All she'd lost was her heart.

"He'll need clothes for tomorrow," she added.

"I'll take care of it, but are you sure you're okay? You look a little rocky. Do you want me to get Emily?"

"No. Please, don't." She didn't want to talk to anyone else tonight. "I'm going to take a shower and go to bed myself."

"Your sister's been trying to reach you. She left a number."

"I'll call her in the morning."

The last person she wanted to talk with tonight was Hayley. She'd know immediately that Leigh was upset and she'd suspect the reason. Leigh didn't want to hear an "I told you so," even if Hayley was too kind to say it out loud.

"You know, Leigh, your grandfather was one of my closest friends." George's light blue eyes searched her face intently. "I would do anything at all for you or your sister."

Impulsively, she reached up and hugged him, blinking back tears at his heartfelt words.

"I know. Thank you." She sniffed, stepped back and offered him a watery smile. "You and Emily have always been here for us and I can't tell you what that means. Thank you, George. I'll see you in the morning."

"Sleep well."

"I'm going to try."

WHEN THE KNOCK came at his door, Gavin wasn't surprised. It had actually taken her longer than he'd expected, but he wished she hadn't come. Walking away from her once had been hard enough. He only hoped he had the strength to send her away again.

He squared his shoulders and reached for the door handle. "Leigh—"

"George," his foster parent corrected, pushing his way

inside and sweeping Gavin with a penetrating stare. ''Leigh told me about the fire. She said you'd been hurt.''

Only rarely had Gavin witnessed this particular expression on George's face, but on those occasions, he'd learned it wisest to tell him whatever he wanted to know.

''Just a couple of minor burns and a superficial cut, that's all. I had them treated at the scene.'' He held up his bandaged hand.

George barely gave it a glance. ''Leigh said she wasn't hurt.''

Ah, that explained the intensity. The words had been a question rather than a statement. He was worried about Leigh. George had always shared a close bond with the Hart family and he and Emily had been extremely protective of the twins since their mother disappeared.

''She wasn't hurt, George, but it was a rough day.'' He gave his foster parent a quick sketch of the events in Saratoga Springs. ''She's really worried about Mrs. Walsh. But I've got to tell you, Leigh's got guts, George. You should have seen her facing down Earlwood.'' He shook his head in remembered disbelief. ''And the way she charged into that fire with me... She's something else. Which is exactly why we have to watch her.''

For the first time, the older man relaxed. ''She's like her mother—and the rest of the Hart family. Good, strong genes in the Harts. They're smart, beautiful and intensely loyal.''

His stare was penetrating. Gavin felt as if he was missing something here, but George's expression suddenly turned rueful.

''I'd better be getting back downstairs. Our guests should be about ready to leave by now. I'll go down and hurry them on their way, then I'll get you some clothes. And don't worry, I'll tell Emily what happened after they're gone. You know where we keep the extra toiletries, so help yourself to whatever you need. We can talk in the morning.''

''Thanks, George. I appreciate this.''

''You're family, Gavin.''

Emily and George had always tried to make him feel that way, even when he'd tried his best to keep them at a distance. They'd accepted him and loved him when he'd been far from lovable. Gavin didn't know exactly when it had happened, but he'd come to think of them as family.

Standing beneath the shower's spray a few minutes later, Gavin tried to put his powerful mix of emotions in perspective. He didn't know much about love, but he knew a lot about wanting—and he wanted Leigh. In trying to do the right thing tonight, he suspected he'd hurt her feelings, but better a few bruised feelings now than a broken heart later.

Leigh was the sort of woman a man took home to meet his mother. Only, Gavin didn't have a mother. He wasn't a hearts-and-flowers kind of guy. That's what she needed, not someone like him. He was all wrong for her—but he still wanted her.

Overhead, a trumpet of thunder announced the arrival of another summer storm. Gavin sighed. He had a feeling he was in for another long, sleepless night.

Chapter Ten

Leigh steeled herself, then entered Gavin's bedroom on a clap of thunder. She came to an abrupt halt. He'd obviously just come from the shower. Beads of water trickled over his skin. And there was plenty of skin to see. He was standing there stark naked.

She wasn't sure which of them was more surprised, but Gavin reacted first. He wrapped the towel he'd been rubbing briskly over his hair around his waist and cinched it there with a curse.

"You said to come in," she protested. Her eyes skirted back up across the sparsely curling hairs on his bare chest.

"I thought you were George."

Her gaze returned to the towel, then back to his face. She mustered a smile and tried for nonchalance. "Not even close. He's taller."

Gavin didn't appear amused. "What are you doing here, Leigh?"

"Enjoying the show?"

He scowled at her. "Leigh, George will be back any minute with some clothes for me. I don't want to embarrass any of us."

"Don't worry, you don't have a thing to be embarrassed about." She was the one who was embarrassed. "I'm not going to stay. I just came to tell you something."

Twisted threads of lightning shot across the sky past the bedroom window. Thunder trembled in their wake. She barely repressed a shudder.

"I hate storms."

Gavin raked his fingers through his wet hair. "Is that what you came to tell me?" he growled.

"There's no reason to snap at me. It's not like I haven't seen it all before."

He took a step in her direction and it was an effort to stand her ground. When she realized she was clutching the seams of her robe together, she released the material and dropped her hands to her sides.

"I came to tell you that you're fired. I'll ask the court to appoint a new executor in the morning. Sorry I disturbed you. I just thought you'd want to know." She gave him a saccharine smile and opened the door. "Sleep well."

Gavin swore. "Leigh! Get back in here!"

George was coming down the hall as she shut the door on his bellow.

"If I were you," she told the startled man, "I'd toss those in his direction and keep going. Apparently, storms make him cranky."

Gavin flung his door open. "Leigh..."

"Good night again, George." She escaped into her room and closed the door. Her knees felt weak and her heart was beating like crazy, but at least she hadn't lost her nerve.

Their voices were indistinct through the door, but Gavin's low rumble definitely sounded aggrieved. She wondered what sort of an explanation he was giving George. After a few minutes, there was silence.

She wasn't sure if the evening had worked out better this way or not, but overall, she was satisfied with the results. She pulled off her robe and tossed it on the chair before slipping into bed. The next move was up to Gavin.

She'd given a lot of thought to her plan before setting it

in motion. If she'd just made a mistake, her ego was going to suffer a crushing blow, but knowing would be better than continuing to pluck petals from an imaginary flower.

This had to work.

She reached for the light switch. Her door swung open and Gavin strode inside without knocking. His hair was still wet and mussed from being toweled. Beads of water still clung to his skin, sparkling against his shoulders in the light. He was shirtless and shoeless, but being dressed in only a pair of unsnapped trousers didn't make him one bit less formidable.

"Was that supposed to be a joke?" he demanded.

Rain beat against the window.

"No," she said sadly. "You're fired."

He studied her and she resisted an urge to pull the covers up higher. Her blue nightgown was perfectly respectable.

"I think you're serious."

"I am."

"You're firing me because I wouldn't share your room?"

"Of course not." He didn't get it. "I'm firing you because I don't intend to compromise your principles any further."

"I hurt your feelings."

"Well, of course you hurt my feelings, but that isn't what this is about. You said you were too tired to think straight. I'm not. I gave this a lot of thought and decided not to wait until morning to make all my decisions."

His eyes narrowed.

"This arrangement isn't going to work and you know it. I wanted to tell you right away so you could start thinking about who I could ask for as a replacement."

Another rumble of thunder punctuated her sentence. It didn't quite drown out the rumble of sound coming from low in his chest. His expression was inscrutable. She couldn't tell if he was furious or amused. Maybe he didn't know, either. He pinned her to the bed with a probing look that made her want to squirm. She held herself rigid.

"I can't decide whether to throttle you, or kiss you senseless."

Her pulse raced. "Let's go for option three. You go back across the hall and we sleep on it."

"I don't think so."

The whiskey-soft drawl of his words sent desire licking along her veins.

"I have to hand it to you. I've never had any woman go to so much trouble to get me into her bed."

Thunder and lightning exploded overhead. Leigh choked back a startled scream as the room was plunged into darkness.

"Do you prefer the left side or the right side of the bed?" he asked as if nothing had happened.

The sound of his zipper being lowered came as a shock.

"What are you doing?"

"Giving you what you want."

Her breathing was so fast and shallow she wondered if she might hyperventilate. She heard his pants hit the carpeting. Her mouth went dry.

"You have no idea what I want," she said shakily.

He came around the bed, his torso silhouetted against the window in yet another display from the heavens.

"You're right. I don't. Understandable given that you're a contrary woman, and I'm simply a man. In case no one told you, men and women don't think alike."

He pulled back the covers while the thunder protested. She shivered as his bare leg slid alongside hers.

"Are you…are you naked?"

"That's the way I generally sleep," he answered.

Anticipation zinged straight down her spine. Every nerve ending in her body seemed tuned to him.

"This is not what I want."

"Too bad. It wasn't what I wanted, either. When you get a little older, you'll realize life seldom gives us what we want."

She sat all the way up as he settled down against the pillow.

"I am not a child!"

"Then stop acting like one. It's late and I'm tired. I'd like to get some sleep before morning."

Astonishment overrode her indignation at the rebuke. "Sleep? You're going to sleep? Here?"

Outside, the storm showed its approval by offering several spectacular displays of lightning.

"I admit it's not going to be easy if you don't stop talking."

"You can't! You wouldn't!"

"Can, and will."

"What about George and Emily?"

"They'll have to use their own bed. This one isn't big enough to hold them, too."

He adjusted his pillow and rolled on his side away from her.

"Good night."

For what felt like a long time, she simply sat there in the dark, barely noticing the storm outside. He'd called her bluff and she didn't know how to handle the situation. None of the scenarios she'd envisioned had anticipated this reaction. An argument? Yes. A discussion? Possibly. Sex? Okay, that's where she'd expected her bluff to lead. That, or an outright refusal to take her dare. But this—

How was she supposed to fall asleep with him naked in her bed? Her mind churned with ideas and possible alternatives. As the storm began to move off, she discarded them all and conceded defeat. Pride wouldn't let her leave, even though she knew she wouldn't get a wink of sleep.

She slid back under the covers, staying as close to the edge of the bed as possible, and stared up at the darkened ceiling. The taste of defeat was bitter and it was her own fault. She loved him. She'd always loved him, but she didn't have a clue how to make the stubborn, irritating, infuriating man see how good they could be together.

In the back of her mind she could hear her mother's voice saying, "All in good time." It had been one of Hayley's least favorite expressions, but Leigh had seen her mother's wisdom proven right more than once. Gavin may have won this skirmish, but she wasn't ready to quit. He cared about her, she knew he did. And he wanted her. She'd just have to give her plan more thought.

GAVIN AWOKE to the sound of thunder. The storm had returned or sent another one to take its place. Beside him, Leigh stirred restlessly. She'd tossed off the covers and was making soft sounds of distress.

"Shh. It's only thunder. Everything's okay. Go back to sleep."

He pulled her against his side, adjusting their positions until she was curled spoon-fashion against him. She settled there as trusting as a kitten, without waking.

Soul-searching wasn't part of his nature, yet he seemed to be doing a lot of it since Leigh had walked back into his life. Was this what love was all about? An intimacy that had little to do with sex and everything to do with caring? He rested his chin on top of her head and closed his eyes, inhaling the scent of her shampoo.

Too bad love and relationships didn't come with textbooks like the law. In the morning they were going to have to discuss this crazy relationship of theirs and he wasn't looking forward to it. Just looking at her was enough to tie his logic into knots.

He'd have to get up and go back to his own room soon,

but he'd better wait for the storm to pass. He was surprised he'd slept at all, and wondered what time it was. It felt like early morning. He could afford to lie here a little bit longer. It was nice holding her like this. Comforting. He'd get up in just a minute.

When he opened his eyes again, the room was filled with daylight, and his hand was cupping the firm, round fullness of Leigh's right breast. He could feel the hardened nipple pushing against his palm. Her body was still curved against his. Their legs were tangled with one of hers trapped between his, and her buttock was pressed firmly against his erection.

She was awake.

Instantly, he released her and rolled away. She turned to look at him, her features still soft with sleep. The urge to kiss her had him pushing aside the covers.

"You're wearing briefs," she said as he stood. "You said you slept naked."

He searched for the borrowed pants, finding them on the floor where he'd dropped them the night before. "I said that's how I generally sleep. I also generally sleep alone."

"So do I, but I don't like to sleep naked. I get cold."

It was on the tip of his tongue to tell her she wouldn't get cold if she shared a bed with him every night, but he bit back the comment in time.

"We need to talk."

She sat up against the headboard looking deliciously soft and rumpled. His stomach gave a funny little twist.

"I think I said something along those lines last night," she told him, shoving aside a spill of hair.

"Get dressed. We'll talk downstairs."

He opened the door before he could give in to one of the detrimental impulses that would have involved kissing her senseless and climbing back into that bed with her. And he came face-to-face with Emily, her fist raised to knock against the door.

"Oh!"

Mentally, he cursed. Outwardly, he nodded. "Sorry, Emily. I didn't mean to startle you."

"Oh. Well."

She looked from him to the bed where Leigh still sat looking soft and dreamy, the marks from the pillow still visible on her cheek.

"I, uh, came to tell Leigh her sister's on the phone."

Leigh shoved aside the covers and swung her legs off the bed. The nightgown had ridden a good distance up her thigh. Gavin heaved a mental groan.

"Emily? Would you tell her I'm getting dressed? I'll call her back in a little bit."

Emily recovered her composure. "All right, dear. Nan will have breakfast ready for you and Gavin in thirty minutes. Will that give you both enough time?"

"Fine with me," Leigh said.

"I'm not hungry, Emily."

"I know, dear, but you know Nan. If you don't eat, she'll grumble about it all day. I'll see you downstairs."

Gavin looked at Leigh.

"I'd say she took that pretty well, wouldn't you?"

"Emily doesn't like scenes," he told her. "She has more effective weapons, like guilt and pointed questions."

"Gee, you make breakfast sound so inviting I can't wait. We aren't children, Gavin."

He let his gaze travel over her womanly shape. "No, we aren't. But don't blame me if you feel like one after she gets through with us."

"We didn't even do anything!"

"Uh-huh. Think she'll believe that?"

"But it's the truth."

"Get dressed, Leigh. We've got a lot to do this morning." He stepped into the hall and shut the door.

His burns and the cut made themselves known as he entered the bathroom. He nicked himself twice while he was shaving with the unfamiliar blade, but he dressed in record time and hurried downstairs. Amazingly, the kitchen was empty. He heard Nan and Emily conferring in the laundry room and he counted his blessings that he wouldn't have to waste any more time on explanations.

Taking one of the spare keys from the hook over the counter, he slipped outside and headed for Emily's car. She could add borrowing the car without asking to his other sins.

The roads were practically empty, so he made good time driving into town. As expected, fire had destroyed the building completely, even doing damage to the ones on either side. He didn't need anyone to tell him he wouldn't be salvaging much from the remains of his apartment.

He parked behind his car and got out. Caution made him examine the vehicle before touching it. Since his building had exploded, it was only prudent to make sure his car wouldn't be next. There were no signs it had been tampered with and his keys were still in the ignition, but he didn't breathe a sigh of relief until he saw that the computer was still in the trunk.

George appeared almost immediately after he parked his car in front of the Walken house. He strolled across the porch to watch as Gavin lifted the computer from the trunk.

"Need a hand?"

"I've got it, thanks. But if you would close the trunk, I'd appreciate it. I had to leave Emily's car across from my building. I'll have to get it back to her later."

"I can drive her into town this afternoon to pick it up."

"Thanks. You wouldn't happen to have a spare keyboard I could borrow, would you?"

"No, but you're welcome to use the one on my computer."

"Thanks, again."

Gavin waited for George to say something about Leigh. George simply held the door open for him. Emily and Nan stood in the hall with anxious expressions. There was no sign of Leigh.

"Leigh hasn't come down yet?" he asked.

"I think she's been on the phone with her sister," Emily said.

Her concern was as tangible as an admonishment.

"We're getting married," he told them.

Emily's lips parted in an "O" of surprise. Gavin was feeling a little surprised as well, even though he knew the thought had been there from the moment he'd opened the bedroom door this morning and seen Emily standing there about to knock.

George rocked back on his heels, but he looked thoughtful rather than surprised. Nan's seamed features split in a happy smile.

"Well now," she said cheerfully, "I'd say that calls for something extra special for breakfast this morning. Give me a few minutes and I'll see what I can do."

"Let's wait until tomorrow, Nan. I'm really not hungry this morning, and Leigh and I have a lot to do. Right now, I need to get this computer cleaned off." He headed down the hall toward George's office.

"Congratulations," George said quietly as he followed Gavin inside.

He set the computer down and faced the one man he'd come to admire more than anyone else he'd ever known. "I know she could do better—"

George shook his head. "No," he said with conviction. "She couldn't."

Gavin swallowed. Hard.

"People will think I'm marrying her for her money."

"When did you start caring what other people think?"

"I care what you think," he told George honestly.

The older man perched on the edge of his desk and smiled. "Last night I told Emily we'd see a double wedding."

Gavin realized his mouth was open and clamped it shut.

"As a rule, I don't offer unsolicited advice, Gavin, but I'm going to make an exception right now. I've watched you both grow into fine adults, but you each have a weakness that could destroy your chances together. Leigh thinks her sister is the strong one. As a result, she doesn't always trust her own instincts. And you dumped that chip off your shoulder, but held on to the misplaced guilt that put it there. As a result, trust comes hard to you."

Gavin shifted uncomfortably. "So you're saying we should trust each other?"

"You can't love without trust. So what's with this computer?"

As Gavin told him what R.J. had discovered, his conscience was being shredded by George's words. He didn't want to examine the reason behind his announcement too closely, knowing he wouldn't like what he'd see. What had seemed like the right thing to do at the time was looking pretty stupid and self-centered at the moment.

George whistled. "Dennison had a secret room, too?"

"I gather you didn't know?"

"He never mentioned it."

"So you don't know if there are any more of them?"

"Now, there's an unnerving thought. Do you think there are?"

Emily entered with a smile and a welcome mug of hot coffee for Gavin. "Nan says she's making a special omelette and you'd better eat it."

His lips twisted wryly. Emily only thought she was the

one in charge around here. Nan had ruled the house since before his arrival. But his humor dissolved in the blink of an eye when Leigh stepped into the room.

"Did you reach your sister?" Emily asked excitedly.

Leigh questioned him with a darting glance as she answered, "Yes."

"I'll bet she was as surprised as we were at the news." Emily hugged her fiercely. "We are so happy for you. Both of you. Have you set a date?"

Her startled gaze fastened on his. He hoped she could read the apology in his eyes.

"Sorry, Leigh. I should have waited to make an announcement."

"That would have been nice," she agreed. She smiled for Emily's benefit. "We haven't had a chance to make *any* plans yet."

He was grateful she hadn't denounced him, even as he wondered why.

"And I'm holding out for a formal proposal," Leigh continued. "You know, champagne, soft lights, music, a ring..."

Gavin winced. Emily relaxed.

"Good for you, dear. Stick to your guns. It never does to make things too easy for the male of the species."

George rolled his eyes, but he stood and slipped an arm around his wife. Gavin decided he'd better stop this conversation before the situation got any worse.

"We have a few things to take care of first, Emily. Like seeing what's on this computer."

"After breakfast," she said firmly. "You know how Nan is about meals."

"It generally pays to concede early and often to the female of the species," George advised with wry humor, giving Emily an affectionate smile.

Gavin was dismayed to see Nan had gone all out, setting

the dining-room table with china, even putting out small glasses of wine for a toast.

"There wasn't time to chill the champagne," she informed them.

"That's all right, Nan, it's the thought that counts," Leigh told her. "And this is lovely and thoughtful, isn't it, Gavin?"

"Very."

He endured their toasts and good wishes, all the while wondering what was going through Leigh's mind. When Emily and Nan enthused over wedding plans, Leigh went along as if it were perfectly normal.

It was a relief when the telephone rang with a call Emily had to take.

"Thank you, Nan," he told the cook, anxious now to get Leigh away so they could talk. "You're still the best cook in the county."

Nan scolded him with a shake of her frizzy gray head and turned to Leigh. "You're going to have your hands full with this one."

"I already do," Leigh agreed.

"What are you doing?" he whispered as they were finally able to head back down the hall.

"Planning your execution," she told him mock sweetly. "At the moment, I'm leaning toward a slow death by painful torture, but I could be satisfied with immediate gratification. Strangulation comes to mind."

George joined them before he could respond, so he forced himself to focus on the distraction presented by the computer. With George and Leigh hovering, he cleaned up what he could of the accumulated dust and dirt before connecting George's keyboard and turning on the machine. The cursor appeared, but the computer refused to boot.

"Is it broken?" George asked.

"I think the hard drive's been wiped," Leigh said thoughtfully.

Gavin tried again with the same results. "I think you're right. Why would your grandfather erase the machine then hide it away like that?"

"I don't know."

"Maybe it wasn't her grandfather who hid the computer," George offered.

Gavin met Leigh's startled gaze.

"I never thought of that possibility," he said.

"Me neither."

"Gavin?" Emily called, coming to stand in the doorway. "Wyatt Crossley's here. He says he needs to see you and Leigh about last night."

"Use the front room," George said. "We'll see that you aren't disturbed."

They went in to where Wyatt waited for them.

"How's the hand?" he greeted Gavin.

Given everything else he'd had to deal with this morning, Gavin had pretty much ignored the pain coming from the small burns and the cut.

"Things could have been worse. How's Earlwood?"

Wyatt's jaw tightened. "He didn't make it."

At Leigh's softly indrawn breath, Gavin sought her hand.

"Do they know what happened?" he asked.

Wyatt shook his head. "The fire's still under investigation. It appears to have been caused by a gas leak in the back room. Once the gas accumulated, it wouldn't have taken much to set it off. Any spark would have done the trick, even something as simple as turning on the light switch."

"Keith would have smelled the gas," Leigh protested.

"People take foolish risks all the time, like going to investigate instead of getting out and calling the fire department. It's just a lucky thing the two of you weren't already upstairs when the explosion happened.''

Gavin thought about the movement he'd seen behind the building. Whether it had been an animal or a human, his decision to drive around front had saved their lives.

''Any chance it was arson?'' Gavin asked.

Wyatt straightened alertly. ''We won't know until they finish the investigation. You have a reason to think it might have been?''

''Nope.''

''Of course not,'' Leigh said quickly.

Too quickly. Wyatt's expression turned speculative. He looked from one to the other and settled on Gavin. ''You tick off anyone in particular recently, Gavin?''

''You mean besides the team we beat last week?''

Wyatt gave him a dry look, but didn't pursue the question. ''Last night you mentioned Earlwood had some money problems. Where'd you hear about that?''

''I couldn't say for sure. I may have overheard it in a conversation at The Inn one night. I know I suggested he might have tried to blow up the place on purpose last night, but it doesn't make sense when you think about it. He wouldn't have collected enough insurance money to make the risk worthwhile—unless he owned the building.''

''Rapid Realty managed the building,'' Wyatt supplied. ''Someone's checking to see who actually owned it.''

''Rapid Realty is one of Nolan Ducort's firms, isn't it?'' Gavin deliberately didn't look at Leigh. ''Did you know Ducort and Earlwood were friends?''

Wyatt stilled. ''No, I didn't. Is that important?''

''Probably not, but the two of them went to school together. They used to hang out with Martin Pepperton.''

Wyatt's eyes narrowed as he made the connection to Pepperton's murder.

''Something you want to tell me, Gavin?''

"Nope. Just making conversation."

"Uh-huh. Interesting topic. I gather you didn't hang with them?"

"Wrong socioeconomic bracket."

"Yeah." Wyatt looked at Leigh.

She shook her head. Gavin found the soft sway of her hair strangely distracting.

"I didn't hang with them, either. They were years ahead of me in school," she told him.

"Leigh, we need to tell him that two days ago I filed a court order on your behalf against Ducort."

Leigh froze. Wyatt's gaze fastened on him.

"Ducort has a stake in R.J.'s company. R.J.'s doing some work at Heartskeep," Gavin told him neutrally. "I caught Ducort hassling Leigh."

"Why would he do that?"

Gavin didn't flinch at the hard tone or the steely look in his friend's eyes. Wyatt had a job to do. Gavin knew he took that job seriously.

"If I wasn't a member of the bar, I might have told you I consider him a dangerous piece of sleaze who'd probably be in jail if his family wasn't so well connected."

Wyatt tensed, so he was probably aware that his uncle and Ducort's father were old school friends.

"Any particular type of sleaze?" Wyatt asked.

"If you ask around, you may discover why smart women give Ducort short shrift," Gavin told him. "He thought Leigh might be his type."

"I'm not," she said firmly.

"He doesn't like being told no," Gavin added. "I made sure he got the message."

Wyatt grimaced. "Will he be filing charges against you?"

"Hey, I'm an officer of the court," Gavin reminded him.

"I made sure there were witnesses. Bram Myers escorted him to his car."

Wyatt's grimace deepened. "Was he annoyed enough to want a little of his own back?"

"Anything's possible. You asked me who I'd ticked off recently and I'd have to say he's the shortlist."

"Uh-huh. Was Ducort still running with Pepperton and Earlwood?"

"You'd have to ask him, but I'd say it's a good bet."

"Two of three are dead now," Wyatt said.

"Makes a person wonder, doesn't it?"

Wyatt sighed. "You've got my cell-phone number. Give me a call if you come up with any other interesting little tidbits, will you?"

"Always happy to help."

As they started for the hall Wyatt stopped. "I almost forgot. About your apartment—they weren't able to save anything, Gavin. I'm sorry."

"I know. I drove over this morning to pick up my car."

"If you need anything..." He let the sentence trail off.

"Thanks, Wy."

Gavin and Leigh followed him as far as the front porch.

"Think you'll be able to play ball with that hand? Assuming we don't get rained out again," he added as he opened his car door.

"If I can stand wearing the mitt, I'll play."

"Consider moving to left field where you won't have to catch as many balls," Wyatt suggested.

"Let's see how much it bothers me first."

"Okay. And, Gavin? Watch your back."

"Thanks. I plan to."

"He manages my softball team," Gavin told Leigh as Wyatt pulled away.

"So I gathered. Do you really believe Nolan caused that gas leak?"

"I don't know, but I like the idea a whole lot better than thinking Earlwood tried to blow us up."

"It's an old building. Maybe the pipe *was* faulty."

"Maybe."

"You don't believe that."

"Do you?"

Leigh tucked a strand of hair behind her ear without answering. "What are we going to do?"

"Like Wyatt said, watch our backs. We'll keep our eyes open and stay alert. I'd like to drive over to Heartskeep and have a look inside that filing cabinet."

Her eyes were troubled as she looked at him. "Don't you think we'd better have a little talk first?"

"We can talk on the way over."

"I think the conversation we need to have is going to take more than five minutes, don't you?"

Chapter Eleven

Nolan hung up the telephone and cursed steadily. He stared down at the bill of sale on his desk and hoped Martin Pepperton was being roasted slowly over the flames of hell.

The bastard had transferred the worthless horse to Nolan just as he'd said. And to add insult to injury, now Pepperton Farms wanted to charge Nolan an exorbitant amount of money for boarding the cursed animal, unless he sent someone to collect the horse.

If that wasn't bad enough, word had spread that he was the champion-bred colt's new owner. Tyrone Briggs was inundating him with calls to buy the worthless beast. Nolan pounded his fist against the desk, sending pens and loose papers flying. He was stuck.

Damn it, he would have given the animal to Briggs if Martin hadn't switched horses in an effort to pay Briggs back because of some colt Martin had bought from the man months ago. Nolan didn't know the whole story and he didn't care. Martin had become obsessed with getting even. He'd concocted this insane plot against Briggs and had landed Nolan in the middle of a living nightmare.

What was he going to do? The situation was going to blow up in his face just as he'd known it would when Martin had concocted the scheme in the first place.

Closing his eyes in despair, Nolan tried to see a way out.

Everything was falling apart! As soon as the cops got wind of this transfer they'd be all over him with questions. He'd told them he hadn't seen or talked to Martin in weeks. These papers made him a liar.

Nolan groaned. He opened his eyes and stared sightlessly at the expensive painting on the wall across from him. He'd even volunteered—*volunteered!*—the information that he'd been at the track the day Martin was shot. If the cops found out that Martin had created false records for this horse he supposedly sold Nolan, they'd see the horse switch as a motive for murder.

What if his alibi fell apart?

What if Leigh Thomas came forward and told them what she'd seen?

Fear sank its icy tendrils even deeper into his guts. He hadn't meant to shoot Martin. It had been self-defense! But who was going to believe that now?

What was he going to do? He had to think.

He shoved back his chair and began to pace. He had two tricky deals he was trying to negotiate right now. A lot of money was at stake. One whiff of this sort of trouble and he'd lose them both. He couldn't afford that. His cash-flow situation was critical.

He rubbed at his gritty eyes. All these sleepless nights were starting to show. If he could get some rest, maybe he could think before everything came apart.

Last night had been a mistake. He'd thought it was a calculated risk. He'd done his research carefully. Insurance investigators could be tenacious little bastards when something like a building blew up, but an old building like that in bad repair…

Hey, gas leaks happened. As long as he didn't leave behind any evidence and no one got killed…

Except Keith Earlwood *had* gotten killed, according to the radio this morning.

Nolan rubbed his bruised knuckles, struggling against a

rising sense of panic. No one was supposed to die. Why had the dumb bastard stayed inside?

The building was one of a handful Nolan had acquired and had had no use for when he'd taken over Rapid Realty seven months ago. The building needed costly repairs. It had already been on the market for over a year without a buyer, and it was a cash drain that had to go.

Keith's firm had been renting the main floor for a pittance. The apartment upstairs was rented as well, but the combined income wasn't a dent on what it would cost for repairs. Keith wouldn't have been out of pocket when it blew up. The insurance company would have made good on his losses. Same for the renter. Nolan had even made sure no one was home at the time.

So why hadn't Keith left? He hadn't hit the bastard that hard.

Oh, God, what if Earlwood had talked to the cops before he'd died?

No! Nolan rubbed his jaw, badly shaken by the thought. If Keith had said anything to the cops, they would have been here by now.

He should never have used Earlwood to keep tabs on the Thomas bitch and Jarret. He'd known better, but it was driving him crazy trying to figure out why she hadn't gone to the cops. There had to be a reason. He'd hoped it would be one he could turn to his advantage. Now, instead of answers, all he had were more questions.

Leigh Thomas had nothing to do with the racing community, yet she'd been talking to one of Martin's trainers inside the restaurant yesterday. She and Jarret had gone straight from there to the racetrack. It had to mean something!

Damn it! Why hadn't she told the cops he'd shot Pepperton? What was she waiting for? What was her angle?

More importantly, what was he going to do about her?

Nolan sank back down in his chair and stared at the papers on his desk.

What was he going to do about any of this? If only he could think.

Keith's death could work to his advantage. Lots of people knew Earlwood needed money. If the cops did figure out someone had loosened the gas fitting, they'd probably assume Earlwood had done it to collect from *his* insurance company.

Nolan stared at his bruised knuckles. He hadn't meant to swing on Keith, but when the little weasel had shown up as he was leaving and began demanding money, Nolan had lost it. Keith's confrontation with Jarret had started him thinking. He had actually found the guts to come right out and accuse Nolan of Martin's murder. Nolan had to admit, for a minute there, he'd actually wanted to kill the stupid, sorry son of a bitch.

But he hadn't! He had to remember that. Earlwood had cracked his head a good one when he went down against the desk that last time, but he'd been breathing. He'd even opened his eyes when Nolan told him exactly what would happen if he went to the police.

Nolan leaned back in his chair and closed his burning eyes. His head was throbbing in pain. Aspirin wasn't touching the headache. He was tempted to fix himself a drink even if it was ten o'clock in the morning. But he couldn't take the risk. He had to stay sharp for his meeting later this afternoon. He had to think. There had to be a way out of this horse deal.

His muscles were coiled so tight with tension he felt as if he might explode. The horse was the big problem, right? So what if he simply got rid of the animal?

Nolan sat up and opened his eyes. If he got rid of the substituted horse, no one would know it wasn't the animal these papers said it was.

His heart began to pound in excitement. That was the

answer! Get rid of the horse and stick with his original story. He hadn't talked to Martin in months. He didn't know anything about these papers. He'd never paid Pepperton a cent for any racehorse. What would he want with a horse?

It would work! He knew it would work. *If* he could find a way to get rid of the horse.

Too bad he couldn't shoot it. Martin's gun was still out in his car. A barn fire was out of the question. The way his luck was running, the animal would survive.

Nolan stood and walked to the window. What if the horse was stolen? What if he hired a couple of thugs to take the horse and turn the rotten animal loose somewhere?

Looking down at the ownership papers, Nolan rubbed tiredly at his eyes and grinned. He was liking this idea a whole lot. Simple, uncomplicated, perfect.

Now if he could just remember the name of that groom Martin had fired a short while ago. The guy would probably jump at the chance to make some easy money and get back at the Peppertons.

The plan was going to work, he could feel it. All he had to do was steal the damn horse and get rid of Leigh Thomas and Gavin Jarret. Too bad they hadn't hit a tree when he'd run them off the road the other night, but he still had Martin's gun.

"WE AREN'T GOING to get any privacy around here," Gavin told Leigh as he started the car. "We'll have to go Heartskeep."

"I'm sure we'll get plenty of privacy there with R.J.'s men running in and out."

"Sarcasm doesn't become you. It's a big house."

"Whatever you say."

He looked over at her, but Leigh was staring out the window. She wasn't going to make this easy for him.

"Are you angry?"

That sent her head swiveling in his direction.

"Why would I be angry, Gavin?"

Her calm was getting to him. He really couldn't decide what she was thinking.

"I figure you must have quite a list going by now."

She remained silent, but he sensed he'd amused her. That was a start.

"I shouldn't have called your bluff last night," he said gently.

"I wasn't bluffing."

He nearly drove off the road, looking at her. Her expression was as serious as her tone had been. He shouldn't have started this conversation in the car. He needed to be able to focus on her—to see her expressions.

"What are you doing?" she asked as he swerved onto the narrow shoulder.

"Parking the car!"

"Here?"

"Yes." He put the car in park, released his seat belt and turned to face her.

"You really want another attorney?"

"I did until you told the Walkens we were getting married."

He struggled to make sense of her words. She sat there looking perfectly composed. If she was kidding, it didn't show.

"What does that mean?" he demanded.

"It means I'm not going to fire you."

He drummed his fingers against the steering wheel. "I guess it would be a little awkward if you fired your husband," he said sardonically.

"We aren't getting married," she scoffed. "You told the Walkens what they needed to hear. It would have been nice if you'd warned me. That breakfast was more than a little awkward, but I understand. And don't worry, it won't be hard to get out of this mess. We'll have to wait a few weeks to make it look good, but then I'll tell them that I changed my mind. Simple.''

Pressure tightened his chest. ''Simple?''

''Don't fret, I won't make you look like the bad guy, Gavin.''

''What the devil are you talking about?'' He gripped the steering wheel in frustration. ''I should have made love to you,'' he muttered.

Her lips parted in surprise. He saw the flash of hurt in her eyes and felt a stab of guilt. He hadn't meant to hurt her.

''I admit that would have been nice,'' she said blandly, ''but it's probably better this way. I'm not much for casual affairs.''

''Nice?'' He latched on to the word while his fingers squeezed the hard plastic steering wheel. ''You think making love with me would have been nice?''

Her eyebrow lifted in phony surprise. ''It wouldn't have been nice?''

He leaned toward her and was rewarded by a spark of real emotion, even if it was apprehension. ''Maybe you don't remember what it was like seven years ago,'' he said softly, ''but I haven't forgotten a thing, Leigh. When I make love to you again, there won't be anything *casual* about it. And I promise you, it's going to be a whole lot better than *nice*.''

Those expressive blue eyes showed a kaleidoscope of emotions that ranged from shock to hope to defiance. It was the hope that pleased him, even as she lifted her chin defiantly.

''Sorry. I didn't mean to dent your masculine pride.''

''Lady, you've been walking all over my pride and you know it.''

''Isn't that better than compromising your principles?''

''That's the second time you've thrown that in my face.'' He cupped her cheek with his hand. ''I didn't mean to hurt you, Leigh. I was trying to establish some objectivity where you were concerned. It was a wasted effort.''

Her lips parted in surprise and he lowered his mouth. Soft and sweet, her lips clung tenderly while a slow heat simmered inside him. She arched her neck, inviting a response, and he gave it, sampling the delicate line of her throat, savoring her feminine shiver of reaction.

His other hand slid across her rib cage, tracing the curve of her breast, feeling the bud of her nipple straining against the fabric that confined it.

And his cell phone rang.

The tinny notes jarred them from the sensual haze that had enveloped them. He rested his head against her forehead, reluctant to let her go.

''Are you going to answer that?''

''I could toss the phone out the window instead,'' he suggested, lifting his head.

She smiled. ''Wyatt would arrest you for littering.''

''In another minute or so, the charge would have been lewd behavior.''

He reached for the phone. ''Jarret.''

Leigh watched as he straightened in his seat.

''No, I'm in my car.''

They were still blowing hot and cold with each other, but the heat was definitely winning.

''Okay, Susan. Give the auditors access to whatever they want. I'll be in when I can, but cancel anything I have scheduled for the rest of the week. No. No new appointments until next week. You can give out my cell-phone number if anything urgent comes up, otherwise leave a message at the Walkens'. Right. Thanks. You, too.''

''I gather that was your office?''

''My paralegal. Marcus did give Eden access to the household account, but he's the one who made all the large withdrawals. They can see the pattern. He transferred money to his private account after each bogus bill was paid in, then he withdrew the money in cash.''

''What does that mean?''

''For starters, it means that if he were alive, your father would have to account for all that missing money.''

''Jacob said he was broke.''

''Maybe he was. Maybe he had a secret vice.''

''Six hundred fifty thousand dollars is a lot of vice.''

Gavin's lips twitched. ''He could have put the money in some account that hasn't come to light yet.''

''I'll bet that's why Eden was so quick to clear out his belongings. She's looking for the money, too.''

''You won't find a taker for that bet here.'' He put on his seat belt and started the car. ''But if that money still exists, we need to find it first.''

''Hayley and Bram are on their way back. We can ask them to help us look.''

''Good.''

She hesitated, reluctant to ask the next question. ''What should I tell Hayley? You know, about being engaged.''

His body tensed. He didn't look at her. ''What do you want to tell her?''

''What does that mean?''

''It means there's a lot of chemistry between us.''

Her heart started racing once more as he picked his words carefully.

''This doesn't have to be a phony engagement.''

She barely noticed the ruts as he turned into the driveway leading to Heartskeep. Her insides were jouncing around for other reasons.

''Are you asking me to...marry you?''

''You don't have to sound so shocked by the idea. I realize this isn't the best time or place to be having this conversation, but since you brought it up—'' he shot her a quick glance ''—why don't you consider the idea? I think we'd suit each other pretty well. I'd sign a prenuptial agreement, of course. I'm not interested in your money, Leigh."

Dazed, she gaped at him. "You're serious!"

"Yes." His eyes suddenly narrowed as he stared through the windshield. "Now what?"

Leigh followed his gaze blindly. As he braked to a halt, her brain slowly came to terms with what her eyes were seeing. Men were running toward the back of the house. Before she could assimilate that, Gavin was out of the car, striding toward the one man who wasn't running, but was standing there scowling after the others.

"What's going on? Where's R.J.?"

The man turned his head and spit. "Trying to catch Lucky before that crazy woman tries to kill him again."

"Eden's here?" Leigh asked, running up behind them in time to hear the man's words.

"Out back. I'm surprised you didn't hear her screaming in Stony Ridge."

Gavin set off at a dead run.

"I'd go through the house if I were you," the man said to Leigh. "It's quicker."

She nodded and sprinted up the steps. The front door was unlocked. No doubt Eden had walked right in. She didn't have a key anymore, and R.J. wouldn't have knowingly given her access.

Leigh raced through the house. She reached the kitchen expecting to see a repeat of the earlier scene between Eden and Lucky, but this time, there was no one in sight. The kitchen door, however, gaped open. Books spilled across the kitchen table as if dropped there by someone in a hurry.

Leigh glanced at them as she started past, and jerked to a stop. The last time she'd seen those books they'd been on the shelf in Marcus's bedroom. Eden had returned to finish what she'd started. So why on earth was she out there chasing Lucky again? Didn't she realize a dog that size could tear her arm off if she made him mad enough?

Leigh hurried outside as Eden burst from the far opening to the gardens. Her face was chalky pale except for two bright red spots of color. *Terrified* was the only word for her expression.

Leigh ran toward her. Had Lucky bitten her?

Where was the dog? She didn't hear him barking. In fact, she couldn't hear or see anyone else at all. Everyone must have run into the maze.

"Eden? Are you all right?"

Eden stumbled. She stared at Leigh without comprehension. Then she ran to her car. Leigh sprinted to intercept her.

"Eden?"

The woman jerked to a halt. Her eyes were wild.

"Stay away from me! Stay away!"

"Eden? It's okay. It's Leigh. Take it easy. Are you all right?"

Eden lunged at her. Completely off guard, Leigh stumbled backward. Eden jumped in her car and twisted the key in the ignition before Leigh could regain her balance.

"Eden! Wait!"

The car rocketed down the driveway. Plumes of dust shot into the hot, humid air. Footsteps pounded up behind Leigh. She heard Gavin swear as the car careened out of sight.

"Why didn't you stop her?"

"With what? Do you see any bazookas lying around? Because that's what it would have taken. What's going on? She looked like she'd seen a ghost!"

Leigh heard someone inhale sharply. R.J., Lucky and several of R.J.'s men spilled out into the parking area. There was a chilling soberness in their expressions.

"R.J.? What happened? Did she hurt Lucky?"

R.J. had a firm grip on the dog's collar. In his other hand, he held a stick. Her head swung to Gavin for an explanation. His dark expression loosened a jolt of pure fear inside her.

"Lucky was digging in the garden again," he said softly.

Unaccountable fear spread with each beat of her heart. "That's okay. I told you he couldn't hurt anything."

No one moved. Everyone watched her. There was pity on several faces. R.J. released Lucky. The large dog trotted over to her, his stubby tail swishing in greeting. He was filthy. Mud and dirt clung to his fur, especially in front. His legs were coated with the evidence of his misbehavior.

"Leigh."

Gavin took her by the shoulders.

"Lucky didn't just dig a hole. He dug a pit. He broke the sprinkler system."

"I don't care! Gavin, you're scaring me."

"He dug up a bone." Gavin tipped his head toward R.J. without looking away. "It's a human bone."

The words formed a rushing sound inside her head. She couldn't tear her eyes from his. They were dark whirlpools of sympathy.

"What are you saying?" she whispered. But she knew. Before his lips parted, she knew.

"Someone buried a body under the sprinkler system."

Her mind went numb. Her voice came out as hollow as her insides felt. "Show me."

"There's nothing to see, Leigh," he said tenderly, gently. "It's a big muddy hole—"

"Show me!"

She wrenched free and started toward the maze. Her gaze landed on the stick in R.J.'s hand. Not a stick. A bone. A human bone.

"Leigh, you don't want to go back there," R.J. said.

The other men were sidling away. She tore her gaze from the bone and moved past them, practically running.

"Let her go," Gavin commanded.

"She shouldn't go back there, Gavin," R.J. said. "There's nothing to see."

SHE WAS IN THE MAZE when Lucky trotted past to take the lead. Leigh was aware of Gavin at her back. He didn't speak and neither did she. Her body felt frozen despite the temperature out here in the sun. There was a horrified acceptance inside her that had no voice.

Somehow, even before Lucky trotted down the dead-end path, she knew exactly where he was going. Life and death were coming full circle. Roses had once bloomed profusely in this spot.

Marcus's favorite place in the maze.

He'd planted his first roses here. He'd tended to them for the past seven years with a fanatical care that no one had understood.

Until now.

The roses were gone, destroyed along with Marcus. Water and mud covered the ground from the broken pipe. Someone had found the cut-off valve, but not before water had flooded the good-size hole Lucky had managed to dig.

Leigh walked toward the hole.

"Careful," Gavin cautioned. "The ground's slippery near the edges."

He was right. There wasn't much to see. Simply a hole filled with muddy water. But somewhere in that muck were the remains of a human being.

Lucky sat on his haunches and looked up at her. She stroked his head lightly. "Good boy, Lucky." She turned toward Gavin.

He watched her through inscrutable eyes.

"This is where he died, you know," she told him. "Marcus was shot to death in that very spot. There's a sort of poetic justice at work here."

Her words seemed disembodied, as if they came from someone else entirely.

"Leigh—"

"Marcus killed our mother. We always knew that. We didn't know he buried her here. We should have. When he planted his first rose, we should have known. Mom always liked roses.''

''Let's go back to the house, Leigh.''

''Don't you see the irony? He died over the very spot where he buried her.''

''Let's go.''

She turned from the muddy hole at the urging of his hands. She looked up at him and saw the knowledge in his eyes.

''At least you aren't trying to pretend it isn't my mother's grave.'' Shouldn't she be feeling something other than this utter sense of calm? ''We always knew Marcus killed her. No one believed us, but we *knew*!''

''The police are on their way,'' Gavin said. ''I called them as soon as R.J. realized what Lucky had found.''

''It could be someone else, Leigh,'' R.J. said.

She'd forgotten about him. Her gaze went to the object in his hand. It still looked like a stick. A dirty white stick.

''It's okay, you know. That isn't her.'' She nodded toward the bone. ''That's just the remnants of what she was. My mother's here.'' She pressed her fist against her chest. ''She'll always be here. It's just good to finally know.''

Her voice quavered and broke. She let Gavin slide his arm around her.

''I'm okay. We can go back to the house now. I need to call my sister.''

Chapter Twelve

Leigh didn't need to call Hayley after all. Her sister and Bram had already arrived. Someone must have told them what Lucky had found. Hayley was running toward the maze, Bram at her side.

Gavin watched the women embrace. It was almost a relief to see the tears start to flow. Leigh's unnatural calm had reminded him all too vividly of his own lack of emotion the day his family had died. He didn't want to see her internalize her grief the way he had. Tears were supposed to be healing. He hoped that was true.

"Do you think it's Amy Thomas?" Bram asked him.

"It will take time to be certain, but I'd say it's pretty likely."

"Hayley always believed her father murdered her mother."

Gavin nodded. "I know. The police should be here soon. Think we can get them inside?"

"Hayley's going to want to see."

"Yeah. So did Leigh. There's nothing to see."

"That won't matter."

"I know."

THEY SAT at the kitchen table while the backyard and the maze filled with police and technicians.

R.J. and his crew were questioned and sent home. Leigh and Hayley hugged him and told him how glad they were that Lucky had found the grave.

Gavin called his office and let Susan know he wouldn't be in after all. Then he called the Walken estate, relieved that it was George who answered the telephone. He let him know what had been found and suggested he turn off the house phone and rely on cell phones for a while. The media would be all over this news.

The sorrow in the older man's voice was deep and genuine. Gavin promised to keep him informed.

He spotted Wyatt out back several times and was grateful that Chief Crossley didn't put in an appearance. Gavin went to meet Wyatt when he finally headed for the back door.

"How are Leigh and Hayley?"

"Stoic," Gavin replied. "They've been waiting for more than seven years to find their mother."

Wyatt grimaced "I know."

"Come in. Bram's making coffee."

Wyatt shook his head. "I can't just yet. Are they up to identifying some jewelry we found?"

"I think so. Just keep your uncle away from them."

Wyatt muttered something derogatory under his breath. "Don't worry, he knows how this makes him look. I'll be back. You planning to stick around?"

"Yes."

"Okay. I've got more bad news. I'll let you decide when to tell them. I had a call from the Saratoga police department. They located Livia Walsh. She suffered a massive stroke while shopping several days ago. She's been in the hospital unable to speak or move. They've been trying to locate her daughter."

Gavin swore softly. "I hope they have better luck than I've had."

"I'll be back shortly."

Hayley was holding court when Gavin joined the group at the kitchen table.

"You know what really galls me?" she asked. "Marcus actually told me Mom was buried there, but I was too dense to realize what he was saying."

"What are you talking about?" Bram asked.

"When I first got here, Eden told me Marcus had dementia. I went out to the maze to talk to him and found him on his knees in that very bed of roses. I thought he was talking to himself. He patted the ground and said something like, 'Your roses are doing well this year, Amy.' I thought it was a manifestation of his illness, but it wasn't. He knew she was under those roses because he put her there."

Leigh shuddered. Gavin touched her shoulder lightly. She gazed up at him, then leaned into his side.

"We had the police digging in the wrong place," she said.

Gavin came around beside her and sat down, jarring the pile of books sitting near the edge of the tabletop.

"Eden knew Mom was buried there," Leigh told her sister. "That's why she was so upset with Lucky. She was afraid he'd find the grave."

"She helped Marcus kill Mom?" Hayley demanded.

"Easy," Bram said. "We don't even know for certain it's your mother's body yet."

Hayley rounded on him. "How many missing bodies do you think are buried around here?"

"Bram's right," Gavin interjected. "We should be careful about what conclusions we go jumping to, Hayley."

"Eden knew—" Leigh began.

"You can't prove that."

"You saw her, Gavin." Leigh said. "Everyone saw the way she acted. She chased Lucky with a knife! And I saw her face when she left. She was scared to death!"

"Reactions aren't proof. Not in a court of law."

"What do you need?" Hayley demanded scathingly. "Pictures of Eden standing over the body with a shovel in her hand?"

"That would help," he agreed mildly, understanding their anger and frustration. "The legal system needs tangible evidence, Hayley. And before you jump down my throat again, I'm on your side! I don't know if Eden helped put the body there or not, but I'd stake my reputation that she knew it was buried out back. Unfortunately, knowing something and proving it are two different things entirely."

"That isn't right," Hayley complained.

"Would you want to go to jail based on someone's interpretation of your reaction to a situation? A lawyer will say she ran away because she was horrified, not because she had prior knowledge."

"You're saying that she's going to walk around free?"

"Gavin's not the enemy, Hayley," Bram said gently.

"It's okay. I understand her frustration, Bram. It's one of the reasons I decided not to go into criminal law. Innocent people go to jail. Guilty people go free. It stinks, but those are facts."

"How do we prove her guilt?" Leigh asked.

Gavin covered her hand with his. "With hard evidence and patience. The police may find the evidence they need buried with the body."

Hayley snorted. "After all this time? I'm surprised there's even bones to dig up!"

"That's where the patience comes in."

"It's not my long suit," Hayley told him.

Bram clasped her hand. "We know."

In the silence that descended, Gavin told them about Livia Walsh. Leigh's eyes brimmed with tears.

"Someone broke into her house while she was lying there helpless in the hospital?"

Gavin stroked her arm in sympathy. "Looks that way."

"We have to do something to help her," Hayley said.

Gavin spied Wyatt heading for the back door and rose to let him in. Bram rose as well. Gavin made introductions all around. Hayley eyed the bags in Wyatt's hands.

"Before you show us anything at all, I can tell you there are two pieces of jewelry our mother wore all the time. One was a plain gold wedding band, the other was a very distinctive, custom-made necklace with two large emeralds. Grandpa had it designed for her right after we were born."

"Grandpa had most of her jewelry custom made," Leigh said. "She had pictures and appraisals on file with her insurance company for everything."

"That will help," Wyatt said, walking to the kitchen table. "How did you know this was jewelry?"

"Because I doubt if there's much else left after all this time."

He didn't answer that, pushing aside the pile of books Eden had left there. "I'll have to ask you not to touch these until our people finish with them."

Using what looked like an elongated pair of tweezers, Wyatt removed a delicate object from the first bag. Mud and dirt covered the necklace, but there were two large stones that could have been green, set in a distinctive setting of gold.

Leigh made a small, choked sound and closed her eyes. Gavin slid an arm around her shoulders. She was shaking.

"That's Mom's necklace," Hayley said. Her voice broke. She turned away and buried her face against Bram's shoulder. Leigh inhaled deeply, opened her eyes and nodded. She looked at the remaining items and confirmed their ownership as well. "Mom always liked jewelry."

"I'm truly sorry," Wyatt said.

"No, it's better this way," Leigh said, wiping her eyes. "We always knew she was dead."

"How did she die?" Hayley choked out.

Wyatt shook his head. "We don't know yet. It will take time to determine, I'm afraid."

Hayley told him what Marcus had said while tending the roses. Leigh related Eden's behavior.

"Is she going to get away with whatever part she played in what happened to our mother?" Hayley asked flatly.

Wyatt looked around the circle of faces. "Not if I can help it. I know my uncle never took your accusations seriously, but I'm not my uncle and this is my investigation."

"He's still your boss," Hayley pointed out.

"The same way Marcus was your father."

For a second, there was absolute silence. Hayley looked at Leigh. Gavin wasn't sure what passed between them in that look, but he felt some of the tension ebb from Leigh's shoulders. Hayley turned back to Wyatt.

"How can we help?"

"We have to go over the case again. I'll need you to think back to that time and try to remember everything you can that preceded your mother's trip to New York City and everything that happened immediately afterward."

"We've gone over everything so many times we could do it in our sleep," Hayley told him.

Wyatt shook his head. "Not the way I'm going to do it. I want every detail—what you had for breakfast, what the weather was like, what you were thinking about when you left for school. It's going to take time. I'm going to be thorough. I want you to start thinking back. We'll look for patterns and inconsistencies. You think you remember everything clearly, but memory is never static. It would be best if the two of you don't talk about what you remember between yourselves or with anyone else. I'll give you each a call to set up an interview. I'm sorry. I know it's a pointless thing to say, but I am."

"Thank you," Leigh said.

When Wyatt left, Hayley turned to Gavin.

"I hope your friend is as good as he thinks he is."

He thought about that for a minute. "I think he may be."

"I like him," Leigh told her.

"So do I," Bram agreed.

He reached down to collect the empty coffee cups and jarred the table. One of the books Wyatt had nudged aside slid to the floor. A slip of paper fell out and skimmed across the floor to land nearly at Leigh's feet. She bent to retrieve it and froze.

"Gavin!"

> I know what you did. Leave twenty thousand dollars behind the left stone lion by nine o'clock Thursday evening.

The note was typed across a sheet of blank, white paper, unsigned and undated. The large font made the message clearly legible to all of them.

"Don't touch it! Bram, see if you can catch Wyatt before he leaves," Gavin ordered. "Don't touch the book, either," he advised Hayley when she would have retrieved it from the floor.

"But there's another note sticking out of one of the pages. More than one," Hayley corrected.

Gavin met Leigh's gaze.

"I think we just found out what happened to the missing six hundred fifty thousand," he said.

"Is this what Eden has been looking for?" Leigh asked.

"I don't know. Maybe. But I'm more inclined to think she was looking for the money itself, not the reason it was missing."

The back door opened and Bram and Wyatt stepped inside. After reading the note, Wyatt herded them all into the library. When he finally joined them there, he told them his people had recovered seven notes in all with various monetary demands. One was a demand for fifty thousand dollars.

"No wonder Marcus died broke," Hayley muttered.

"It will be interesting to see if we can relate these demands to the money withdrawn from the bank accounts," Gavin mused aloud.

Wyatt nodded. "You and I will need to sit down and go over those accounts. Any thoughts on who might have been blackmailing your father?"

"Take your pick," Hayley said. "The field's wide open. Marcus wasn't exactly loved by anyone."

"So I've heard."

"What about Eden?" Leigh asked.

"She married him," her sister argued. "She didn't need to blackmail him."

"I know," Leigh agreed. "And Jacob said she was really upset that Marcus was broke, but that could have been an act. When I asked Jacob if she needed anything, he told me Eden had been putting money aside for years... remember, Gavin? If she was afraid Marcus had kept these notes, it would explain why she was so frantic to remove all his belongings from the house."

Gavin sought Wyatt's gaze. "Not to make your job any harder than it already is, but what if the notes were typed by Marcus himself? They aren't dated. He could have been the one who was doing the extorting. Maybe from Dennison Hart."

Into the shocked silence, Wyatt muttered something under his breath. "You've got a devious mind, Counselor."

"Just playing devil's advocate."

"I don't need that kind of help. I'll keep an open mind. We'll need access to the house, I'm afraid."

"Look anywhere you want," Hayley invited. "But you'll need to find Eden if you want to look at anything that belonged to Marcus. Those books and his furniture were all she left behind.''

''I have people looking for her as we speak. Gavin, is there any way this could relate to last night's explosion?''

''What explosion?'' Hayley demanded.

''I'll tell you later,'' Leigh said. ''It wasn't an accident?''

''I don't know yet, but the way Gavin seems to be drawing trouble...''

Gavin spread his hands. ''Hey, I'm just the family attorney.''

''So you keep telling me. You four have anything else you want to share with me?''

Gavin looked at Leigh. She shook her head.

''All right. I'll be in touch.''

''And you didn't tell him about the room R.J. found because...?'' Bram asked quietly after Wyatt strode off down the hall.

''I asked him not to mention it,'' Leigh said. ''I want first look inside that file cabinet.''

''Good thinking,'' Hayley agreed. ''Let's go!''

''Shouldn't we wait until the police leave?'' Leigh asked. ''It might be a little difficult to explain what the four of us are doing in an empty bedroom closet.''

''Sounds kinky,'' Bram said in an effort to lighten the mood.

Hayley nudged him in the ribs. ''It's getting late. Why don't we go over and talk to Emily and George? We can come back here tonight after everyone is gone.''

Bram raised his eyebrows. ''You want to come back here after dark?''

''We can't. R.J. still has the power out on that side of the building,'' Leigh reminded them.

''We could use flashlights, or move the filing cabinet to one of our rooms,'' Hayley suggested.

Gavin shook his head. ''The police will be here all night.''

''It's supposed to rain again tonight.''

''That doesn't matter. They'll have tents and tarps. After seven years, the recovery will be along the lines of an archaeological dig. There are a lot of bones in the human body and they want to recover all of them if they can. They'll be sifting that entire area for anything they can find. Besides, Hayley gave them blanket permission to search the house for evidence. If I know Wyatt, he's going to make a thorough job of the search.''

''Should I have said no?''

''No, you did the right thing, Hayley,'' Gavin told her. ''He would have come back with a court order and made the search anyhow. This way, you're cooperating with the investigation, which is always preferable.''

''So the filing cabinet has to wait until tomorrow?'' Hayley asked.

Gavin nodded. ''Or until the police are done with their search upstairs. We can't remove anything from the house at this point that might contain potential evidence.''

''Wyatt's not going to be happy that we held back information, either,'' Bram said mildly.

''We won't. We're just going to delay telling him. If we find anything pertinent, we'll let him know right away.''

But he knew Wyatt would be annoyed, particularly if there were other rooms like the one R.J. had found still concealed in this dark barn of a place.

Hayley and Bram stood to leave.

''The press is probably camped outside the front gates,'' Gavin reminded them. ''R.J. disconnected the telephone line before he left so we wouldn't be inundated with calls. We'll have to rely on cell phones.''

Hayley groaned. ''I forgot about the media.''

"We'll use my truck and take the back road," Bram suggested.

"I'm not sure we can drive around to the barns from here anymore. The road's overgrown. It hasn't been used in years."

"My truck can handle it. You two want to ride with us?"

Leigh looked at Gavin.

"Go with them," he told her. "I'll use my unofficial status to hang around a while longer."

"I'll stay with you." She turned to her sister. "Before you go, I need to tell you something. Gavin and I are getting married."

"What!"

Leigh didn't look at him. "Emily and George know. So does Nan. We haven't told anyone else."

"Including me!" Hayley didn't bother to cover her hurt.

"I know. I'm sorry. It only happened this morning—after I talked to you."

"It's my fault, Hayley," Gavin interjected. "I told Emily and George without consulting her. Sorry. I should have waited for Leigh to tell you first."

She eyed Gavin with suspicion before turning that suspicion on Leigh. "Do you know what you're doing? No offense, but this is awful sudden."

"No, it isn't," Leigh said. "It's taken more than seven years."

Hayley's lips parted in surprise. Gavin went still.

"Be happy for me, please?"

"Oh, Leigh, of course I'm happy for you!" Hayley enfolded her in a tight hug. "It's just that you caught me by surprise. I never expected an announcement like this."

"I know."

"I want details," she said, pulling back.

"Later," Leigh promised. "I didn't want you to hear about this from Emily or George."

"I would never have forgiven you." She turned to Gavin, who was being congratulated by Bram. "Don't hurt my sister."

Gavin looked her straight in the eye. "It's the very last thing on earth I want to do, Hayley."

Leigh felt her throat constrict. Hayley looked suitably impressed. She tossed her head and returned his gaze. "I never had a big brother before. This should prove interesting. Welcome to the family."

"He's a good guy," Bram said at Leigh's side.

"I know. The two of you are very much alike."

Bram looked startled. "I'll take that as a compliment. Come on, Hayley," he said more loudly. "I want to get out of here before that rain comes in. It's already starting to get dark out, so it must be on the way."

Gavin touched her shoulder as they watched Bram and Hayley leave. "Was that announcement your way of giving me an answer?"

Leigh met his gaze. "No. It was expedient."

"Expedient. Interesting word choice. So, your answer is no?"

She gave her head a shake. "I thought lawyers were supposed to understand fine distinctions."

"Sorry, I'm feeling dense right now."

"You told me to think about it. Us. So, I'm thinking about it."

For what felt like an eternity, he didn't respond. "Fair enough."

There was a tentative knock on the kitchen door before it swung open and Wyatt stepped back inside.

"I thought you left," Gavin said.

"No, I'll be here most of the night. We're trying to get the scene under cover before it starts to rain. I saw Hayley and Bram leave and was wondering about you."

"All right if we hang around for a while? Leigh needs

to collect some papers and files—things we need to go over. We can run them past you first if you want.''

Wyatt gave him a steady look. Leigh kept her features as inscrutable as possible.

''I can't let you take anything that might pertain to the case, Gavin.''

''I want my mother's murder solved more than you do,'' Leigh said forcefully. ''The last thing I'm going to do is conceal potential evidence. We only want to look at some of my grandfather's papers. Since he died before my mother even disappeared, I hardly think they're relevant to your investigation, but if it turns out they are, you'll be the first to know.''

Wyatt searched her face as if he knew she was hiding something. His nod was slow in coming. ''All right, Leigh. Let one of the officers know when you're ready to leave.''

THE FOOLS HAD BEEN caught.

Nolan cursed through his panic as he sped away from his vantage point overlooking Pepperton Farms. They would talk, of course, they were bound to. He was glad now that he'd hired them over the telephone. It had cost him a precious ten thousand dollars for nothing, but at least they couldn't identify him.

There was bound to be an investigation into the horse now. Nolan felt everything closing in on him. He should have approached someone else, only there hadn't been time to search for anyone else. The two men had worked there. They knew horses and they both had a grudge against Pepperton Farms and Martin in particular. The little guy was a friend of the groom's, an ex-jockey running to fat. Nolan had been lucky to find them in the first place. There was no way he could have known they'd be so incompetent. If he could have done the job himself, he would have, but horses were big and they had teeth for biting and hooves for stomping.

He'd never forget the sound of that horse's hooves hitting Martin's flesh as he'd left the barn that morning. The memory made him shudder every time he thought about it. He never wanted to get that close to a horse again.

Nolan thought of a few more choice words and used them.

He was scared. The acrid taste of fear was bitter in his mouth. He wanted to howl in rage and frustration. He couldn't eat and he couldn't sleep. Leigh Thomas was a threat to his very existence. The only way to deal with a threat was to eliminate it. He should have done that from the start.

Nolan rubbed tiredly at his eyes and thought about Martin's gun. If he shot Leigh and put the gun in Jarret's car, the cops might buy a lover's quarrel. Even if they didn't, there would be no way to tie her murder to him. It was the only thing left to do.

Except, the whole idea made him sweat. Ironic, really. He was already responsible for three other deaths, yet he was afraid to kill one small woman.

Because the other deaths had all been accidents. Killing Leigh would be a deliberate act.

He had no choice! It was her or him. His family's wealth and connections wouldn't be enough to keep him out of jail this time. Not if the cops realized he'd shot Martin or caused that gas leak. Leigh had to die.

He turned his car in the direction of Heartskeep. There was supposed to be a back road to the estate somewhere off one of the side roads between Heartskeep and the Walken place. It wasn't marked and he wasn't sure exactly where the road was, but he wouldn't be seen if he could find the entrance.

Of course, the road was probably an overgrown mess.

He'd just had his car cleaned and waxed. The low-slung sports car wouldn't be able to handle anything too challenging. He should drive to the car dealership he'd just purchased and borrow another truck or SUV, but now that he'd made up his mind to do this, he didn't want to wait. Every second he delayed brought him that much closer to total ruin.

If the road looked bad, he'd leave the car and walk in. That was a better plan anyhow. No point taking the risk of getting stuck. He'd park where the car couldn't be seen and walk to the estate. If Leigh wasn't there, he'd wait. Sooner or later she'd show up. She always did.

If only the rain would hold off just a little bit longer.

Chapter Thirteen

"That was good thinking, telling Wyatt the files belonged to your grandfather," Gavin praised.

"It's the truth. At least, I think it is."

"We'll need a flashlight."

"There should be one in that kitchen drawer," Leigh told him. Only there wasn't. "Well, I have one in my bedroom."

"All right." Gavin started for the back stairs and stopped, obviously remembering her dislike of them.

"It's okay," she told him. "I'll never be comfortable on them, but I can handle it." Especially if Gavin was with her.

"I don't think there are too many things you can't handle," he told her.

Warmth suffused her.

"Leigh, do you trust me?"

"Yes. Why?"

He smiled. "I trust you, too. Let's go before Wyatt comes back."

Wondering what that was all about, she followed him up the dark, narrow stairs. At the landing, he paused.

"Hold up a minute."

She watched him run his hands along the dark wood.

"What are you doing?"

"Looking for a second entrance onto the balconies. And I'm guessing... Yep. There it is."

Leigh peered up and down the hall nervously as a section of wall swung inward beneath his hand.

"We've lived here all our lives and we never knew this was here. How lame is that?"

"You weren't supposed to know."

"I still feel stupid."

Reluctant, yet also curious, she followed him onto the balcony and caught her breath. The dining room stretched below, lit only by the fading light from the skylights overhead.

"It's so strange." She whispered, even though there was no need to whisper. Heights had never bothered her before, but this felt disorienting, even eerie. A cold chill settled in the pit of her stomach.

"Be careful," Gavin cautioned. "There's a step down to the railing."

He showed her, walking over to peer over the side. Leigh drew blood, digging her nails into her palms to keep from ordering him back. Above them, the scudding clouds continued to turn the day to early twilight.

"We should have left lights on down there."

Leigh had never been any good at hiding her emotions. She knew her desire to leave was written all over her. Gavin frowned.

"Hey, are you okay?"

"We should get the flashlight." The open space around them was growing darker by the second. The clouds were changing from gray to black, filling the skylight above their heads.

"All right. Just let me show you how to open this door."

Leigh bit her lip to keep from telling him she didn't care. A sense of impending danger filled her. She told herself she was simply reacting to the sudden barometric drop in pressure. She always had reacted strongly to storms even as a child.

Anxious, almost desperate to be away from there, she let him show her the all but invisible depression that triggered the door. She opened it, then closed it again quickly to show him she understood how the mechanism worked.

"What do you want to bet that was modeled after the original design?"

Leigh didn't care. She wanted to go. She wanted light. She wanted away from here. But Gavin was studying the wall next to the staircase. He ran his fingers over the paneling on one side and then the other.

"What are you doing?" She could no longer contain her agitation.

"The wall's too thick."

"What?"

"Unless the fireplace has a double flue—one on either side of this landing—then the wall is too thick over here."

He tapped both sides, listening hard. Finally, he returned to the side next to the stairs. "The chimney flue is opposite the stairs. So what do we have next to the staircase?"

"Gavin, it's getting really dark."

He ran his fingers carefully over the paneling. "I thought as much. Got it."

Leigh didn't have to ask what "it" was. The wall beside the staircase opened without a sound to reveal a second, much narrower set of stairs. She didn't know why Gavin couldn't hear the pounding of her heart from where he was standing. Only, he wasn't simply standing. With a smile of satisfaction, he stepped inside.

"What are you doing? You aren't going down there!"

"Don't you want to see where the stairs lead?"

Absolutely not! Every fiber of her body was screaming at her to get away from here.

"Aha!"

A single, weak lightbulb perched above a minuscule landing part of the way down these much narrower, much steeper stairs.

"I figured if the room R.J. found had electricity, this would too."

"It's a staircase for skinny midgets."

Gavin grinned up at her. "I believe the politically correct terminology is 'little people'."

"Okay, fine. You found a staircase for slender little people. Can we go now?"

Like the hidden room, the walls were unfinished, which didn't make them the least bit inviting.

"We'll have to go single file, obviously. Want to bet these were originally part of the back staircase?"

It was on the tip of her tongue to tell him she didn't care. She wasn't about to go down those steps, but Gavin was already heading for the landing. He was like a kid at Christmas. Couldn't he sense the wrongness here?

"Now, that's interesting," he said, pausing on the landing.

Leigh fought her common sense and stepped inside. The strain of the past few days was getting to her. Gavin would think she was an idiot if she told him she couldn't do this. She started down. The door closed at her back.

"Gavin! The door closed!"

"No problem. There's another one here at the bottom. Hey, are you okay?"

She shook her head mutely. Panic held her motionless. Her heart was thudding so fast it felt as if it might explode.

"Leigh? Are you claustrophobic?"

She couldn't answer. She couldn't breathe. He swore softly and started back up to her.

"Take my hand."

"I can't."

He stared at her.

"Look at me."

His eyes were all she could see.

"You said you trusted me."

"Oh, God." Somehow, she found the ability to hold out her hand.

"That's right. Keep looking at me. You're okay."

"I can't...breathe."

"Sure you can. You're breathing just fine. Come on. We're going to be careful because the stairs after the landing are pitched even more. Whoever designed this didn't have a lot of room to work in. I wonder what it was originally used for."

Leigh didn't care. If he hadn't taken her hand, she doubted she would have made it down the stairs. It was all she could do not to hyperventilate. Maybe he was right. Maybe she was claustrophobic. She never had liked small places.

At the bottom, he pulled her into his arms. She laid her head on his chest and closed her eyes, breathing deeply of his scent.

"I'm sorry," Gavin said contritely against her hair. "I didn't realize."

She lifted her head and offered him a tremulous smile. "It's okay. I'm okay."

"You're a lot better than okay, Leigh. There's a door right here, see? It must exit next to the dining-room fireplace."

She focused on his words, glad that he didn't release her completely when he turned to show her the door.

"There're built-in shelves there," she managed to say.

"I remember. Bookcases always hid the secret entrances in old horror movies."

"And the hero and heroine usually discover the secret passage right before the bad guy shows up."

Gavin tilted up her chin and kissed her lightly.

"This isn't a movie. But you're the bravest person I know."

"Just goes to prove you need to get out more," she replied and was rewarded by the flash of his grin.

"Do you want to see where this passage leads, or go out into the dining room?"

He released her to look along the wall until he found another wall switch. Another weak light flickered to life at the end of the narrow passage.

"There's another room!"

Gavin nodded. "Right above us is the upstairs landing."

"But why is this here?" She followed him in the space. "I mean, why would someone hide a room here? What could it have been used for?"

"Beats me. Your ancestors weren't into smuggling, were they?"

"Not that I know about." Her heart was still racing, but the dreadful sense of panic was fading away.

"There's stuff on those shelves under the stairs. Look. Even a wine rack." He lifted a dusty bottle and blew on the label.

"That's the dinner wine my grandfather used to like."

The shelves held much of the family silver, she realized. Most was carefully wrapped and labeled. The large chafing dish and a pair of silver candelabra sat unwrapped, dark with tarnish. Leigh moved closer. The large silver chest that held the silverware sat on the floor next to the wine.

"At least we know Eden didn't steal the family silver."

"Not yet," he agreed. "Or at least, not all of it. But someone's been in here recently."

He pointed down. Leigh saw a path had been worn in the dust. She followed the trail to the corner and the outline of another door.

"Must lead to the kitchen," Gavin said.

"Not just the kitchen, the pantry. Remember when Mrs.

Norwhich thought she saw someone close the pantry door?"

"You're right."

While Gavin examined the exit, Leigh's gaze was caught and held by something that gleamed brightly on one of the shelves. She uttered a soft cry and reached for the small gold treasure chest.

"What's that?"

He'd opened the door, Leigh saw. On the other side it was actually a shelving unit in the kitchen's walk-in pantry. She held out the small chest so Gavin could see it.

"I told you about this. Grandpa used to keep candy in this for us."

Lovingly, she brushed her fingertips over the surface before lifting the lid. The scent of chocolate still clung to the velvet lining, but the contents weren't candy.

Gavin lifted out a cardboard box that had been jammed inside the chest. The box had been mailed to her grandfather three weeks after his death. Leigh recognized the return address immediately.

"McGarvey's is a jewelry store in New York. Ian McGarvey made all Mom's custom jewelry. Grandpa must have ordered this for her before he died. I wonder why Mom didn't say anything."

"Maybe she never got the package," he said quietly.

Fury sent her fingers to the cardboard. "Someone opened the box."

That Marcus might have kept something like this from her mother was unthinkable. Four velvet jewelry boxes sat inside. A small slip of paper was taped to the outside of each box.

"This one says Amy," she told him.

Leigh set down the chest. She could barely swallow as she opened the box. Gavin gave a soft, tuneless whistle. Even in the dim light, the necklace and matching earrings were exquisite. Heavy, for such delicate pieces, they had to be twenty-four-carat gold. The design was softly elegant, yet richly detailed. Three large, square-cut emeralds had been woven into the design. Smaller versions of the gems had been worked into the matching dangling earrings.

"Wow. If those stones are real—"

"Mr. McGarvey doesn't work with imitations."

Leigh closed the jewelry box and lifted the next one. Her name was taped to the top. "Oh!" Her necklace replicated exactly one-third of the design of her mother's necklace. There was only one emerald in the necklace and each earring.

Grief blurred her vision. Only Gavin's voice kept her from surrendering to the awful pain that threatened to swamp her.

"Why are there four boxes?"

She blinked back her tears, closed the box and reached for the next one. Hayley's name. Inside, was an exact replica of hers. The last box said Alexis.

"Who's Alexis?"

Leigh shook her head. The contents of the final box were identical to hers and Hayley's. She stared at Gavin, bewildered, and suddenly very, very frightened.

"Do you have another sister?"

"Of course not."

"Did your mother have a sister?"

"She was an only child."

"Then who's Alexis?"

"I don't know!"

There was a crash of thunder so loud the house seemed to reverberate with the sound. The lights winked out with terrifying abruptness.

"I think the storm arrived," Gavin told her dryly. "Can you put the jewelry back in the box?"

"I...think so." She was shaking badly. There wasn't the

faintest hint of light anywhere. "We can't leave them here."

"We aren't going to. If Mrs. Norwhich saw someone disappear in the pantry, chances are, Eden knows about this room. I'm surprised she hasn't cleaned out the silver by now, but she probably expected to have more time. I don't think she anticipated that we'd change the house locks."

Leigh put the jewelry inside the box and closed it by feel. "Gavin, I can't see a thing." She hated the thread of fear she could hear in her voice.

He ran his large, warm hand down her bare arm. The surge of comfort and safety brought a huge sense of relief. Their fingers meshed.

"It's okay. The door to the pantry's still open. I can get us out."

"If you tell me you can see in this void, I'm going to kick you." Her lips felt stiff and her voice held a tremor, but she tried to infuse the words with a touch of humor so he'd know she wasn't going to go to pieces no matter how scared she felt. She was rewarded with a low chuckle.

"Nope, I can't see a thing, either, but I've got a good memory. Can you manage the chest with one hand? You can hold on to my other hand."

She gripped his fingers tightly. "I can carry the chest."

He transferred the box to her arms. "I'm pretty sure there's nothing on the floor between us and the door, but I'm not so sure about the pantry."

Slowly, they inched their way forward.

"Mrs. Walsh never kept things on the floor. I don't know about Mrs. Norwhich."

"We should be safe enough. The door wouldn't have opened if something had been blocking it."

"There's a cheery thought."

Gavin squeezed her fingers lightly. Leigh knew the moment she stepped into the pantry. There was a different feel to the air. Her chest no longer felt quite so constricted.

"Uh, Leigh? Where's the door to the pantry located in relationship to where we are?"

Leigh thought for a minute. "I think we're in the far right corner if you were in the kitchen facing the pantry. The door is almost centered, so if you walk in a straight diagonal line, you should run right into it."

"A straight diagonal line? You wouldn't want to lead, would you?" he teased.

"Not really. No."

He continued inching forward, abruptly coming to a stop. She felt him groping for something and the room was suddenly flooded with light.

"But the lights went out!" she protested, even as relief washed over her.

"A power surge, obviously."

"Not in there." Leigh pointed to the dark opening.

"Must have been too much for those weak lightbulbs. Wait here for a second while I see how to close this door."

It took him several minutes to find the mechanism. Unlike the others, this switch was built into the underside of a shelf.

They stepped into the kitchen to find rain beating fiercely against the windows. A particularly strong wind gust suddenly pushed the back door open. As Gavin hurried forward, he slid on a wet spot on the floor. He caught himself on a counter. As he closed the back door, Leigh focused on a muddy trail that led across the kitchen floor to the library side of the house.

Gavin gave a quick shake of his head when she would have called out to him. He crossed to her side.

"Wyatt?" she mouthed, afraid to whisper.

"I'll see. If something happens, run outside and get one of the officers."

"No!" she whispered fiercely. "Gavin, wait!"

She wasted her breath. The problem with strong, independent men like Gavin and Bram was that they always assumed they could handle anything. Leigh applauded his bravery, while cursing his stupidity. If the footprints didn't belong to Wyatt or one of his men, anyone could be inside the house with them.

Leigh set the treasure chest down next to the refrigerator and crept to the corner where Gavin had disappeared. She peered down the hall, but it was too dark to see anything.

A cold ball of fear ghosted through her. She'd never enjoyed hide-and-seek, and she hated this. Her instinct was to run out in the rain and drag an armed police officer back inside, but she was afraid he'd shoot Gavin by mistake.

Something squished behind her. Leigh whirled at the small sound.

"Hello, Leigh."

Nolan's triumphant whisper nearly stopped her heart. He was soaking wet and held something in his hand that he pointed at her head. Leigh fled down the hall. She heard him curse as he came after her. Gavin would hear them. He'd come to get her. But he wouldn't realize Nolan had a gun. Leigh changed direction. She cut straight across the dining room to the far hall.

"Gavin, Nolan has a gun!" she yelled.

"Bitch!"

She rounded the corner. She'd never make the back door before he caught her. Without breaking stride, she plunged up the steps, leading Nolan away from Gavin.

His hand caught her ankle as she reached the landing. She kicked back, hard. Her foot connected, but she stumbled and fell.

A hand reached for her out of the darkness in front of her. Her scream died as Gavin yanked her to her feet and thrust her onto the balcony, placing himself between her and Nolan.

"He's got a gun!"

Gavin lunged for Nolan's out-thrust arm. As they came together, the gun spat a burst of flame and noise harmlessly into the air.

Gavin gripped his gun arm. As they struggled, Nolan forced him back. Gavin's foot missed the step down that led to the balcony's railing. When he stumbled, Nolan shoved him back.

Leigh reached for Gavin's flailing arm, terrified that momentum would send him over the waist-high railing. Instead, he hit it with a resounding crack that jarred both of them. Nolan grabbed her other arm, wrenching her toward him. Off balance, Leigh had no chance to struggle before he shoved the muzzle of the gun against her cheek.

"I'll kill you! Come near me and I'll kill her!"

His voice was high and shrill like a woman's. He yanked her against his sopping clothing, holding her with a bone-punishing grip that threatened to cut the circulation to her arm. The smell of the gun was acrid in her nostrils.

"Let her go, Ducort."

Gavin's voice was gritty, but amazingly calm.

"Not a chance."

He squeezed her so hard, she couldn't prevent a gasp of pain. Gavin's fists balled at his sides.

"I need her dead."

Shocked, she realized he was serious.

"I don't know why you haven't gone to the cops yet, but you're the only witness. I'm not going to jail for Martin's murder."

"What are you talking about, Ducort?"

"Didn't she tell you, Jarret? She was there when he died. I don't know what her deal was with Pepperton, but I saw her plain as day, just like she saw me."

"You killed Martin Pepperton?"

"It was an accident! The crazy son of a bitch pulled a gun on me! When I tried to take it away, it went off. It wasn't my fault! Tell him how it was, you bitch!"

"I wasn't there, Nolan!"

He gave her a shake that would have sent her flying if he hadn't been holding her so tightly. "Lying whore! You looked right at me!"

Gavin moved to intercede, but Nolan thrust the gun back against her cheek. "Don't move. None of that matters now. This will still work. A lover's quarrel. She shoots you and turns the gun on herself."

Her body turned to stone. He was insane. He was really going to kill them.

Gavin cast a quick glance down toward the dining room. He shook his head.

"The cops won't buy it, Ducort."

How could Gavin sound so calm?

"They will. Someone else must have seen her at the track that day. After the cops match the bullets to the one in Martin, they'll know this is the same gun. They'll learn what their deal was. Maybe they'll even tag the two of you for Earlwood's death. I heard you were there when the place went up. Too bad you didn't go up with it and save me the trouble. You should have left Jarret to rot in jail for old man Wickert, Leigh."

"Did you kill him, too?" Leigh gasped.

"Not intentionally. We were going to frame Jarret for theft. To pay him back for taking you away that night. It doesn't matter now. None of it."

He pulled the muzzle from her cheek, swinging the gun toward Gavin.

Everything happened at once.

"Police! Drop your weapon," Wyatt yelled from below.

At the same time, Leigh threw her weight against Nolan, and Gavin launched himself at them.

Several shots exploded.

Nolan screamed. He attempted to twist away from her. He missed the step and grabbed for Gavin. There was another shot. He and Gavin staggered back against the railing. The wood gave under their combined weight with a loud, cracking, splintering sound.

Leigh grabbed Gavin's arm with all her strength. The railing fell away. Nolan fell with it into the darkness below. Leigh and Gavin crashed to the floor, precariously close to the gaping hole. Gavin landed on top of her, emptying her lungs.

"Leigh! Are you hurt?" he demanded, rolling to one side and pulling her with him.

She struggled to suck air into her lungs, dimly conscious of voices and beams of light coming from the dining room.

"Leigh!" Gavin crushed her against his chest. "I'm sorry. I'm so sorry."

Footsteps pounded toward them. The balcony trembled under their weight. A flashlight pinned them in its beam. As Leigh struggled for air, she was stunned to see Gavin's face wreathed in pain. Tears filled his eyes as he looked at her. "Where are you hit?"

She managed to shake her head. "Not. Winded."

Wyatt and another officer reached them. "Are you all right? I'm sorry, Gavin. I couldn't get a clear shot."

"We're okay," he said gruffly, pressing her against his chest. "Ducort?"

"He landed across the back of a chair. He's unconscious. I think his neck's broken. We've got an ambulance en route. Can you stand? We need to get off this balcony before the whole thing comes down."

"I STILL DON'T UNDERSTAND," Emily said the following morning as Leigh sat with her and George at their kitchen table. ''Are you saying the police think Nolan shot Martin Pepperton because Martin sold him a horse?''

Leigh shrugged. ''Basically, that's what it boils down to. Wyatt Crossley said Nolan talked before he went into surgery. According to Nolan, Martin switched the paperwork on two racehorses. One horse called Sunset Pride was worth a lot of money, the other horse wasn't, but looked just like Sunset Pride. Martin wanted Nolan to sell the worthless lookalike to a man named Briggs because Martin had a grudge against Briggs.''

''That's crazy,'' Emily exclaimed.

''Not only crazy,'' George agreed, ''but stupid. Pepperton should have known that scheme would never work.''

Leigh nodded. ''That's what Nolan told him, but Nolan said Martin was so high on drugs he wouldn't listen. Wyatt says the autopsy report confirms the drugs, and the gun Nolan says he took from Martin was registered to Martin.''

She looked up at the sound of footsteps coming down the hall toward them. Emily shook her head.

''That still doesn't explain why Nolan thinks you saw him shoot Martin Pepperton.''

''I've no idea.''

''I think we found the answer,'' Hayley said.

She strode into the room holding a file folder. Leigh's gaze immediately sought Gavin, who stood behind her next to Bram. Gavin was holding her grandfather's treasure chest. Leigh had forgotten all about it until now.

At their grim expressions, fear skittered down her spine once more.

''What's wrong?''

Hayley shook her head and looked to Bram. Gavin set their grandfather's chest on the table. He walked around to her side and lifted her chin with aching tenderness.

''How do you feel?''

He loved her. It was there in the depths of his eyes, in the gentle warmth of his touch. Everything else faded away.

"Fine."

"Your arm?"

"A bruise. What about you? George said the three of you went back over there this morning." She couldn't prevent a tiny shudder.

Gavin brushed a strand of hair from her face. "You were sleeping so soundly, I didn't have the heart to wake you when I left. I thought you'd still be sleeping, considering how late it was when we got to bed."

"I woke up a few minutes ago," she admitted. "What else happened? What's wrong now?"

His eyes darkened and he looked to Hayley and Bram. "While I distracted Wyatt in the kitchen, your sister and Bram slipped upstairs and grabbed some files from the hidden room."

Emily made a small sound of concern. "Don't you think you should tell Wyatt about that room, Gavin?"

"We will now," he told Emily. "We don't have a choice."

"Remember the picture I found in the drawer in Grandpa's office downstairs?" Hayley said. "Bram thought it had been computer generated, a picture of one of us that someone had altered."

"I remember. We were going to look for the source of it on Jacob's computer. Were you able to figure out the password, Bram?"

Hayley shook her head. She took the seat beside Leigh. "We haven't tried that computer yet." There was deep pain in her eyes.

"The picture wasn't a composite, Leigh," Bram said. "Though it was probably a digital shot."

"I had a quick look at the files in the car on our way back." Hayley spread open a folder on the table. Gavin's hand rested on Leigh's shoulder and they all stared at the pictures that spilled across the table. Pictures of Hayley, but not Hayley.

"I don't understand. Who is that?"

Emily, George and Nan crowded around for a better view.

"Grandpa hired a private investigator to find out. His report is in there. We weren't twins, Leigh. We were triplets. Marcus gave her away. He just took our sister and gave her away."

Leigh stared at her while her body turned to ice. "What are you saying?"

"There's a copy of her birth certificate. Look at the date. Look at the time. A home birth with Marcus as the attending physician. She's our sister, Leigh! Marcus gave her away—or more likely, sold her to these people."

"Oh my God," Emily whispered faintly.

Leigh looked to Gavin for confirmation, while horror took root in her mind. He nodded grimly.

"She was born first. She would have had to have been for him to pull this off. We were both delivered by C-section at the hospital."

"Mom would never have let him!"

"Mom didn't know! Don't you see, Leigh? He must have drugged her or something. He delivered her first baby in the normal way. Then he drove Mom to the hospital to deliver us in front of witnesses. Mom never knew."

Hayley choked on her tears. Leigh realized she was crying too. Tears slipped down her cheeks as she lifted the nearest photograph. Her features stared back at her. This wasn't someone who looked like them. This person was an exact replica. Only the hairstyle and the clothing set her apart.

George and Emily were both talking at once. Bram was

speaking low in Hayley's ear. It was Gavin's voice Leigh heard.

"Alexis."

She stared at him, then slowly nodded. "Yes. Alexis."

"What?" Hayley demanded.

"Her name is Alexis. That's why Grandpa ordered new necklaces and matching earrings. Three stones for three granddaughters. Hayley, Leigh and Alexis." She blinked up at Gavin and her tears fell faster.

"How could he do that?" Nan demanded. "How could Marcus give away his own child?"

George held Emily tight against his chest. His face mirrored the horror they all felt.

"I don't know," Bram said, sounding ill.

"We have to find her!" Hayley demanded.

"I'll call Wyatt," Gavin said.

"No!" Hayley protested before he could move. "You can't tell the police. *We* have to find her."

Leigh wiped at her tears, struggling for composure. "Hayley's right."

"Leigh, we can't do that. We have to tell Wyatt," Gavin said. "Alexis is the reason your mother was killed. I'd bet on it. She must have found these files after your grandfather died."

"This is why she went to New York," Hayley agreed. "It's why she seemed so upset those last few days. She would have wanted to see Alexis for herself."

Leigh knew her sister was right.

"Once she confirmed the truth," Hayley continued, "she would have come back here and confronted Marcus."

Leigh agreed. That was exactly what their mother would have done.

"Dear God," Emily whispered.

"We have to find Alexis first," Hayley said emphatically. "She shouldn't learn about our existence through a media blitz. We'll call the investigator, find out where she lives, go and see her.''

''Now, wait a minute. There's an address given in this report,'' Gavin admitted, ''but it's more than seven years old.''

''Hayley's right,'' Leigh told him. ''We have to do this. Please, Gavin. A day or two can't make any difference to Wyatt's investigation. Marcus is dead.''

''But the police—'' Emily began.

''No, Emily,'' George intoned. ''They should be the ones to find her and tell her the truth. She shouldn't learn about this from strangers.''

''Give us three days, Gavin,'' Hayley pleaded. ''If we can't find her by then, we'll give the files to Wyatt.''

''I hate to play devil's advocate here,'' Gavin said softly, ''but there's one thing you haven't considered. What if Alexis already knows the truth?''

There was shocked silence as every eye focused on him. Gavin gazed at each stunned face before coming to rest on Leigh.

''Remember how Nolan Ducort claimed that you saw the murder? What if it wasn't you, but Alexis he saw that day? It seems to me that if your mother went to New York to see if this was her daughter, she would have approached her, or at the very least, approached Alexis's parents to confirm her daughter's identity?''

Bram nodded. ''That makes sense. Maybe Marcus didn't kill your mother after all.''

''Or maybe he had help,'' George said grimly. ''Her adopted parents had almost as much to lose as Marcus.''

Everyone began to talk at once except Leigh. She held Gavin's gaze. ''Alexis doesn't know. I can't explain why I'm so sure, but I am. She doesn't know about us. I don't know what happened in New York or out back in the garden, but Alexis doesn't know about us. She thinks she's alone.''

Gavin touched her cheek. ''Three days,'' he told her. ''And if I get disbarred, you'll have to support me.''

Leigh threw her arms around him. ''I love you.''

Gavin felt as if a gate inside him had opened, allowing years of carefully contained emotions to flow freely for the first time. Leigh loved him.

''Let's call the private investigator now,'' Hayley said.

''It's Sunday,'' George pointed out. ''I doubt anyone will answer on a Sunday afternoon. Don't you think we should take the time to read through everything in this file first?''

IT WAS HOURS LATER before Gavin drew Leigh outside on the back-porch swing. Another storm was sweeping across the Hudson River. Cloud lightning flashed in the distance.

''How are you holding up?'' he asked.

''I'm okay. I keep wondering what she's like. How do we tell her what Marcus did?''

''You and Hayley will find a way.''

''How could he be our father? What sort of a monster was he?''

''I don't know.''

She sought his hand and he pulled her against his side. For a long time, they simply sat there in silence watching the storm approach.

''George said something to me the other day… Actually, he said several things, but they made a lot of sense.''

''George usually does,'' she agreed.

''He said a person can't love if they can't trust.''

''Is that why you asked me if I trusted you when we were checking out the balcony yesterday?''

He nodded. ''You didn't hesitate. You said yes. But he

said the trust you lacked was in yourself. You compare yourself to your sister and feel like you come up short."

"Is that what you think?"

"No. I think you know who you are."

"I do now. When I compare myself to Hayley, I see differences. Sometimes I wish I could emulate her, but that usually gets me into trouble. I'm me, good, bad or indifferent."

"How about spectacular?"

"Spectacular's good." She grinned at him. "I like spectacular. What about you?"

"He nailed me," Gavin admitted. "He said I didn't trust easily because I couldn't shed my guilt over what happened to my family."

"Ah, but not trusting easily isn't the same thing as being unable to trust at all."

"I know." He smiled, pleased she'd seen that instead of telling him he had nothing to feel guilty about. "You said you loved me. Because I agreed to help you?"

She searched his face. His chest constricted, growing tighter and tighter as he waited for her answer.

"I fell in love with you when I was thirteen years old. Mom stopped for gas and I saw you changing a tire. Your eyes haunted me. I wanted so badly to fix whatever had put that shuttered look in your eyes."

His mouth went dry.

"Mom said that of all the kids Emily and George took in, you and R.J. were special. She said if you ever learned how to open your heart, you'd be the sort of man a woman could always depend on, but she wasn't sure it was a lesson you were going to learn."

"She told you that?"

"Yes. My mother was wise in a lot of ways. She knew how I felt about you."

"You were thirteen! A kid!"

She smiled. ''I doubt she thought I was going to nurse those feelings for the rest of my life. She was trying to teach me how to look beneath the surface of a person. At least, I think that's what she was doing. Was she wrong?''

''Do you mean, have I learned that lesson? Am I the sort of man a woman can depend on?''

''I already know I can depend on you.''

''So you want to know if I've learned how to love? I don't know, Leigh. All I can tell you is that those minutes up on that balcony last night were the worst minutes of my life. When I thought you'd been shot, I was devastated.''

She closed her eyes. His stomach contracted. ''I'm saying this all wrong.''

''No, you aren't.'' She opened her eyes and they were filled with love.

He pulled her into his arms. ''I love you, Leigh.''

''I know. I think I knew the day you told me about your family. You don't trust easily, but you trusted me with something that was vital to who you are.''

''God, but I love you. I know you wanted a formal proposal—''

''No. I only want you.''

''You deserve it all, the dinner, the moonlight, the flowers—''

She laughed up at him with her eyes. ''You on bended knee? Can we get pictures? Hayley will never believe it otherwise.''

''Brat.''

''Hayley's the brat. I'm the quiet one, remember?''

''A malicious falsehood. I know better.''

For a long time, he simply held her, content to feel her against his chest. ''People will say I'm marrying you for your money, you know.''

''So what? They'll say I bought you for your looks and charm. Let them talk. It gives them something to do.''

''Then you'll marry me?''

''Anywhere, anytime.''

He fished in his pocket and pulled out the ring George had given him early this morning.

''Where did you get this?''

''George took it from the safe-deposit box for me yesterday. It was my grandmother's ring. Ironically, it's an emerald, not a diamond, but I thought you could use it as a place holder until we have a chance to select something more to your taste.''

''No, not irony—fate,'' she corrected, staring at the brilliant green stone. ''This was meant to be my ring.''

Her eyes filled with tears as he slipped it onto her finger. The ring was only a little bit loose.

''I don't want anything else. All I ever wanted was you.''

Rain splattered against the porch. ''Are you crying?''

''Tears of happiness,'' she assured him.

''We'd better go inside before we get soaked.''

''I don't mind.''

Neither did he. Nothing had ever felt more right than sitting here in the rain holding Leigh like this.

''Gavin?'' she said after several minutes had passed. ''If we're right about Alexis, I'm off the hook, aren't I? She's the one who should inherit Heartskeep.''

''The missing heir,'' he agreed. ''The third twin.''

Leigh's answering smile was wistful before her expression filled with new resolve.

''Good. All we have to do is find her.''

''We will. I promise you. We will.''

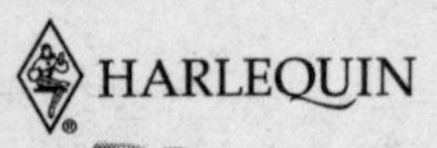

INTRIGUE®

COMING NEXT MONTH

#741 A WARRIOR'S MISSION by Rita Herron
Colorado Confidential
When Colorado Confidential agent Night Walker arrived to investigate the Langworthy baby kidnapping, he discovered that the baby was *his.* A night of passion with Holly Langworthy months ago had left him a father, and now it was up to him to find his son—and win the heart of the woman he'd never forgotten.

#742 THE THIRD TWIN by Dani Sinclair
Heartskeep
Alexis Ryder's life was turned upside down the day she came home to find her father murdered, a briefcase full of money and a note revealing she was illegally adopted. Desperate to learn the truth, she had no choice but to team up with charming police officer Wyatt Crossley—the only man who seemed to have the answers she was seeking.

#743 UNDER SURVEILLANCE by Gayle Wilson
Phoenix Brotherhood
Phoenix Brotherhood operative John Edmonds was given one last case to prove himself to the agency: keep an eye on Kelly Lockett, the beautiful heir to her family's charitable foundation. But their mutual attraction was threatening his job—and might put her life in danger....

#744 MOUNTAIN SHERIFF by B.J. Daniels
Cascades Concealed
Journalist Charity Jenkins had been pursuing sexy sheriff Mitch Tanner since they were children. Trouble was, the man was a confirmed bachelor. But when strange things started happening to Charity and Mitch realized she might be in danger, he knew he had to protect her. Would he also find love where he least expected it?

#745 BOYS IN BLUE by Rebecca York (Ruth Glick writing as Rebecca York), Ann Voss Peterson and Patricia Rosemoor
Bachelors At Large
Three brothers' lives were changed forever when one of their own was arrested for murder. Now they had to unite to prove his innocence and discover the real killer...but they never thought they'd find *love,* as well!

#746 FOR THE SAKE OF THEIR BABY by Alice Sharpe
When her uncle's dead body was found in his mansion, Liz Chase's husband, Alex, took the rap for what he thought was a deliberate murder by his pregnant wife. But once he was released from prison, and discovered that his loving wife hadn't committed the crime, could they work together to find the *real* killer... and rekindle their relationship?